# Praise for
# *The Ghosts of Gwendolyn Montgomery*

"*The Ghosts of Gwendolyn Montgomery* is full of vibrant characters, sublime mysticism, and captivating twists that includes a world-renowned goddess. Readers are in for a wild ride!"

—Luanne G. Smith, bestselling author of *The Vine Witch*

"With orishas, angry ghosts, and a breach between worlds that can only be sealed by a badass mystical heroine, *The Ghosts of Gwendolyn Montgomery* is a gritty New York feast."

—Veronica G. Henry, bestselling author of *The Canopy Keepers*

"A beguiling and sensual page-turner, *The Ghosts of Gwendolyn* delivers an engrossing tale that taps into the supernatural and mystical while remaining rooted in the bonds of friendship and family. The ties between Gwendolyn and Fonsi will ring true to anyone that grew up among neighbors who become play cousins, and the pull of personal history runs deep. This propulsive novel intertwines horror, romance, and reconciliation with a deft touch of humor. Destined to be a book club favorite."

—Rasheed Newson, bestselling author of *My Government Means to Kill Me*

# THE GHOSTS OF GWENDOLYN MONTGOMERY

*A Novel*

## CLARENCE A. HAYNES

LEGACY
LIT

New York   Boston

This book is a work of fiction. Names, characters, places, and incidents are the product of the author's imagination or are used fictitiously. Any resemblance to actual events, locales, or persons, living or dead, is coincidental.

Copyright © 2025 by Clarence A. Haynes

Cover design by Dana Li
Cover art by Natasha Cunningham
Cover photos by Getty Images

Cover copyright © 2025 by Hachette Book Group, Inc.

Hachette Book Group supports the right to free expression and the value of copyright. The purpose of copyright is to encourage writers and artists to produce the creative works that enrich our culture.

The scanning, uploading, and distribution of this book without permission is a theft of the author's intellectual property. If you would like permission to use material from the book (other than for review purposes), please contact permissions@hbgusa.com. Thank you for your support of the author's rights.

Legacy Lit
Hachette Book Group
1290 Avenue of the Americas
New York, NY 10104
HachetteBookGroup.com
@LegacyLitBooks

First Edition: June 2025

Legacy Lit is an imprint of Grand Central Publishing. The Legacy Lit name and logo are registered trademarks of Hachette Book Group, Inc.

The publisher is not responsible for websites (or their content) that are not owned by the publisher.

The Hachette Speakers Bureau provides a wide range of authors for speaking events. To find out more, go to hachettespeakersbureau.com or email HachetteSpeakers@hbgusa.com.

Legacy Lit books may be purchased in bulk for business, educational, or promotional use. For information, please contact your local bookseller or the Hachette Book Group Special Markets Department at special.markets@hbgusa.com.

Print book interior design by Taylor Navis

Library of Congress Cataloging-in-Publication Data
Names: Haynes, Clarence A., author.
Title: The ghosts of Gwendolyn Montgomery : a novel / Clarence A. Haynes.
Description: First edition. | New York : Legacy Lit, 2025.
Identifiers: LCCN 2024060291 | ISBN 9781538768518 (hardcover) | ISBN 9781538768532 (ebook)
Subjects: LCGFT: Paranormal fiction. | Novels.
Classification: LCC PS3608.A9456 G48 2025 | DDC 813/.6—dc23/eng/20250110
LC record available at https://lccn.loc.gov/2024060291

ISBNs: 978-1-5387-6851-8 (Hardcover); 978-1-5387-6853-2 (Ebook)

Printed in the United States of America

LSC-C

Printing 1, 2025

*To my mother, Naomi Haynes; my grandmother, Alma Haynes; and all the women with magnificent power who haven't been sufficiently seen—this one's for you.*

# THE GHOSTS OF GWENDOLYN MONTGOMERY

PROLOGUE

# FIRE

She opened her eyes, terrified. Something was burning. Badly. The stench...

Giselda rolled over to her left. Her godmother, the woman who'd raised her for years, was sprawled out. A crisp, smoldering thing. Flesh parched. Eyes gone. The green gown she wore reduced to cinders.

"Madrina!" Giselda yelled. She scrambled over and grabbed her godmother's right shoulder only to recoil. Her fingertips scorched from hot skin.

"Madrina," she said again, her voice now a whimper. Giselda put her hands to her mouth, felt the hot metal of her flower ring pressed against her upper lip. Tears blurred her vision, though she could see several candles had been overturned.

The carpet was burning.

She looked down at her blistered fingers. Power had lingered there moments ago, before a white flash of light filled the den. Then came the loud explosion and shrieks from Madrina and a swirl of colors and finally...darkness.

Giselda coughed from the smoke. The large cloth tapestry on the wall had caught fire as well, images of orishas overtaken by flames. She sat there, paralyzed.

"*Levántate!*" someone yelled. "*Get your ass up! Don't you dare let yourself burn in here, after all I've taught you.*"

Madrina's voice, in Giselda's head.

She surveyed the burning room, thankful that her cousin Fonsi wasn't in the house, that he was still at the botanica with Estelle. She had to leave, alert the neighbors. Giselda rose from the floor holding her breath, her legs trembling, heart pounding as she stared at Madrina's lifeless body. She pushed open the door, dashed into her bedroom to grab her backpack, and ran outside as she yelled, "*Fire!*" That's when Giselda knew that her time using her gift was done. That she would never mess with that horrible in-between place ever again.

CHAPTER ONE

# RED RUNWAY

Thick white gardenia petals fell from conference room ceilings as Gwendolyn ran through meeting after meeting, fielding inane questions about her A-list clientele. Yellow petals tripped her up when she hopped onto the D train at 125th right as a rat scurried from a garbage bin on the subway platform. Pink petals covered countertops as she and her boss Jessica ordered margaritas like no tomorrow. The accompanying aromas were sweet and citrusy with undertones of something light, metallic.

But the vision of James, the new dude in her life, was what left her breathless. Red petals covered the couple as they rolled around in flowery fields, their intertwined bodies sweaty. Petals clung to James's chest and back and behind, Gwendolyn's nails raking his skin, her lips on his neck. His head was buried in her shoulder as he moaned and whimpered. He was close, she could tell, and so was she, but she didn't want to stop, refused to stop. She'd waited far too long.

James raised his head, panic in his eyes. "Gwendolyn!" he yelled, his breathing ragged, his body immersed in viscous shadow. The field of flowers turned gray and dry.

Something heavy pressed against Gwendolyn's body. Invisible but familiar. Deadly.

James screamed.

She jumped from her pillow.

Gwendolyn blinked, noticed the overcast skies through her window. She rolled over and scanned the tiny electronic clock on her nightstand. *6:57 a.m.* She'd woken up just in time. Her alarm was about to ring in a few minutes.

She got up and stepped into the bathroom, groggily handling her business. Minutes later, Gwendolyn swapped her silk purple bonnet for a pink shower cap before hopping into the glass-enclosed shower. She lathered up her body and tried to assess her dream before the memory faded away. The flowers represented what was on the horizon, one of the main elements of the big museum event just hours away. A premonition of future success. But her vision of James panicking? She wasn't sure what to make of that.

As she ended her shower, Gwendolyn realized her limbs were stiff, leaden, as if a weight were dragging her down. *No, not today*, she thought. *No time.*

She rubbed lotion on her damp skin, put on makeup, and styled her braids into the twisty updo her hairdresser Shana had shown her how to create a million times yet which still took her forever to get right. As usual, her arms ached when she entered her walk-in closet. In the corner was a small altar she'd adorned with a glass of scented water, a large bowl of honey, and five sliced oranges that surrounded a two-foot statuette of a woman in a shimmering yellow dress. Her hair was free, flowing, her arms outstretched. Gwendolyn bowed her head to the woman, placed two fingers to her lips, and then placed them on the figure. Her morning ritual.

Gwendolyn swiveled around and zipped open a suit bag she'd hung in a corner, revealing a cream blazer and matching skirt along with a silk beige camisole whose neck was embroidered with peacocks. A LaMarque original. Gwendolyn added layered necklaces and a sunflower ring to the outfit and gazed at her reflection in a floor-to-ceiling mirror. Brown skin, mauve lipstick, and nude nail polish contrasted with couture linen. Her MO before a big event was to hype herself up, twirl and shimmy, and when she was feeling really silly, shout "Yaaaaaaaaasssssss queen." But this morning? Wasn't in the mood.

"Snap out of it, girl," Gwendolyn mumbled as she carried white pumps into the living room. Her eyes caught the edge of *Media Today* on her coffee table, the industry weekly loaded with insider film and TV news. She'd just become the first Sublime Creative employee ever featured in the magazine's Rising Stars section. "I'm only doing this for you and the agency," Gwendolyn grumbled to Jessica after she'd agreed to the interview. The thought of too much public attention made her nervous, the reason why she'd chosen a career working behind the scenes in the first place. But Gwendolyn's reputation had become well-established for those in the know, a byproduct of stellar work.

In just a few years, having zero connection to the entertainment world, she'd become a PR go-to woman with the ability to create the most exquisite on- and off-screen personas (aka "brands") for her clients. Whether they were regional rappers who unexpectedly found themselves social media darlings or meek actors who strutted down red carpets with badass designer looks, Gwendolyn was the mastermind behind their ascent. The quality of all the events she planned and oversaw…graceful, immaculate, some said majestic. She'd worked her ass off, deeply grateful to Jessica, who'd hired Gwendolyn at one of the lowest points in her life.

As a result, Sublime had gone from a boutique PR/management agency focusing on indie creatives to New York's top Black-owned firm fueled by mainstream artists and influencers. But Sublime still held far too precarious a place in the industry, considering the stiff competition. The company was weathering a downturn, with Jessica having to implement cost-saving measures. No more business travel. No more expense account lunches. Jessica and Gwendolyn were even working without assistants, relying on associate staff for help. Layoffs were on the horizon if things didn't turn around, and fast.

Gwendolyn grabbed her purse and raincoat, hot coffee top of mind if she was going to make it through a major fashion event. She stepped onto the corner of 118th and Adam Clayton Powell as she made her way to her favorite neighborhood café. The sidewalk was damp, the air unseasonably warm and humid from early-morning rain. People with their heads buried in phones stole a glance at Gwendolyn in her linen suit. *Good*, she thought. *Very good. I might feel off, but LaMarque does the damn thing every time.*

She took out her phone to check if any early-morning messages had come through and grinned at the text she'd expected to see. *Morning... Just wanted to say hey, sending good vibes before your big day. See you at museum...*

From James.

\* \* \*

A few months ago, Gwendolyn had added the bullet point "Go Out on Dates" to her never-ending to-do list cloud doc. After five months of zero physical intimacy, work killing her softly, she realized she was slowly, surely going insane. She found herself in a constant state of distraction as she walked Harlem streets, checking out well-groomed dark Adonises with thick legs covered in tailored pants and mustached around-the-way guys in sweatsuit ensembles who had a certain Aaron Pierre je ne sais quoi. Gwendolyn valued her independence, saw herself as a loner. Life worked better for her that way, this she knew, but she also knew she could no longer deny her needs.

*Imma fix this*, Gwendolyn told herself, as she did whenever she had a problem, whether personal or professional. Uncomfortable going to a bar by herself, she focused on the apps, trying to remain open-minded though they felt like a waste of time. Gwendolyn soon met up for coffee with a pompadoured finance guy who talked nonstop for an hour about himself and his pals, constantly spouting "my bros" this and "my bros" that. Two days later, she went out with a cute but unsmiling philosophy professor who looked her up and down for half a minute and asked if she always overdressed for dates. And then came the dimpled Saks Fifth Avenue manager who, ten minutes into drinks, opined about the wonders of erotic asphyxiation. (She ended *that* date immediately.) Having sex with any of these fools simply for the sake of getting some nice, one-night-stand ass...nope, wasn't going to happen. She'd gone down that road before, sleeping with dudes whose vibes were off. Never again. They didn't deserve her body or her time.

Just as she was on the verge of recalibrating her approach, she'd met James H. Watson at a Dance Theater of Harlem benefit event that she'd squeezed into her schedule. He was an understated dream with his fade haircut and purple bowtie and button-down shirt and long mahogany fingers that danced as he cupped his old-fashioned. James humble bragged in a baritone voice that he was a foundation fund manager before asking Gwendolyn all the right questions about herself, his gaze never leaving her face. She in turn shared the highlights of being a Sublime senior publicist, impressing him with her client roster. While James admitted he was a divorcé, having split with his ex-wife only a year ago, Gwendolyn kept it light and shared her standard spiel about her interests and hobbies...fashion, art, classic movies, soul, jazz. The sort of thing that positioned her as an alluring woman of culture. After almost an hour of small talk, she decided to give him The Look, which meant something very carnal needed to happen sooner rather than later.

James fidgeted with his bowtie and asked Gwendolyn if she wanted another drink. On his way to the bar, as he turned around to check her out yet again, he collided with another patron and spilled his old-fashioned all over the woman's mauve drape dress. "I'm sorry!" he yelled as he grabbed a batch of napkins and tried to pat the scowling woman down without being fresh.

*Ohmigosh, he's a goofball*, Gwendolyn thought. James came back with a clementine mocktail, his bowtie crooked. And that's when she noticed how he bounced on the soles of his feet as she spoke about her job, how his baritone became a tenor when he cackled at one of her tired jokes, how nervous he was to be in her presence. Her lust-filled illusions were now supplanted by reality. James was *so* not the smooth operator she'd imagined.

A chaste style of courting began. Gwendolyn realized that something about this profoundly decent human being made her feel centered, more like herself. Their time together consisted of elegant dinner dates and long walks under city streetlights and bashful smiles. James clearly enjoyed talking to Gwendolyn about his background growing up in PG County, Maryland, seemingly content with the scant details she shared about growing up in the Bronx. During their third date, an early dinner at a French bistro, after one too many awkward silences, she mentioned a couple of rappers she repped, something that almost always grabbed the attention of men. Sure enough, James dived into the abiding love he had for hip-hop's Soulquarian movement, how it got him through high school and college. How he'd compiled several notebooks of his own rhymes, though his big sister Anita tried to break it to him gently that his flow was shit. He found out the hard way when performing at an open mic show in DC.

"I mean, my swag...nonexistent," he said. "But one of the big lessons I've learned...well, guess I'm still learning, is to keep it real. Be myself. I think it's why me and my ex-wife didn't work out, both of us acting all the time like we're big and bad and perfect instead of being vulnerable, getting to share who we really are." He looked down at his plate of roasted chicken and potatoes. "I'm not going to repeat the same mistakes."

Gwendolyn nodded and took a sip of her Merlot, resisting the urge to excuse herself and sprint out the back door. This level of vulnerability? Wasn't on the agenda.

But for some reason she didn't run. They had their first kiss that night under a streetlight in Central Park, Gwendolyn's sense of time swept away as desire bloomed. She enjoyed the feel of James's stubble against her cheeks and the sound of his guffaws when he was excited. How his fingers intertwined with hers, the palms of his hands soft and tender. (Gwendolyn thanked the heavens that the man knew how to moisturize.) How he caressed her back and asked, "Is this okay?" How he beamed when she leaned in and whispered, "Yes." How he buried his head in her neck and stayed there, the two lost to the night's shadows as Gwendolyn thought, *What am I doing?*

As a publicist, she studied people all the time, and it was clear that sex with James would no longer be a hit it and split sort of thing. He certainly wasn't pushing, seemed to be infinitely patient, not minding the silences where Gwendolyn could've been sharing more. But nonetheless, the prospect of things getting complicated lingered the more they hung out. *Is this really a good idea?* she asked herself over and over on the taxi ride home after their fourth achingly lovely date.

But one night, Gwendolyn kicked caution to the curb after an excruciating day. She'd spent almost fourteen hours contending yet again with foolishness from her most famous client, fellow Harlemite Clive Sergeant, whose career was heading toward its nova phase. Clive knew his worth, was aware of his immense popularity and how charming his fans found him to be with his green eyes and crooked smile. So why follow rules meant for commoners?

The actor had set up his European cocaine dealer in a private trailer on set while shooting *The Senses*, a gritty Hestia Studios drama based on New York's underground gigolo scene during the late '70s. Dealing with Clive's numbskull work behavior? Not Gwendolyn's job, but there she was, imploring the actor to consider that sometimes, every now and then, adhering to the law and acknowledging other people's boundaries made life easier. And then she spoke to the enraged showrunner, begging her not to fire Clive and to think of the multiple Emmy nods on the horizon for the production, of the nuanced *Vulture* thought piece that would spotlight his bravery as a fearless biracial actor who'd dared to do full-frontal sex scenes. (Intimacy coordinator on hand, of course.) And on top of that, Gwendolyn had to speak to the scary drug dealer, delicately asking him to leave set and think about his life choices, about the risks he might be posing to whatever visa or green card situation he had going on with the U.S. Gwendolyn thought the scowling man with black shades and long beard and knife tattoos topping each of his fingers was going to shank her in the side then and there, the way he'd growled. She'd spent hours cleaning up Clive's mess, running between trailers after takes, skipping lunch, downing cups of coffee from craft services…

And so, when she'd left the set, barely able to keep her eyes open from the migraine settling in, she thought of nothing but the kind, beautiful man who'd been pursuing her for weeks. Of her need for comfort. Pleasure. To be appreciated and taken care of. She'd called James while in the car to say she was coming over, taken the elevator to his eighteenth-floor apartment in Chelsea, and jumped on him as soon as he opened the door.

With a silly smile plastered on his face, he'd welcomed her energy, no questions asked, the two weaving around like snakes on the living room floor. They engaged in raw, carnal foreplay that left chairs overturned and cushions askew and clothes strewn everywhere. The two endured carpet burns on their backs and behinds before Gwendolyn said, "Maybe we can take this to the bedroom?" James looked up, nodded maniacally, and hoisted Gwendolyn up as she wrapped her bare legs around his torso, their kissing slick, hungry.

Being on an actual bed with thousand-count sheets and plush pillows brought things to a whole new level. James placed his head in between Gwendolyn's legs, his wet tongue meeting her own wetness, her moans echoing through the apartment. Their lips touched yet again. She tasted herself on him, ripe, sweet. Like honey. "Is this okay?" he asked once again when he pulled out a condom, waiting for Gwendolyn's consent before putting it on and slowly, gently entering her, his gaze never leaving her face. Deep, deep motion began, James making the loudest, weirdest noises during sex Gwendolyn had ever heard, a cross between a husky in heat and a beagle who needed to be let outside. But even with the canine sounds, oh, how glorious the connection was. The unyielding care and devotion to her body he displayed, eyes locked, sweat on sweat, kiss after kiss on skin.

Late into the night, Gwendolyn lay in James's bed, newly energized, watching him walk into the bathroom. The silly smile was back on his face. She took in his smooth, glistening nakedness, his lithe limbs, his tight backside. She could go another round. And another. *This is what I've been missing*, she realized. Sadness sank into her bones.

James settled back into bed and held her close. "I put aside an extra towel and washcloth," he said. "And toothbrush… I know you have stuff to do tomorrow, but you can spend the night if you want. I hope you will."

Gwendolyn felt the tug, knew it would be more sensible to take herself home, but she didn't want to be by herself. Could finally admit she was tired of being by herself after so many years. *I like this*, she thought. *I like him. It's okay.*

She didn't want to let go.

Gwendolyn moved deeper into his arms, the first time she'd spent the night with a man for as long as she could remember.

The next morning, with Gwendolyn not needed at the agency or an event, James ordered croissants and coffee so the two could have a work breakfast. He'd been the consummate gentlemen, providing a steady supply of healthy snacks, even laundering her clothes. Gwendolyn wore his navy-blue robe all day and tried her best not to grab the man for more play. Sublime had looming deadlines after all.

When James slipped away to another room to speak to a client, Gwendolyn surveyed his apartment, a minimalist affair with its industrial-style kitchen unit and beige futon and a large mirror placed right by the door. In some ways similar to her bare-bones aesthetic, though James was way more comfortable with basic IKEA furniture and random keepsakes. He'd framed each of the elementary school crayon scrawls of his nieces, setting the pictures above a desk that sat in the corner of the living room. One of his massive bookshelves contained family photos, his undergrad degree from Howard, and snow globes representing different locales. *The places he's traveled?* she wondered. He even had a few action figures in military uniforms standing next to miniature vehicles. *G.I. Joes?*

After finishing his call, James noticed Gwendolyn taking in his place. He gestured to the shelves. "My work can be intense, so with some of my stuff I like to remind myself not to take everything so seriously, you know? Remember to have fun."

As evening descended and Gwendolyn got ready to leave, she explained that the next few days would be insane as she prepared for Sublime's big fashion show at the Brooklyn Museum. "Will you be my guest?" she asked. James immediately hopped up and down, threw up his arms, and performed a bootie dance.

"I'll take that as a yes," Gwendolyn said, and gave him a kiss before she headed home. *Maybe this can actually work*, she thought as she rode the subway. The prospect of having someone she cared about at one of her events, comforting. A possibility she hadn't imagined.

* * *

Gwendolyn snapped out of her mind fog and hooked a right into Faith's, the local café that made the most delicious coffee she'd ever had. Faith's walls were lovely to behold, the space doubling as a gallery for local artists. New work had been hung up since her last visit, a series of portraits that collaged acrylic hues with photos of people in languid poses.

An elderly man stood at the counter, his frame hunched over a metal cane. The barista on duty had turned around to prep an order. Seconds later, a slim dude sporting a baseball cap and shades got in line behind Gwendolyn. He reeked of weed. She stepped slightly away to avoid his smell seeping into her hair and suit and took in the medium-sized canvas where a large brown woman in a sheer black dress reclined on a stone bench. Her long, curly locs were interwoven in a forest of golden leaves and sunflowers surrounded by a swarm of bees.

Gwendolyn realized that she'd seen this image before, on a postcard she'd picked up during her last visit. The colors and textures were so inviting, so reminiscent of her hidden place, that she'd felt compelled to visit Faith's when she'd glanced at the card resting on her kitchen counter last night. In the café, she stepped closer to the art as she caressed the petals of her ring. In the painting, letters flowed along the woman's hair in a florid script that spelled out *A Curlicued Canvas*. Gwendolyn's gaze drifted down to the righthand corner of the canvas, where she saw a signature... ARTURO VASQUEZ.

The man in front of Gwendolyn moved away from the counter and she stepped forward, recognizing the barista who'd started about a month ago, a guy with glasses, olive skin, and cascading hair that grazed his shoulders. Today he looked good in a form-fitting pine-green T-shirt, pecs and shoulders on display, and baggy striped pants. The barista noticed Gwendolyn and his face lit up.

She spotted the barista's slim nose ring—a hoop—and his employee nametag, which read…ARTURO.

"Wait, are you… You're the one who did this." Gwendolyn gestured to the canvas behind her.

He nodded, his curls shining in the overhead light. "You noticed. Wow," Arturo said. His voice had a sing-song quality. She heard an accent. "I told Faith when I started working here that I'm an artist, maybe I could exhibit some pieces. The person scheduled to show their stuff this month canceled last minute, so I jumped in, got the slot. We're having a special reception this coming Tuesday. Postcards for the event are by the door." He leaned forward and extended his hand.

"I'm Arturo. Arturo Vasquez, but guess you know that," he said, releasing a gigantic smile that revealed a large gap in his front teeth.

"I'm Gwendolyn. Great to meet you," she said as she shook his hand. "And yes, I grabbed a card the other day." Arturo's nails were covered in black polish. A small lion's head ring rested on his index finger.

"So whattya think?" he asked.

"Oh, I think it's great how well you take care of your hands considering you paint."

Arturo frowned, looked at his palms, and smiled again. "Noooooooo, I mean, whattya think of the art?"

"Oh, apologies," Gwendolyn said. Heat rushed to her cheeks. She veered into professional mode. "I like. *Absolutely* impressive. Amazing colors, textures, interesting collage technique…saw some chiaroscuro in a couple of pieces. Gotten any sales?"

"Actually, yeah, this one in the back. You mentioned collage. I did something a lil different and—"

Someone cleared their throat, loudly. Gwendolyn turned around to see Weedhead scowling, his chapped lips bent. "Yo, lady, I got somewhere to be," he said. "Chitchat with Pedro Pascal Jr. here another time."

Arturo locked eyes with Gwendolyn, just for a second, before he jutted his chin toward the man. "Sir, apologies. I'll be with you shortly."

Gwendolyn remembered she had somewhere to be as well. "Right," she said. "Medium hazelnut coffee with milk, no sugar. To go, please. And congratulations, Arturo."

"Noooooo, congratulations to you, Gwendolyn. Couple people around here say you're some kind of hotshot corporate lady even though you keep it on the QT. I mean, it's not my business, but I can tell how well you're doing for yourself, inspiring others. We need people like you in the community." He placed his hand on his chest. "Coffee's on me."

Gwendolyn pursed her lips, wondering if she needed to do a better job of maintaining a low profile if folks she didn't know were trying to get into her biz. Still, this was fine. Maybe. Arturo's flirting, obvious, harmless compared to the occasional catcalls she got on the street. There was something about him besides his good looks. A warmth. Visceral, easygoing. But it wasn't like she'd go on a date with him even though she and James weren't exclusive. A guy like Arturo? Too artsy, probably living with his parents, getting thirsty gals to undress and pose for him all the time amid moist foliage. Nope, not for her.

Another barista rushed in from the back and went behind the counter, preparing her order. Gwendolyn scooped up the beverage and gave Arturo a small wave of thanks. "I'm here every Thursday and Friday," he said. "And remember, this coming Tuesday, the reception."

"Appreciate the invite," Gwendolyn replied. She made her way to the exit right as Weedhead sent her another scowl that screamed *uppity bitch*. She barely resisted the urge to turn around and shout, "You stink!"

A black sedan was waiting for her outside. 8:05, right on time.

"Morning, Ms. Montgomery," Bo said as he opened the backseat door.

Bo was Gwendolyn's occasional weekend driver, going out of his way to sync his schedule with hers as much as he could. Gwendolyn refused to deal with the subway any time she had a milestone event, the squeaking rats on the tracks more than she could bear when she needed to be sharp and focused. So she splurged on a car service, never charging the additional expense to the agency. She'd texted Bo the previous night with the location of her morning pickup, knowing she would stop by Faith's. A former firefighter from Hoboken who wore his light brown hair in a buzz cut, the buffed man was always punctual.

"Morning, Bo," she said. "You good?" He nodded and gave her a thumbs-up, his grin gigantic. Gwendolyn took a seat, coffee in the backseat's cup holder, vintage purse on the side, phone in hand as she checked her texts and emails. Jessica was at the museum, making it her business to always be on-site when it came to big Sublime events. Their two stars were already there as well. Veronykah had finished soundcheck with her band and was now conducting the incense-lighting ritual she needed to get her personal aura right pre-performance. (Convincing museum administrators that the singer wouldn't be violating their fire codes? A long, quiet hell.) Gwendolyn had spent the previous night with LaMarque and his models, the manic fashion designer running through his show for the umpteenth time, his operatic voice booming through the halls.

Gwendolyn opened her work account only to see LaMarque's latest eight-paragraph email of concerns. *Okay, okay...breathe*, she reminded herself as the acrylic painting she'd been staring at floated in her mind. She suddenly imagined Arturo with his nice hands and tight tee and shiny nose ring reclining across from her in the sedan's backseat, pants rolled up, beverage in hand, discussing the merits of acrylic collage while bees buzzed overhead. She blinked the vision away, cheeks flushed.

They drove from Harlem to Crown Heights under overcast skies as Gwendolyn continued to check emails. Within thirty minutes of leaving

Faith's, the awning of the Brooklyn Museum loomed overhead, the interior lobby's floating brick arches a familiar sight. Museum staff dashed about as Gwendolyn scanned the area to make sure everything and everyone was perfect. A bright neon sign on an upper wall gave off a glow, the phrase SONG OF WINTER SKIES encircled by lavender irises and primrose.

Gwendolyn spotted James entering the lobby in a slender sky-blue suit with a white boutonniere that matched his shirt. He cradled a bouquet of white and yellow violas in the crook of his arm.

"Oh, James." She dashed over as he saw her and dramatically presented the bouquet. "You didn't have to do this… Thank you." She leaned into his chest, the brief snuggle time wonderful. She'd missed him.

"My pleasure. Nice to see you, lady."

Gwendolyn gestured to a pair of front-row seats. "I'm going to do a walkthrough," she said. "Sit, relax, chat up some of the other guests. I'll join you soon." Moments later, her heels clacked through the lobby as she inspected the runway and adjoining stage with an assortment of instruments, the band no doubt hanging with Veronykah in the back. Staff and crew were in position to guide the crowd. Scores of people filed in…fashion reporters, influencers, stylists, celeb performers. Some folks sported flowers in their hair or on lapels while wearing light-colored clothes, just as their invites had requested.

The band soon took the stage and dived into an assortment of Billie Holiday songs, classics like "You Go to My Head" and "April in Paris." Content that everything was in order, Gwendolyn sat beside James. Jessica stood by the backstage entrance in an aquamarine pantsuit. She gave Gwendolyn a wink and thumbs-up, her unspoken message to her star employee: *You got this. Congratulations, sis.*

A collective murmur filled the space. Clive Sergeant entered the lobby, strutting in front of his bodyguard, the actor in full-on black. Photographers snapped away as he bent low in front of Gwendolyn and kissed her hand before taking a seat one row over. Minutes later, at 9:55, staff members closed the doors. The live band switched from Lady Day to "Sky Kissing," a smoldering slow jam lighting up streaming charts across the country. Veronykah Cahmet, clad in another LaMarque original, stepped onto the circular stage. The singer's beaded gown was drapey, loose. Her makeup glittered. Crystals lined her cheeks. Photographers swiveled toward her, cameras flashing.

Veronykah's melismatic *ooooooooooooooo* filled the lobby. Her alto was wispy, layered with a seventies soul vibe as she wove through her signature song. The room of jaded actors and fashionistas and high-profile execs began buzzing. This was exactly what people had come to expect from Sublime events…really Gwendolyn's events. Something special, indescribable. Still, she was nervous. Goosebumps suddenly appeared on her legs as a slight chill swept through the space.

Black and brown models of all shapes and sizes strutted down the runway one by one, clad in browns and blacks and navies that represented LaMarque's fall/winter collection. The band eased into their next set. A model in a white sweater and long skirt sweeping the ground strode forth, followed by another in a mohair jacket and baggy trousers.

The lights slowly faded. People gasped as they were swathed in darkness and a special blacklight enveloped the lobby. Many radiated a blurry spectral white depending on what they wore.

Veronykah's beaded gardenias and jeweled cheeks reflected the blacklight onto the ceiling, birthing a sea of twinkling stars. Luminous rays of gold and jade and lavender swept the crowd. Some photographers adjusted their camera settings and snapped away. Influencers had their phones up, video lights on.

The show with its surprise special effects was going exactly as planned. Gwendolyn sighed in relief even as she pulled her jacket tight around her body, the chill in the air palpable. *Has the museum turned on the AC?* she wondered.

More winter symbols were projected onto the ceiling—a snowy owl, a fox, a wolf, snowdrops and pansies—all rendered in impressionistic designs sewn onto pieces of the collection. The figures sparkled, taking Gwendolyn's breath away, as if they'd come to life. She saw *Vogue* blurbs floating in her mind: "exceptional…" "an effervescent, elegant spectacle…" "LaMarque has arrived!" This would be a professional milestone, the designer celebrating the natural world at a show presenting his fall/winter collection. Gwendolyn's idea. Black and brown folks were often showcased in summery fashion campaigns, she'd argued, but why not honor our right to inhabit all seasons?

Gwendolyn's phone vibrated in her skirt pocket. Media hits were coming in, she was sure, notes of praise from people tuning in to the live broadcast. But more importantly, offers to hold meetings, to shore up branding deals for LaMarque and Veronykah. Potential clients peeping the show would soon be reaching out, asking for opportunities to work together. New income was on the horizon. Sublime would be okay, financial woes over.

*Yes.*

James took Gwendolyn's hand and gently squeezed her fingers. She glanced over, saw tears streaming down his face as he gazed upon what she'd created. Confirmation that she'd brought awe and grace to others with her work.

*Yes.*

Gwendolyn felt rejuvenated, able to breathe for the first time in days. Energy pulsing beneath her skin, energy she pushed down by instinct. She could refocus, enjoy the show. Exult in her agency's future success, exult in being with her man.

As the models walked out, craggy red streaks appeared at the runway entrance, flowing onto the floor. Some sort of paint.

Gwendolyn let go of James's hand. This effect wasn't in the production doc.

More crimson paint flanked the runway, as if being poured onto the platform.

"What's going on?" James whispered.

She gave a tiny shrug, mouthing, *I don't know.*

Gwendolyn smelled something. The faint odor of copper.

The models continued their walk, undeterred. One model slipped on the paint and fell to the ground, letting out a tiny shriek as her feet were swept out from beneath her.

Gwendolyn jumped from her seat and dashed to the runway. "Are you okay?" she asked as she leaned over the platform and reached out for the young woman.

A second model fell, pulling down another. And then another.

*No*, Gwendolyn thought. Veronykah kept singing but looked over with a question in her eyes. *Should we stop?*

The special blacklight filling the lobby was too dim for Gwendolyn to discern what was happening. She pivoted from the runway and ran to the control booth, discreetly positioned behind the coat check. The technician responsible for the show's effects was still as a rock, dumbfounded.

"Turn on the lights!" she shouted as she grabbed him by the arm, the air now so cold that her breath had begun to mist. The man glared briefly at Gwendolyn and flipped two buttons on his console. The entire museum flooded with light.

Gwendolyn's heart pounded. She could see. Everyone could see.

Veronykah stopped singing. The musicians stopped playing.

A statuesque man with long platinum hair in a flowy pantsuit rushed onto the runway from backstage and bent down to assist a fallen model. LaMarque, his face crushed.

Gwendolyn was just as horrified. The show, a catastrophe. The runway... the walls... the models... all covered in scarlet paint.

No, that wasn't right. Not paint.

Blood.

The metallic scent in the air should have told Gwendolyn all she needed to know. The same scent that had permeated morning dreams.

She blinked, looked down. Her linen suit, splattered.

Gwendolyn fought a wave of nausea. A multitude of sounds filled her ears as she absorbed everything around her. LaMarque was onstage cursing, the blood-soaked models in tears. Jessica leapt onto the runway to help.

Veronykah's jaw scraped the stage.

Clive ran toward the museum's exit, bodyguard in tow.

James was frozen in his chair, head buried in his chest.

Thick, streaking crimson... everywhere. Cold numbing Gwendolyn's fingers.

Something appeared on the back wall of the runway. Smeared, dripping. Hard to read.

She squinted.

It was in Spanish. Letters large and jagged. Grotesque.

TRAIDORA

*Traitor.*

## CHAPTER TWO
# LA PLAYA

"Your husband doesn't want to move on."

Fonsi took a deep breath and suppressed a yawn, lamenting that he hadn't run outside earlier in the afternoon to get a coffee. His client's vanilla-scented perfume tickled his nose as they sat in the small room located at the back of his shop. "He's concerned…about you," he added. "He doesn't want you to be alone."

Mrs. Johnson sat on a large wooden chair underneath a bright bulb. The woman's eyes brimmed with tears. Her mouth, a flat, grim line.

"I…I know what you're saying," she said. "My kids, they grown but they been coming by to check in on me, telling me I can stay with them now. But I just want to be alone, sit with my memories of Chester. I ain't ready to move on either." She squeezed Fonsi's hands, which she'd held on to as soon as she'd sat down.

Fonsi used to be taken aback when his clients took his hands during sessions in the backroom of his botanica. He thought that they didn't grasp how these appointments worked, that they'd watched too many films depicting séances where people talked to the dead while surrounded by ancient artifacts, palms clenched together in a chain of magic. There was some truth to this, but Fonsi had never needed to link hands with anyone to do basic medium work, didn't need any of that additional woo-hah that came from the fakes. He simply needed an object that the dearly departed had used on the regular, that held sentimental value.

Over time, Fonsi realized that most of his clients understood exactly how his gift worked, especially since he overexplained everything. (He was getting better with that.) They took his hand because they needed the support, to feel grounded. Because they perceived him as someone who wouldn't reject their overtures of intimacy. And they were right. Fonsi had learned long ago how to place others' needs before his own.

Ever since he'd taken over La Playa Espiritu, a botanica that catered to a range of spiritual beliefs, word had slowly spread around the neighborhood that there was this really chill dude who could low-key communicate with the dead, taking on cases for people who thought they'd encountered ghosts. Fonsi had warned his clients that what he did had to remain a secret even though he knew some people would talk. All good. The whispers about his work were just enough so that the gossip could remain unsubstantiated and his status as a Guardián hidden, which took precedence over everything else. He could earn extra dough, help folks out, and give them peace of mind without revealing who and what he really was.

Irma Johnson hadn't seemed interested in any of the hocus-pocus kept behind closed doors. The stout gray-haired woman who lived two blocks over had visited the botanica now and then for years, purchasing the occasional scented candle or bottle of Florida water. But when she'd come in a couple of weeks ago with that droop to her shoulders and eyes that Fonsi had recognized in so many of his clients, he knew what she was going to ask him—to make contact with someone who'd passed on. The hard-working man Mrs. Johnson had been married to for more than thirty-five years had unexpectedly succumbed to a stroke.

During their first meeting, Fonsi informed Mrs. Johnson that he needed access to some of her husband's prized possessions, that she could bring him pictures if she liked, though it was probably better for him to inspect Mr. Johnson's things in person. "Come on over in the morning," she replied. "Before you open the shop. I'll make you breakfast."

The next day, Fonsi tried to be as courteous as possible as he entered Mrs. Johnson's modest apartment, acutely aware of her grief. Yet as soon as he walked in, he felt it, a slight pressure forming in his head.

Mrs. Johnson had been kind enough to gather several of her husband's things and place them on a large wooden table. A signed poster of James Brown marking his first appearance at the Apollo. The pair of beat-up brown oxford shoes that Mr. Johnson refused to throw away. And an array of power tools... drills, a grinder, and a few other items that Fonsi had no hope of identifying. Mrs. Johnson explained that her husband had been a foreman for various construction sites around the city, beyond proud of his work.

Fonsi surveyed the materials for a moment and declared, "That's what I need." He pointed to the frayed plaid handkerchief that, he came to find out, Mr. Johnson had carried with him for more than a decade. The cloth gave off a buzz, a gentle ringing in Fonsi's ears. He called the sensation his Spirit Sense, in honor of Peter Parker and Miles Morales, his favorite arachnid superheroes. The sound in Fonsi's head was kicking in hardcore as he held the hanky, the way it always did whenever he came across objects to which ghosts tethered themselves. Fonsi had gotten so good with his gift that he could sometimes detect spectral energy from a photo. Being up close and personal with the handkerchief, that was it, he was sure.

Fonsi clutched the cloth, displaying a reverence for the item that would help him forge connection. (He also hoped the grieving woman possessed enough sense to throw the presumably snot-infested thing into the wash before placing it on the table. Just last week, he'd put up with a client who'd brought over soiled panties for a reading.) Fonsi usually needed time with a memento, to let someone's energy seep into his consciousness so he could dream and crystallize messages from El Intermedio, the ethereal limbo that harbored ghosts not ready for true death.

When Fonsi's gift had appeared when he was a teenager, he learned he was a medium who could send his spirit from his body to El Intermedio as he slept. The experience was frightening at first, but he gradually grew more comfortable with his sleep-trips. How his dream self felt weird and weightless. How the walls and trees and clouds he observed seemed solid at first, but upon closer inspection had a wispy quality. Like an illusion slowly falling apart.

And then there were the souls of the dead, spirits who could look like anything depending on their state of mind. Most ghosts Fonsi met when he sleep-tripped closely resembled their appearance at the time of their passing, but others looked off the damn wall, especially those who'd died from terrible circumstances. He tried to be discerning with the type of work he took on. Instances where people were actually possessed by the departed, he would leave to other, older Guardianes and priests who had far more experience with that sort of thing.

But even with his choosiness, Fonsi still stumbled onto disturbing cases. He'd once communicated with a deranged apparition whose bloodshot eyeballs ping-ponged from their sockets into his scarred hands; Fonsi realized after their chat that the man, who'd tethered himself to a kitchen apron, had been tortured with a butcher's knife before his murder. Another ghost he met, who'd tethered herself to a copy of Toni Morrison's novel *Sula*, had stretched her body to gruesome lengths. Her spaghetti-like fingers and legs dragged behind her as she wailed about being so obligated to family that she never pursued her dreams as an author before dropping dead from a heart attack. And then there was the ghost who'd gone way too far with plastic surgery, haunting her Upper West Side surgeon after latching on to one of his scalpels. When Fonsi met her in El Intermedio, her shoulders and breasts and booty were way bigger than the size of her head and waist and legs. Body dysmorphia, ghost style.

He sleep-tripped with all of these spirits and more, in constant communication with those they'd left behind on the other side who sensed their presence. An intermediary who focused on dialogue, understanding, care... what the dead needed so they could find peace and let go. But Fonsi couldn't help everyone. On each visit to El Intermedio, he noticed spirits swirling around with no anchor to the real world but who still refused to accept true death and join the ancestors, who for eons inhabited the thick, murky crimson of limbo as wraithlike things. Spirits who were twisted, hurting. A shadow of who they were.

Thankfully Chester Johnson was far from a tortured soul. When Fonsi had approached Mr. Johnson in his dreams, the old man was sitting on a fluffed purple throne in front of a massive open-air wooden shed full of tools, the day bright, clear. The tools were so clean and spotless that they glistened, the shed aglow from their shine. Mr. Johnson was putting all his energy into maintaining the illusion for their visit, clearly having gotten into the swing of things with how El Intermedio worked, how the dead could shape small portions of the realm based on memories held in their hearts. Fonsi spotted several other apparitions swirling about on the far horizon, keeping their distance, preoccupied with their own affairs. Mr. Johnson paid them no mind.

"It's good to meet you, fella," the elderly man said. "Had a feeling somebody would be coming soon from the other side."

"It's really good to meet you as well, er, Mr. Johnson," Fonsi said, always somewhat awkward when meeting a spirit for the first time. "I hope you don't mind me taking up a bit of your time. I'm here on behalf of Irma." He kept his distance as he spoke. The couple of times Fonsi's spirit form had touched a ghost felt horrible.

"Ah, Irma, my beautiful, beautiful girl," Mr. Johnson said. The old man spoke at length, as if catching up with an old friend. He knew his wife was in pain, still wanted to keep him close. And so allowing himself to enter true death? Off the table, wasn't going to happen.

After a while, Mr. Johnson drew closer. "I ain't no expert, just got here and all," the dead man whispered. "But something about this limbo place feels off. Like something ain't right." He crossed his arms. "Don't matter. I ain't leaving Irma. I'll stick around long as I can."

Fonsi was confused about what Mr. Johnson meant but knew his time with the spirit was up, could feel himself being pulled back to his body. Staying in El Intermedio for long periods of time was beyond him, though he'd constantly pushed himself to get better, to go from a few seconds of vague impressions when he was younger to communicating with the dead for minutes at a time. His cousin Giselda had been his biggest inspiration to be great with his gift.

"Mr. Johnson, before I leave," Fonsi spat out as he was about to be tugged away. "Why the hanky?"

The old man reclined in his throne, looked up at the cloudless sky. "The kerchief's what I used to wipe away my tears at the hospital, when I knew I'd be leaving Irma."

And then he was gone.

Now, sitting in front of Mrs. Johnson in his backroom, Fonsi hesitated, not sure how much he should share with his grieving client. But he really liked Mrs. Johnson, had faith she could be strong. And he was cognizant of the time as he glanced at his cellphone on the bench next to him. Fonsi had another appointment, an extremely important appointment. He needed to leave soon.

"Your husband's not suffering," Fonsi said, picking up the pace of his words, annoyance creeping into his bones. He felt guilt over harboring negative feelings with a client as cool as Mrs. Johnson. "To be honest with you, those who've passed, they often remain with us because they're hurting so much, because they're troubled by something horrible that happened before they died. It's kind of one-sided to say that people who're alive are the ones being haunted by folks who've gone. Ghosts are actually *way* more haunted by all the things they've left unresolved. But I don't think that explains what's going on with Mr. Johnson. Your husband, he's an exception."

Tears streamed down the old woman's face. She looked down at the table.

"He's not in pain," Fonsi continued. "He was fine with passing on. It's just... He feels like he should linger in the home you shared until you're ready to let him go. *Really* ready. I think where he's at now, he can hold on for a bit. He seems strong, but if he holds on for too long... Well, it could change him. In a not-so-great way." Fonsi paused. "I know this is difficult to hear."

Mrs. Johnson met his gaze. "So when I let go of Chester, that's when he'll be able to move on? That's when he'll get his peace?"

"Yes."

Mrs. Johnson stood up, smoothed down the orange cardigan she wore over a cotton seashell-print dress. "Then I guess I have work to do," she whispered. "Chester was one of the most loving men God put on this earth. I'm not surprised, him still doing right by me even from the grave." She looked directly at Fonsi. "But I'm a grown-ass woman. After all he put up with when he was alive, my baby needs his rest."

Fonsi had nothing more to say.

A couple of minutes later, he placed his denim knapsack on his shoulder and walked Mrs. Johnson to the shop's exit. "Thank you so much," she said. "If you'd like, I can leave a little extra something for you next time I stop by. Just waiting for my pension check."

He shook his head. "All good, Mrs. Johnson, keep your money." Irma Johnson was seventy-one years old, a retired MTA worker who was a beloved elder of the community. Even with a struggling business, Fonsi never charged clients over sixty-five for medium work unless they were swimming in cash. "I'm just happy you trusted your gut and came to me. I know you're a church lady."

"Honey, just cuz my behind loves Jesus doesn't mean I don't have sense. I can feel Chester all up in our place. Living with someone all those years, you know when they're around. And far as I'm concerned, you're doing God's work here, just calling it a different name." She leaned over and gently tugged Fonsi's beard. "But really, try and be good to yourself. Don't let life get you down. You're a beautiful young man."

"Er... I won't, Mrs. Johnson. Have a good night." He again felt a surge of annoyance, though he also appreciated her genuine kindness. Most of his clients were far too caught up in personal drama to give two kicks about how Fonsi was doing. A harsh reality that came with his line of work.

Door chimes rang as the old woman left the botanica. He understood what she was implying about his appearance. For weeks now folks in the neighborhood had been concerned, how the quiet botanica cutie pie who could maybe talk to spirits, who'd mostly sported fresh fade haircuts and trimmed goatees for years, had suddenly started to walk around like a mountain man who'd set up a tent in Roberto Clemente Park. Fonsi's uncombed afro had gone beyond retro dimensions, accompanied by a thick beard that engulfed his neck and shoulders. Body hair sprouted from his arms and chest. Ungroomed, uncoordinated. Not the Fonsi they knew. His boy Tariq had declared that the look was bad for business, that customers, after being lured in by bright wooden walls and rows of rainbow-colored candles and vibrant statuettes of orishas and saints, were then scared away by the second coming of Captain Caveman glowering at them from a register.

Fonsi flipped the shop's sign to CLOSED and stepped outside, the yellow awning with the words LA PLAYA ESPIRITU emblazoned overhead. Robyn stood to his left, headphones on, yellow and green beads over a white tee, the kid no doubt bopping to some house music track as they whipped around the store's water hose to clean the shop's sidewalk. Fonsi had practically been a one-person operation for the entire time he'd taken over La Playa, often close to burnout. So he'd been relieved when this Dominican student who grew up around the corner, who considered themself a devotee of Catholicism and Santeria, had declared they needed some extra cash and would be down to work a few nights and weekends while taking classes at Bronx Community. The hire was a strain, as Fonsi had never experienced financial windfall, but he made it work. And he was grateful for the quality of Robyn's work, how they went the extra mile, even creating new window displays every week that captured the eye. Right now, a mermaid statuette of Yemaya, the mother orisha of oceans, and a porcelain figurine of her alter ego, the Virgin Mary, were occupying the window with cue cards explaining their spiritual relationship.

Robyn and Fonsi were on the same page, envisioning La Playa as a place that could combine old-school spiritual traditions with modern ideas around health and wellness. Centering the experiences of the Black Diaspora and Latinidad, always. Bringing Robyn on board, one of the best decisions Fonsi ever made, though he sometimes experienced moments of guilt not clueing them in that he was a medium. Robyn, of course, was quick to notice all the clients who went to the store's backroom—standard stuff for some botanicas, really—but never pressed their boss for more information. A surprise considering the kid's gift for gab and devotion to increasing store revenue at all costs.

"You good, Jefe?" Robyn asked after they took out one of their earbuds and gave Fonsi a pound. "I know it's Thursday, see you making moves."

"I'm good," Fonsi replied. He'd never told Robyn why for the past two months, every Thursday he left the shop promptly at 7:45. Nor did he reveal why he took off the following morning. From the kid's smirk, he could've sworn that Robyn was able to read his mind. Which was technically impossible, but considering Fonsi's gifts...

"And you're set to open the shop, right?" he asked. "Stay through the afternoon? I've updated the morning's TDL on the La Playa shared drive. I left the laptop open in the back, but I can print it out if you want, or download..."

"Yep, yep, I know, I know, I already put the list on my phone. See you. Y, Jefe, puhleeeze, get yourself a cut. Ve a la barbería, pronto."

In their part of the 'hood, unless you were struggling and had no one to hook up your 'do for free or were simply strung out, one never, ever walked outside looking disheveled. Robyn prided themself on getting a sharp cut once a week, though Fonsi had initially been mortified to discover the latest letter design his employee had etched onto the back of their head... LA PLAYA, 4 ALL UR SPIRITUAL NEEDS... with the store's website appearing under the slogan. Fonsi debated taking a pair of clippers and getting rid of the tacky ad himself until he noticed that foot traffic into the store had significantly increased over the past few days. One lady even mentioned that she saw a kid bopping down Grand Concourse with LA PLAYA on the back of their head and thought she should check the shop out. Robyn Guerrera del Rivero, the enterprising spirit Fonsi hadn't realized he needed.

Fonsi waved Robyn's words away as he left the shop, their standard goodbye. He let out a big yawn as he walked down 150th Street, no longer feeling the need to hide his tiredness. He wished he felt more energized for what he had planned for the evening, but it couldn't be helped, not when he'd been seeing two or three backroom clients per day for the past month with no days off. Like clockwork, every year, between Mardi Gras and Easter, requests to communicate with the dead increased significantly. Most would assume that he'd be busiest on macabre holidays like Halloween or Día de los Muertos. But Fonsi's peak time was now, with the spring equinox just a week away, when day and night were of equal duration, the barrier between realms most permeable. And for some reason, there was more ghostly activity happening now than what he remembered from previous years. The extra cash was nice, but he needed time off. Sending his soul from his body to sleep-trip on the regular meant a full-night's rest was elusive, that he was walking around like a zombie.

Clouds covered much of the evening sky. He soon turned north, making quick work of the dozen blocks taking him to the old tenement on 162nd where he rented a studio. Right as he was about to cross the street and reach his building, his phone buzzed.

*Thinking of you. Missing you. I know we're taking a break but hope we can connect soon, Fons. We're grown-ups, we'll figure this out.* ♡♡♡♡♡ *you so much.*

Fonsi tucked the phone back in his pocket. Raphael had been reaching out for a good two weeks now, undeterred by Fonsi's lack of a response. The text perfectly showcased how his ex tended to get his way by wearing folks down with an entitled charm, his self-proclaimed truth becoming everyone else's truth. Fonsi wasn't taking a break. He'd declared to Raphael that they were over, done, kaput. Raphael left him alone for a minute, probably licking his wounds, but had now come roaring back. Which was surprising.

Fonsi shook his head. He wasn't going to let Raphael get to him, not tonight.

He entered his apartment, solemnly placed his hands to his lips, and bowed to his altar, a modest affair that displayed statuettes of the seven main orishas that he'd carved from wood years ago, with a framed photo of his mother nestled between the deities Elegua and Yemaya. Fonsi had put his sculpting talents to use by creating statuettes for La Playa as well, the figures always selling out within days. His way of convincing himself that his time at art school hadn't been a waste.

Fonsi took a quick shower and oiled his body with his favorite shea butter–lavender mix sold at the shop. He hung the damp towel on a huge wicker chair next to his desk, flipped open his Mac, and scrolled to the twelve-hour playlist dubbed "Never Ordinary" that began with Sade's *Love Deluxe*. He clicked play. The eerie synths of "Cherish the Day" filled the apartment.

He crept onto the bed, turned around, and lay on his back, ready, naked, sleepiness gone. He was trying to relax, to ignore the nervousness that crept into his frame whenever he waited for the ghost who'd once written his name on a bathroom mirror... Amede.

A red wooden cube sat on a low table in front of Fonsi's bed, perfectly in line with his legs. The box featured two intersecting lines embedded with calligraphy, the symbol of Papa Legba, the Vodou deity of the crossroads. A memento of Fonsi's trip with Raphael to a part of the Dominican Republic bordering Haiti, one of many trips the two had taken during their whirlwind romance.

The steady beat of "Bullet Proof Soul" drifted into the room as Fonsi experienced delectable presence. A warm fullness in his throat. Gentle strokes along his chest and arms and thighs. Tickles on his forehead and neck. Amede saying hey.

According to Guardián lore, the dead craved texture, to be reunited with the physical world. Hairy, curly terrain preferable over smooth skin any day. Fonsi's forest of curls served as antennae, an enticing playground for contact. So many mystics were considered sloppy, with their uncombed tresses and unshaven crotches and flouncy outfits. But a medium's mission was to make connection, provide connection any way they could with what they had, including their bodies. And so it went: on another Thursday night, the foreign presence who'd stowed away tethered to a box found deep pleasure in his new boo.

Fonsi spread his legs and arched his back as he felt Amede around him, chilled pinpricks followed by intense heat that left him breathless. He opened his mouth and stuck out his tongue, splayed his fingers and toes…anything to make himself big and wide and deep. Anything to receive as much of Amede as he could.

He exulted in the sweat that swathed his body, in his cries of pleasure. Fonsi lost all sense of time just as he had before with his ghost, surrendering completely to the sensations enveloping the crevices of his neck and the outer lines of his torso and the backs of his knees as Amede entered him. His rectum, loose, tight. His nipples, hard, erect. He saw the faint outlines of a long, narrow face. Head bald. Lips full. Fonsi too swept away to know if what he saw was real or…something else.

Hours later, he lay curled up on the cold wooden floor, spent after nonstop lovemaking. Morning's dimness peeked through the blinds. Amede would soon return to El Intermedio, where the disembodied dwelled when they didn't anchor themselves to the human world via mediums or mementos. The spirit would need another week to replenish his power and manifest again. But for now he lingered, akin to a cool breeze.

Fonsi repeated "thank you" over and over and placed his palm over his heart, his farewell ritual for his horny ghost. He continued to feel Amede all around him. A light dampness on the tops of his toes. Amede kissing his feet? A roughness on the left side of his face. Amede's palm, calloused, even as a ghost? He couldn't be sure.

Shame swirled through Fonsi's body yet again when he thought about their time together. He wasn't ready to grapple with the repercussions of what he was doing, of brazenly encouraging a spirit to make contact solely for pleasure. Guardianes were supposed to safeguard the barriers between realms, to help the dead find peace so they could leave the living alone. To actively court a spirit, and into one's bed no less...forbidden. But Fonsi was tired of being treated like trash by the Raphaels of the world, of trying to make himself desirable for flesh-and-blood men who viewed him as a disposable thing. This connection was all his, a private paradise.

He rose slowly, finding his balance as he walked to the window and peered through the blinds. Thick gray clouds filled the sky. After a moment, he turned to go pee and noticed condensation had formed on the bathroom mirror.

He hadn't been in the bathroom for hours. The steam from the previous night's shower had dissipated long ago.

Fonsi looked more closely at the mirror and jumped back. The condensation...another message. The text was easy to understand, letters puffy and thick.

*Beware*

CHAPTER THREE

# CRUEL REFLECTION

"Just so we're clear, Detective, to pull this off someone would've had to bypass security and support staff, make their way backstage, transport a significant amount of..." Gwendolyn glanced over at the dirty runway. "...of whatever this is, and leave the museum unnoticed?"

Grimacing, all Gwendolyn wanted to do was hop onto the raised platform with a gigantic mop, rubber gloves, and buckets of soapy water and wipe away the gruesome sight. But that would be tampering with evidence.

Detective Zachensky shrugged, his argyle sweater partially covered by a brown vinyl jacket. "Ms. Montgomery, none of the models or support staff reported anything suspicious, even though a few people commented on how cold it'd gotten with the AC. To be honest with you, a perpetrator could've easily fled the museum unnoticed. The lobby was dark, folks were distracted. Easy to create havoc."

Gwendolyn nodded. "Right. You're right."

She clasped her hands tightly, ring pressed into flesh as she tried her best to ignore the runway and keep herself from trembling even though the lobby was no longer cold. James had draped one of LaMarque's cream mohair cardigans over Gwendolyn's blazer, each of its sleeves silhouetted with butterflies. So thoughtful. And then of course she'd chased him away.

"I'm sorry, but maybe you should leave," Gwendolyn said after she'd surveyed the disaster that had become LaMarque's show, police on their way. Her tone, curt. "I need to sort through this mess, no distractions. You understand, right?"

"Right," James replied. "Yeah, I'll...I'll, um...I'll call you." He gave a tiny wave, standing there, unsure if he should lean in for a hug or kiss. Gwendolyn steeled her heart, ignored his stricken puppy dog face and how his shoulders slumped. *I'll make it up to him*, she told herself as she gave him a peck on the cheek and walked away so she could consult with staff.

A museum manager escorted the first wave of police into the building while security ushered guests outside. An ambulance soon arrived, with one poor model who'd twisted his ankle being ferried out on a stretcher by paramedics. Minutes later, LaMarque stomped through the lobby with the racks of clothes his staff wheeled forward. "Motherfucka, either arrest me or get the hell up outta my face!" he said when Detective Zachensky asked him to stay on-site. The designer then gave Gwendolyn the evil eye, flipped his blond weave, and stormed out to the vans that would cart his creations away. More than two dozen couture ensembles, ruined.

Once guests had been escorted off the premises, Zachensky requested that Gwendolyn, Jessica, the musicians, and select staff remain behind for questioning and to walk his team through the scene. Uniformed officers had searched the lobby area, the runway cordoned off by yellow tape. A department photographer was busy snapping away. Cops were also inspecting the building's upper levels just in case the perpetrator had attempted to hide upstairs. Thankfully the letters Gwendolyn thought she'd spotted on the wall were gone.

"The bigger mystery for me has to do with logistics," Zachensky continued. "Where would someone have gotten all this blood, if that's what this is? A slaughterhouse? They would've needed to have gathered a full tank of the stuff, maybe pump it in from somewhere outside, have a vehicle. And then the logistics of making a clean escape from the museum with no trace... None of the pedestrians we talked to outside mentioned seeing anything suspicious, no conspicuous vehicles. Even had officers check the sewers. Nothing. Real sicko, whoever did this. Smart, sneaky as hell, but *real* fuckin' sicko." Zachensky cleared his throat. "Sorry for the language, Ms. Montgomery. I grew up visiting the museum with my folks. It's disgusting to see it like this."

"No apologies necessary, Detective," Gwendolyn said. "And you mentioned forensics are on their way, correct, to verify this is really..." She gestured at the runway. "...blood?"

"Yeah, we usually have a full house at the precinct so we can get forensic investigators on the scene pronto, but some kinda stomach flu's hit the office. Several people out sick... One of my colleagues just started puking at his desk like one of those vultures who vomit up food to defend themselves. Saw it on a *National Geo* documentary. I mean, poor Joey had just eaten this jalapeño dip..." He held up his hand. "I digress. We managed to get a photographer here but our two remaining investigators are all over the borough handling cases. One's in the Rockaways and another over in East New York. Not that far, but she still needs a minute to get here."

While Jessica was busy talking to museum administrators, Gwendolyn stood in front of the band's stage with the detective. The musicians were sitting on the floor in front of the drums, smoking joints that smelled like Vicks. Oddly, none of the cops seemed to mind the stink or breach of rules considering the circumstances, even though Gwendolyn felt like she might gag. (Weed, the bane of her existence for the morning.)

Mike, the senior manager, had been sending voice memos to the off-site museum director nonstop since they'd started to confer with the police. He spoke a mile a minute, on the verge of tears as he coughed from menthol marijuana. Gwendolyn barely understood the words catapulting out of his mouth, like "updating insurance policies" and "thousands of dollars in damage" and "closed for days" and "creepy as hell" and "*Craaaaaa-aaaaaap!*"

Zachensky scowled at the administrator as if he wanted to slap the man. "Uh, we've taken statements from you and Ms. Uggams," he said, turning back to Gwendolyn. "I don't know if you have more stuff you need to handle with the museum, but far as I'm concerned, you're free to go. We'll be in touch over the next coupla days as we continue the investigation. And if we discover anything major we'll reach out right away, of course. I don't want to say it was an inside job, but I gotta tell you it's hard to see how someone pulled this off without having access to logistics."

Gwendolyn retrieved her card from her purse and handed it to the detective. "Thank you for everything, Mr. Zachensky, including your honesty. If you need me to come in to the station, anything at all from Sublime, don't hesitate to reach out." She needed to sound forceful, clear. "What happened here can't happen again."

Zachensky tapped the card against his chest before placing it in his pocket. "I'm with you. And Ms. Montgomery, though I wish it were under better circumstances, it's a pleasure to meet you. My sister-in-law's an entertainment publicist too, been praising the quality of your agency's events for years. Top-notch, like magic, she says."

"Oh, it's absolutely wonderful to hear that, Detective," Gwendolyn said, words belying the anxiety that blossomed in her chest. She hated being recognized. That *Media Today* profile… What had she been thinking? "And please tell your sister-in-law, colleague to colleague, I appreciate her support." She shook his hand. "Thank you again."

As the detective joined a quartet of officers, Veronykah walked over, having changed into loose-fitting jeans and an off-the-shoulder sweatshirt. Her bejeweled accents, gone.

"I'm so sorry," Gwendolyn said as she embraced the singer, Jessica joining the group. "If the police can't solve the case, I'll hire private investigators. We'll get who did this, I promise."

"Girl, ain't your fault some crazy fool wrecked the show," Veronykah said. She swiveled to her band members. "Guys, this nasty shit y'all puffing smells like sinus medicine... Put it out!" The musicians yanked the joints from their mouths and awkwardly scanned the area, realizing they had nowhere to dump the stubs.

Gwendolyn felt her shoulders relax, grateful for Veronykah's kindness. Even with her eccentricities and pre-performance rituals and tendency to break into song wherever, the vocalist/composer was Sublime's most grounded client by far. Gwendolyn made a mental note to send her flowers as soon as she got back to the office.

"I'm gonna help the boys finish packing up our stuff, then we're outta here," Veronykah said. "I'll text you, 'kay?"

"Great," Gwendolyn said. Through the huge glass entrance, she spotted news vans parked directly outside. She looked down at her blood-splattered suit.

*I'm not talking to the press, not like this.*

"We need to leave through the back," Jessica said to the museum manager, who was self-administering breathing exercises. "Gwen, why don't you..."

"On it," she said. "Texting Bo now, telling him we'll send over coordinates."

Jessica swiveled back to their client. "Gwen and I need to get back to the agency, Veronykah. I know you're not a diva, that you have every right to walk out the front door like a normal person, but as recognizable talent, I'd like for you to exit discreetly. Sublime will issue an official statement to the press about what happened here. And for God's sake, stay off social media. Let's synchronize stories, present a united front."

Veronykah squeezed Jessica's hand. "You got it."

In a few minutes, after having left through the museum's back exit, Gwendolyn and Jessica were standing on Washington Avenue just a few yards away from the entrance to Brooklyn's botanical gardens, waiting for Bo to make his way around. Gwendolyn spied the blossoming trees that graced the entrance, remembering her dreams from the morning. Jessica retrieved her inhaler from her big brown purse and took a deep breath.

"Ohmigoodness, are you okay?" Gwendolyn asked. "Your asthma… With all of this madness, I forgot…"

Jessica waved away the concern. "Just doing my standard dose, nothing to worry about. That was really crazy, huh?" she said. "Crazy and disgusting, just like the detective said. Who'd want to do something like that?"

"It *was* crazy," Gwendolyn said. "And I completely agree with you about how to handle this. When we get back to the office, we should craft an official announcement on behalf of LaMarque and Veronykah about the 'unfortunate, terrifying incident' at the museum. But also emphasizing how 'their combined artistic vision for a beautiful world remains unscathed.' Veronykah will be down for whatever we propose. LaMarque, another story. I'll call him tomorrow, give him time to cool off. And I have that museum manager Mike's intel. We have to figure out if they want to issue a joint release. I can also reach out to…"

"Stop," Jessica said. "Gwen, just… stop. Take a moment. Breathe. Are you all right?"

She blinked. "Of course. Why wouldn't I be?"

Jessica placed her fingers to her left temple, grazing her short afro cut, agitated. "Because what went down in there was disturbing as hell."

Gwendolyn listened, doing her best to breathe as her boss advised, to keep her body from shaking once again, hoping Jessica wouldn't say that she'd seen a bloody message laid out in Spanish.

"I'm fine," Gwendolyn said. "What happened was unfortunate, sure, but we'll fix it. Someone wanted to hurt Sublime by sabotaging a premier event. We need to figure it out, make sure the police get the asshole who did this."

Jessica held up her hand. "Okay, hold up, Gwen, what makes you think this is about the agency? Someone could've easily been targeting the museum...or a guest or client. It's hard to imagine anybody coming after Veronykah, beloved as she is, but you never know the skeletons folks have. And LaMarque has most certainly pissed off tons of people."

"Point taken, but we still need to be proactive, safeguard our assets. Make it clear we'll do what we must to protect our clients."

"Sure. You're right, Gwen, as always," Jessica said with a slight Brooklyn accent. "But take a moment, decompress. You've been busting your ass nonstop over this event. I want you to relax, no obsessing. And our ride's here." Jessica gently elbowed Gwendolyn as she pointed to the black sedan pulling up to the curb. "Bo, babeeeeeee... Good to see you, sir."

The big man jumped out of the car. "Ms. Uggams, yeah, really good to see you, too. Saw cops swarming around outside the museum. One of 'em filled me in on what went down." His eyes turned into saucers at the state of Gwendolyn's clothes. "Oh man, Ms. Montgomery..."

"I'm fine," she said. "I just got covered in gunk from the runway. But I'm not hurt. Really."

"We appreciate you, Bo, always," Jessica said. He opened the sedan door, his eyes still trained on Gwendolyn. She felt too vulnerable, too exposed, as if she were a grubby child. A feeling she detested.

Gwendolyn sat in the back of the sedan and pulled out her phone, ignoring the multitude of emails that had flooded her inbox over the last hour. She popped in her earbuds and visited the website for MCURY News, which specialized in domestic and international coverage. A reporter on live video stood in front of the museum. "Police say they'll release an official statement later, but so far they have no idea who might be behind such a gruesome prank..."

Gwendolyn logged on to social and kept her phone close to her chest so Jessica wouldn't realize she was doomscrolling. She was unsurprised to find that the influencers and fashion reporters who'd been at the show had shared tons of pictures and videos of the bloody runway. Most described an exquisite experience that had gone suddenly, irrevocably wrong. A top influencer with 652K followers had already asked, "How can LaMarque's once pristine brand ever recover?"

Gwendolyn watched in real time as hundreds of likes and reshares popped up across a range of channels. Reel restitches with emojis and avatars floated across her screen, with one video of the slipping and sliding LaMarque models stitched to a clip of Naomi Campbell falling at a Vivienne Westwood show due to outrageously high platform shoes. Another clip showcased a blood-drenched Carrie in her tiara and gown at prom followed by a delighted Wednesday Addams surveying the school dance where sprinklers rained crimson.

*Great.*

In twenty minutes, they'd crossed the Manhattan Bridge and reached Sublime's Soho main office. Gwendolyn bade Bo goodbye and told Jessica she'd be in the office momentarily, that she was going to her gym across the street to clean herself up. Gwendolyn ignored the stares of the front desk workers as she scanned herself in and headed straight downstairs for the women's locker room, which was empty. A mercy. She removed the mohair cardigan, glanced at her reflection in the mirror overlooking a sink, and stopped dead in her tracks.

A bird's nest had replaced the morning's perfectly coifed 'do. Her stained, bedraggled designer suit, the linen that had glowed just hours ago...no words for what it looked like now. She'd been actually walking around in public like this, covered in vile, smelly blood from an animal. Or a person. *This* was what Bo had been glaring at.

Nauseous, Gwendolyn turned away from the mirror, took off her suit and camisole, and dumped them into the trash. After she'd showered and toweled off, she pulled her hair back into a ponytail and put on the spare T-shirt and sweats she kept in her locker. She jogged back over to the office, overcome once again by an urge to fix what was quickly becoming the biggest fiasco of her career. She got in the elevator, swiped her pass, pressed 3, and seconds later walked into the humongous loft that housed Sublime's main operations. Jessica had occupied the space for more than two decades, finagling with the landlords for a deal each time she renewed her lease. A huge studio portrait of Jessica in red lipstick and a wide-legged leopard-print jumpsuit loomed over all. Her décolletage...like whoa. Everything hanging out. "I've earned the right to look sexy as hell in the business *I* built," she proclaimed when Gwendolyn side-eyed her boss after the picture went up. Jessica's ample bosom hovering over her employees' heads? A lawsuit waiting to happen in Gwendolyn's vigilant mind.

A couple of people greeted her with tiny waves from their cubicles. Most had become used to how she entered the loft and made a beeline to Jessica's office. Gwendolyn Montgomery, courteous, respectful, too busy for small talk. Gwendolyn Montgomery, razor sharp, picks up the slack, will do anything for Sublime.

She plopped down on the leather sofa adjacent to Jessica's main desk. The two entered each other's offices at will, their physical ebb and flow central to maintaining the business. No need for formal etiquette when there was nothing to hide. "All right, so I took a gander at what they're posting on the feeds," Gwendolyn said. "I'll start the release, send it over to you for approval in half..."

Jessica shook her head. "No, you're going home." Her voice was warm but authoritative, boss in the room. "I'll have a couple of the associates work on our statement and look it over this afternoon, coordinate things with the museum. And I could tell you were checking out social in the car. Your poker face is atrocious."

"Jessica…"

She took Gwendolyn's hand. Even with her raunchiness, when Jessica was focused, she gave off *I am supreme mother* energy, able to make you feel like she was cradling you in her arms and crooning Vesta Williams's *Women of Brewster Place* theme song while pointing out missteps. She did this with all her employees, but everyone knew she adored Gwendolyn. That she viewed her star senior publicist as the magnificent, capable daughter she wished she'd had.

"I know telling you to chill is like asking you to do a hula dance barefoot with knives on hot coals, Gwen, but relax, for real," Jessica said. "I know what it is to put pressure on yourself until you drop. Ain't worth it, girl. Take a break. A much-deserved break after all this bullshit. I'm worried about you."

Gwendolyn shook her head. "This was my event. I should handle what happened."

"And you will, in that indomitable way of yours. But not today. I know you like to walk around all cute and be Ms. Professional 24/7, but enough's enough. Be easy."

Gwendolyn rose, head held high, eyes trained on the elevator. Indignation rose in her chest. "I'll see you Monday," Gwendolyn murmured. She refused to look at her boss. "I'll be working from home all weekend. Reach out whenever."

"Don't leave here mad, okay? You'll feel better in the morning, I promise. Call me tonight if you like. Or maybe you're going to see James? I spoke with him at the show. Such a sweetie. I mean, clumsy as hell, straight-on collided with one of LaMarque's clothes racks when he was leaving. But nobody's perfect, right?"

Gwendolyn said nothing more as she left. With James, maybe an apology was on the agenda. How they'd left things at the museum, her snippy attitude...not the best look. Surely he understood that she wasn't fully herself.

With Bo long gone, she started to head uptown, unsure if she should jump on the train or take a taxi. The fresh air felt good as she strode by the small department store selling an array of products imported from Japan, neutral-hued garments and accessories taking up window space, followed by the small designer boutique with a selection of mannequins in head-to-toe stonewashed denim. Gwendolyn still marveled that the wide-legged cuts she'd sported as a teen were back in style. She walked and walked, eventually passing an array of coffee shops and the huge used bookstore and gigantic multiplex she used to visit with the cousin she hadn't spoken to in over a decade.

Gwendolyn dodged several people hunched over their phones, slow-moving specters oblivious to the world around them. This happened almost any time she walked Manhattan streets. She thought she should've gotten over the feeling of being invisible long ago, but something about having to dodge folks who cared nothing about her existence still stung. She soon reached Union Square, her feet no longer able to endure the torture of walking in heels. The gray of the sky, too depressing. She peered up at the clouds, remembering forecasts had predicted sunny skies. Gwendolyn decided to splurge and hailed a cab. Within minutes, the ride turned torturous. When she was walking, distracted by city sights and clueless pedestrians, Gwendolyn could easily avoid thinking about the crimson runway. But sitting still, stuck in a car, she kept on playing over and over in her head what had happened at the museum, seeing the bloody TRAIDORA flashing in front of her. Maybe she hadn't been seeing things.

*What if the police spotted the words? In one of their photos? Or what if it shows up on social media?* The thought sucked her breath away, like her chest had caved in. She stared at her phone, imagining that Zachensky was about to call her at any moment and ask her to come in for questioning. That he'd determined she was withholding information.

By the time Gwendolyn entered her apartment, she felt heavy, a familiar weight returning to her body, a weight that threatened to bury her too many times. It was all she could do to drag herself to her bedroom and change into shorts and a tee. She lay down and peered out the window. The sky had turned an even deeper charcoal gray.

As she drifted off, Gwendolyn thought of the woman in yellow in her closet and asked for strength and guidance.

CHAPTER FOUR

# THE BREACH

"All right, spill it, mofo, who you fucking? You got that I'm-getting-ass-on-the-regular glow."

"*Must* you be so loud?" Fonsi whispered. He and Tariq sat in the middle of a crowded 2 train that had just entered the subway tunnel right before 149th Street and Third Ave. Tariq was a man of many talents, but voice modulation? Or choosing appropriate moments to bring up personal affairs? Not part of his skill set. No matter how often Fonsi hoped that things would turn out differently, riding the train with his best friend inevitably led to public embarrassment.

"I'm not with anyone, okay?" Fonsi continued. "You're the one who's been telling me how I need to clean up my raggedy behind if I want to start dating again." Fonsi glanced up. A couple of passengers were glaring down at them, including a woman who resembled Mrs. Garrett from the fifth and sixth seasons of *The Facts of Life*. Her flaming scarlet bouffant partially blocked a banner ad for the new TV series everyone was talking about, *The Senses*.

Tariq squinted hard at Fonsi, his lips curled. His trademark stare of disbelief. "You're lying. Know you too well. You're getting ass. You got that perkafied, bouncy look you walk around with when someone's been up in your stuff." He paused. "Wait... Waiiiiit... please tell me you ain't back with Numero Uno Park Avenue Ho."

"We're not having this conversation, Tariq," Fonsi whispered. "And no, Raph and I aren't back together. He's been texting and calling, but I haven't responded, so..."

"Maybe you should block his number, be firm. Make it clear shit's over, after what that mofo did." Tariq paused again. "Unless you're still interested..."

"I'm *not* interested..."

Fonsi wasn't in the mood to be grilled by Tariq. He hadn't envisioned spending his Sunday on a never-ending subway journey marked by scheduled delays and unscheduled delays and damp, piss-laden tunnels. But Tariq's mother, Estelle, was adamant that they had to get to her place over in Queens ASAP.

"You're not telling me something," Tariq said. "I can feel it, bruh. Talk to Ma. She always has good relationship advice."

Fonsi agreed, but he wasn't about to open up to anyone else about his ex. After the last two guys he'd dated ghosted him, Fonsi thought he was the luckiest person in the world to match on the apps with a young gentleman like Raphael Murray. He had it going on with professional pictures highlighting his career as a Realtor. Raphael was clear during their first few dates that he was genuinely interested in getting to know Fonsi, that he found Fonsi's artsy, "of the people" energy refreshing. Fonsi couldn't quite believe his ears, had wanted to pinch himself, to be desired—*thank the orishas*—by a quality dude.

And so Fonsi went along with his new beau's plans as the two got to know each other... Well, sort of got to know each other, Fonsi having sense enough to keep his Guardián work a secret. The two embarked on all-you-can-eat gay brunches and Broadway musicals and circuit parties in Montreal and Mykonos and Ibiza, none of which had been Fonsi's thing before. Time with Raphael took precedence over all. Fonsi closed La Playa for days, ignoring the dent in his finances, pushing aside the guilt that arose when he canceled on clients who wanted to connect with someone they cherished on the other side. He kept his fade and goatee trimmed, sharp, and purchased a variety of sweater/khaki ensembles in neutral colors, a look Raphael deemed suitable for casual and upscale events alike.

"Bruh, this *really* what you want?" Tariq had asked right before Fonsi and Raphael took an impromptu trip to Punta Cana, Fonsi rolling his luggage through the botanica to the cab waiting outside.

"Yes, I'm embracing a new me," Fonsi replied in the most chipper voice he could muster, aware he sounded like a first-episode contestant on *Bachelor: The Gays*.

Punta Cana had been the couple's fifth trip together in two months, Raphael using the excursions to once again satiate his craving for delicious dudes. Fonsi learned the hard way that Raphael had far-ranging appetites that included everything from bootylicious Bahamians to pale, svelte Swedes. As such, Raphael preferred to avoid strictly defining their relationship, keeping their connection open so he could hook up wherever, whenever, however. "Let's not limit ourselves," he said over drinks a couple of months into their romance. "Let's always enjoy what others have to offer." Fonsi nodded, ignoring the pangs of anxiety that ran through his body.

Not long afterward, he'd thanked the orishas again when their trip to Miami was canceled due to inclement weather and he and Raphael were unexpectedly holed up in his apartment, eating Chinese takeout, watching '90s cartoons, talking and kissing for hours. The two slow danced for the first time to Fonsi's cherished slow jams playlist. As the drowsy melody of H.E.R.'s "Damaged" played on, Raphael's head on Fonsi's shoulder, Fonsi lost himself to the moment, caring for nothing else but being with his man.

That night, Fonsi convinced himself he could make an open relationship work. After so many years, he'd *finally* graduated from awkward one-night stands with guys he had little in common with to real commitment, sorta kinda. Progress nonetheless. At first he was thrilled by the fleshy offerings that came from hanging with Raphael, the array of guys found at glamorous apartment parties and dingy saunas. More access to hot (or lukewarm) sex than he'd ever imagined. But then he noticed with these men he desired how they rarely got deep, rarely asked him where he was from or about his interests or work. Rarely even asked his name if they bothered to talk to him, their faces stoic, unsmiling. He looked at Raph cavorting freely with other naked men in their gym's steam room, sucking dick left and right, Fonsi even having his own dick sucked, but more often than not left on the sidelines as he watched his boyfriend enjoy the gay urban smorgasbord that was New York City.

Seven months into their relationship, Raph and Fonsi were the last guests to arrive at a Manhattan penthouse soiree billed as a housewarming, for which Fonsi had brought a crystal fragrance diffuser in the shape of a swirling merman. (He thought the ornament gave off cool vintage vibes à la Madonna's "Cherish" video, even reminding him a bit of Yemaya.) As soon as he walked into the apartment, his Spirit Sense buzzed. Fonsi started to frantically scan the space, anxious that the penthouse might be haunted. It had happened occasionally when he was out and about, a presence revealing itself. He almost always felt obligated to track down the ghost, to see if intervention was needed. His life work after all.

He scoped the joint out, trying to look as nonchalant as possible, barely noticing that all the attendees had formed a circle in the living room before stripping down. The housewarming in fact an orgy.

Raphael and an Asian dude soon took turns pounding six furry white men on a huge sectional sofa after they'd all done lines of coke. Fonsi sat on a hard wooden chair with the diffuser in his lap, clothed, sober, head buzzing from the hidden ghost, ignored yet again. It was then that he looked around, admitted he was totally repulsed, and asked himself, *How the hell did I get here?*

A seventh man came out of nowhere. He was less furry than the others, slender with dirty blond hair and the kind of ennui that came from being born privileged and the right type of cute. He straddled Fonsi's thighs and wiped his nose. "Wanna fuck?" the guy slurred. "Raph says your package is small for a Black guy, but all good. I'm not choosy, 'specially if I top."

Fonsi sprang from the chair—furball and diffuser tumbling down, merman shattering into little pieces—and fled the penthouse as Raph continued to plow away on the sofa. Fonsi hoped that whatever spirit lurked in the apartment was somehow powerful enough to make his horrid boyfriend suffer. Gouge out his eyeballs. Thrash him against a wall. Bite his bony ass with sharp, fang-like teeth.

Once he was outside, Fonsi called Tariq and burst into tears. Tariq had never liked Raph, had called him a fake hootie patootie who treated Fonsi like ten-year-old dollar-store chancletas. But to his credit, not once did he utter the words *told you so*. Instead he invited him to his Morningside Heights place and listened as his pal spilled how unhappy he'd been, how instead of cruising for men in saunas or traveling all over the damn place he just wanted to be held in his boyfriend's arms night after night and listen to slow jams. How in his heart of hearts he knew Raph indeed treated him like raggedy, ten-year-old dollar-store slippers. Fonsi had tried to be a modern, open-minded boyfriend, and for what?

He cried and cried as Tariq cradled him on the sofa. "You ain't never,

ever have to put up with that shit again, papa," he said. "You had the experience, got some takeaways. You tried."

Fonsi felt so cherished in his best friend's arms and wondered why nothing had ever developed between them, the two having known each other since childhood. Some people presumed Tariq was a player with his juicy "ba-dow!" physical trainer body and glistening tattoo sleeves. But he was honest as they came, a loyal, devout pansexual comfortable dating women, men, trans, and nonbinary people alike. A loyal, devout lover boy who'd never thought of Fonsi as more than a pal.

Tariq had his best interests at heart, but Fonsi couldn't handle talking about true feelings, not on a crowded, stuffy MTA car with the *Facts of Life* matriarch staring him down. "I have a podcast about small business management that Robyn told me to listen to," Fonsi lied, pulling out his earbuds right as the train pulled into 125th, the stop marked by the loud screeching of wheels. Tariq nodded, made a peace sign, and pulled out his tablet, no doubt going over his work schedule for the following week. As Fonsi listened to a show he'd blindly selected about prairie dog adoption, he fondled the big denim knapsack he held to his side, wishing he could've brought Papa Legba's box with him.

Ever since Thursday night, he'd carried the artifact with him everywhere. For the first time since their connection, he swore he could feel Amede's energy constantly, offering the faintest of caresses. But to bring the box into the home of a Guardián as spiritually sensitive as Estelle—disaster for sure, practically flaunting in her face how he'd broken one of the biggest rules of their order.

Fonsi and Tariq soon transferred to the E at Times Square and later switched to a Queens shuttle bus that replaced regular train service due to track repairs. Upon reaching the Jamaica Center–Parsons/Archer stop, knowing that they would need to take yet another bus to get to Estelle's house in Laurelton, Fonsi gave up on trying to save money and summoned a rideshare to take them the rest of the way. Minutes later, the yellow Prius pulled up to a large two-story beige house.

"Mis corazones!!!" shouted a woman who came bounding down the front steps, a large man in a Yankees baseball cap right behind her.

"Mamiiiiiiiiiii…" Tariq squealed in delight as he covered his mom's face with kisses, doing the same with his dad.

"Good to see you," Tariq's father said as he pulled Fonsi into an embrace. "How you holdin' up, fella?"

"I'm well, Mr. Bailey. Just tired I guess."

The older man chuckled. The gold crown on his upper right molar, exposed. "Running La Playa no joke, right? Or you still hooking up with that saditty fella who can't keep his behind still?" Mr. Bailey smacked Fonsi's shoulder with a loud cackle. "Let's go inside, y'all," he said. The keys hanging from his belt clinked. "I've put chicken on the grill, made potato salad, greens, maduros. We'll chow down after Estelle talks to y'all. Dinner in half."

The group walked into the living room, a warm space with comfy chairs and wooden floor pieces and a large record player flanked by a wall unit full of vinyl albums. One album was displayed at the front of a perfectly lined stack, an original *Siembra* from Willie Colón and Rubén Blades. Fonsi figured that Mr. Bailey went out of his way to showcase the album whenever he came over, an indirect shout to Fonsi's and Blades's shared Panamanian roots.

"That first song on this album, 'Plastico,' well, let me tell you," Mr. Bailey said the first time Fonsi visited his home many years ago. "Back when I'd just moved up here from South Carolina, I used to be all up in this real nice club, Lela's, over on the west side of the city for its disco and R & B nights. But I could hold my own on their Latin nights, too." Mr. Bailey winked. "So there I was after work, and the DJ put on 'Plastico,' and there she was, getting her swerve on with her girls as that string intro came on..." He gestured to Estelle. "Most radiant woman I'd ever beheld, Lord have *merc-eeee*! So I caught the beat and sashayed over to her best I could, and rest as they say..."

*Sashay* was indeed the right word for Mr. Bailey. He was beyond plump, with big arms and a big belly and a big backside with hips that switched as he walked. He wore his weight in a way that declared rotundness was magnificent, so much so that Fonsi realized, during the months he lived with the Baileys, that the man was prone to walking around the house buck-ass naked. When he did opt to wear clothes for work and social gatherings, it was clear Mr. Bailey's style had become frozen back in the '80s, his standard uniform consisting of blue jeans, primary-color polo shirts, and a glistening Jheri curl that grazed his shoulders. (Fonsi was stunned that activator was still on the market.) And he continued to wear his ring of keys even though he'd retired from custodial work a year ago due to arthritic knees. "Always gotta be ready," Mr. Bailey sometimes said right before he tapped the ring.

Estelle walked over and gave her husband a peck on the cheek. The two were about the same height, her caramel skin a contrast to his darker brown. Fonsi imagined Estelle as she once appeared to Mr. Bailey not long after she'd moved to New York from Puerto Rico. Based on what he saw in old family pictures, Estelle hadn't aged save for some extra pounds and streaks of silver in her black curls. Preferring to wear form-fitting jogging suits and crisp loungewear in pastel hues, she was thinner than her husband but big and curvy in ways that turned (much) younger heads. Mr. Bailey clearly adored his wife. Fonsi could see it in the way his eyes sparkled when he gazed upon Estelle, in how he cackled when he reminisced about running New York streets in their twenties, in how he'd never asked her to give up running La Playa despite the long hours she endured until passing on the shop to Fonsi.

"Addison, pick a couple of albums to listen to while we eat," she said. "Fonsi and Tariq, ya'll with me. We're going to my study."

Estelle led son and best friend through a hallway to the back of the house. "Yo, Ma, Fonsi has something going on with his love life and won't talk to me about it, so I told him to speak to you later." Tariq gave his friend a conspiratorial grin. *Don't think I forgot*, his look said.

Estelle pulled Fonsi close. "Oooh, baby, you know you can come talk to me anytime you want. Visit, call, text... whenever. But I hope you listened to my advice and stopped sending men pictures of your dick and asshole online. It's like a random stranger asking me to spread 'em and take a snapshot of my chocha. It's too *demeaning*. Lead with the fullness of who you are."

"Tía Estelle!" Fonsi shouted. "Is this necessary?"

"Oh puh-leeze, you've heard worse," she said. "And this is a tell-it-like-it-is household." She pinched his left cheek. "It's why you love us."

Estelle's words rang true. For Fonsi, Tariq's family were walking, talking embodiments of the "Way of Absolute Candor," a philosophy espoused by warrior alien nuns from one of his favorite *Star Trek: Picard* episodes. The Baileys' lack of shame about telling it like it is, both torturous and a balm to the soul.

Estelle sat down on a cream papasan chair after the trio reached her study. "Siéntate," she commanded, pointing to the matching couch with red cushions that sat across from an altar resplendent with illustrations of orishas and saints and photos of her ancestors and candles... so many candles. Like Fonsi, Estelle was a medium, though her visions came to her via smoke and light. Whereas Fonsi could communicate directly with ghosts, Estelle's premonitions were broader, vague, more mysterious, though sometimes startlingly precise. In consideration of the potential hazards of working with flame and smoke, her study was well ventilated with sliding doors and multiple air ducts. She sometimes lit an array of scented candles outside and meditated as Mr. Bailey declared to nosy neighbors, "Gotta keep them 'squitas away!"

Estelle's space had been a sanctuary for Fonsi for so many years, during some of the most difficult years of his life. And as tough as she was with her advice, her ability to listen without prejudice was infinite. She was the only Guardián with whom Fonsi shared burning questions about their system of beliefs.

He'd often felt like he should tread lightly when it came to interrogating Guardián philosophies, seeing as how their place in the world was so precarious. People from parallel spiritual beliefs sometimes looked askance at his order, a group of loosely organized mystics who, despite being called upon to deal with disgruntled spirits, hadn't gone through sacred rituals of initiation as seen for instance with Lucumi worshippers. But once Fonsi had a question, he found it almost impossible to contain. What if there really weren't deities on high? he once asked Estelle, shame burning in his chest for even contemplating such a thing. What if the orishas and saints were mere concepts through which Guardianes could focus their gifts? She simply nodded and allowed Fonsi to unburden himself. Estelle rarely needed concrete answers when it came to the supernatural, was much more invested in giving her protégé the freedom to explore.

Now she folded her hands on her lap. "We have a big problem," she said. "The barrier between our world and El Intermedio, it's weakening. A breach is forming."

"A breach?" Tariq said. "Ma, that...doesn't sound good."

"Understatement of the year, mijo, but I've been sitting with the candles for days now, reading what the smoke brings. Just to be sure. There's no doubt, the barrier between our realms is failing."

Fonsi clutched one of the cushions in his lap. *I have to be brave*, he thought, and took a deep breath, trying to will absolute candor into his bones. He had to speak openly about Amede, admit that maybe their dalliance was somehow connected to this. *Better to come clean now...*

"Estelle, this breach, I'm sorry, but this might be my fault. This is embarrassing…"

"You're sorry for what?" Estelle said. "For missing the signs? Fonsi, you work too hard running the shop and, no offense, love, but your head is always in the clouds, always trying to figure out some mystical conundrum or help your clients. You spend way too much time sleep-tripping, not looking after yourself."

Fonsi looked down, unsure of what to say.

"When it comes to reaching out to those who've departed, you'll soon be a master," she continued. "And you're doing such wonderful things for your clients. But either way, this isn't for you to figure out."

"Ah, okay…" Fonsi lifted his head back up. Maybe now wasn't the time for big reveals about ghostly affairs. Candor left his frame almost as soon as it arrived. "Uh, do you know what could be behind the breach?"

"I don't, but there are signs. Look at the sky. It's been gray for three straight days now even though forecasts promised sunny skies by the weekend. And can't you feel it…that something's off?"

Fonsi nodded slightly, realizing that he had indeed felt on edge for the last couple of days, chalking it up to nervousness about Amede. But what Estelle was saying, if he was honest with what he'd been feeling in his body, in the very ether… And then there was the matter of his work in the backroom.

"For the past couple weeks, clients have been coming in nonstop," Fonsi admitted. "It's been overwhelming. Do you think…it's connected to a weakened barrier, as you said?"

"I'm sure," Estelle replied. "Spirits are having a field day tethering themselves to the living world with a more permeable wall. And there's not much we can do, not by ourselves. Mediums like you can communicate with those who dwell within El Intermedio, but to tamper with the nature of limbo itself, repair its fabric? Beyond us. You know that. We need a manipulator."

"Last time there was a breach, that's what jumped off one of those fires in the South Bronx, in the '70s, yeah?" Tariq said.

Estelle beamed at her son. Growing up, Tariq hadn't manifested any supernatural gifts except for the uncanny ability to speak his mind and suss out lies, but she'd been determined that he would know everything about Guardián history, same as if he were a bona fide mystic like his older sister, who'd moved to New Orleans. Tariq's knowledge of their history, top-notch, practically rivaling Fonsi's. "Yes, mijo, one of the South Bronx fires, which led to all that damage and pain not long after I'd moved to New York. And then it was left to us to clean it up." Estelle paused. "But Fonsi knows the story well, right, baby?"

Fonsi remained silent. All Guardianes worth their grain in the arcane knew what went down in 1979. How a cadre of spirits had stowed away on an artifact brought over from Colombia's ancient pyramids by a Medellín native who'd relocated to the South Bronx. That these ghosts, united in their power, had liberated themselves from El Intermedio while creating a burst of heat that ignited the oil-soaked rags lying in the man's tenement apartment. No one knew why the man had oily rags—was he a mechanic?—but the spirits' moment of liberation caused the place to go up in flames.

It had taken multiple mediums to locate the apparitions, who'd floated around the borough lost and bewildered, frightening residents along the way. And it had taken Fonsi's mother, Ignacia Harewood, the only known manipulator in New York, to create a triad with other Guardianes, corral the ghosts back into El Intermedio, and seal the breach. The effort almost killing her.

Irreparable damage had been done. The building where the ghosts had freed themselves burned down to the ground, displacing scores of people. A few died. More casualties of the burning Bronx of the 1970s.

Fire played such a fateful role in his mother's life.

"I figured, us talking about a breach, you would start to think about Ignacia," Estelle said to Fonsi. "Your mother... could be difficult, I know. That's why I had you two come over, wanted us all to sit together, for us to figure this out as a family. To sit together in ritual, as that's our way, as Guardianes." She reached out and held Fonsi's wrist. "So you know we love you."

Fonsi could see from the corner of his eye that Tariq was on the verge of pulling him into a bear hug, his natural response whenever Fonsi's mother came up. He swallowed hard. He was going to push the hurt aside. Be brave. "All right, so to deal with the breach you said we need a manipulator," he said. "But with Mom gone... Didn't you once mention knowing someone back in Puerto Rico with that sort of power? Otherwise that only leaves... well, Giselda."

"Yes, I know," Estelle said. "That dude in Puerto Rico, his name's Humberto. Lives in the mountains, notoriously hard to reach. So that gorgeous cousin of yours, presuming she's still in the states, we need to find her. Fast."

Fonsi shook his head. Now he understood why Estelle had summoned him. "I haven't spoken to Giselda in years and I don't know where she is. I'm pretty sure she doesn't want to be found, especially by us." Fonsi fidgeted in his chair. This was becoming very uncomfortable. "To be honest I don't know if I want to see her after what happened with Mom. After what she did."

"Maybe I'm not being clear, Fonsi," Estelle said. "I know you're still hurting, but it really doesn't matter what you want at this point. Or what Giselda wants. If she's alive, she needs to be found. Manipulators can interact with El Intermedio almost at will, can repair any damage.

You know this. Far as I'm concerned, it's no coincidence that this is happening with the equinox just days away, when the barrier between our worlds is at its weakest. And I'm sure you also know the lore. Any breach left unsealed by sunset on the equinox will remain open indefinitely, or at least until the next equinox, which would be fall."

"Whoa," Tariq said. "This is bad."

"You said it, mijo. The amount of danger we're in, of the terror that'll descend on all our asses if the barrier remains broken…you have no idea just how bad things could get. The dead being able to interact with the living however they want, to engage in their obsessions. To have their *revenge*. Think of those anguished ghosts you've met, Fonsi, floating around in so much pain. If they had no limits, if they no longer had to tether themselves to objects or property. Our city would go under."

Estelle leaned forward, stared Fonsi down.

"I know this is hard for you, baby, but to handle this, to fix whatever's happening with El Intermedio, we've got to find your cousin. We need Giselda."

## CHAPTER FIVE
# SARGE IN THE SKY

"We're thrilled to welcome to the stage actor, producer, humanitarian...our very own Clive Sergeant."

Boisterous applause and shouts filled the Silvercup Studios lawn as Clive jogged to the stage, waving to the audience before sitting down next to his latest showrunner, Olga Olsson. Invited guests consisted of reporters, Hestia Studios execs, and a few of Clive's fellow actors from his forthcoming show *The Ride*. The historical fantasy series was based on Irish author Erin Carrigan's best-selling novels about mystics who possess a special rapport with powerful horses. Considering the balmy temperatures, the production facility had opted to hold the Long Island City event outside even with overcast conditions that perplexed forecasters. That morning, a local TV meteorologist offered his opinion on why the skies had remained dark gray for days despite sunny forecasts, that there'd been moments in history when inexplicable weather patterns persisted for short periods of time.

Gwendolyn clapped along with the gathered attendees. She stood backstage on a call. "They're getting started," she said, earbuds in. "Call you later."

"Let me know how everything goes," Jessica replied on the line. "And good luck."

Gwendolyn hung up and rejoined the cluster of people standing stage left, hidden from view. Zachensky, to her right. Cops were stationed on either side of the lawn. The detective had called in a favor to the local precinct and asked a few officers to patrol the premises. And he'd been kind enough to meet Gwendolyn at the event even though Queens was outside his jurisdiction. (*Standard detective protocol?* she wondered.) Zachensky had called that morning to inform her that forensics had deemed the substance at the museum to be human blood, and so his team was in the middle of combing police records for any reported thefts from city blood centers. After he'd given her the news, Gwendolyn had tried to imagine her body as something akin to titanium steel—tough, impervious, anything to keep herself from trembling or closing her eyes and lying back down. But she still felt heavy, slogging through the day. She'd barely mustered the energy over the weekend to call James and apologize.

Standing on the Silvercup lawn, she tried to focus and hype herself up over her client's latest success with a fledgling franchise. Studio execs at Hestia still loved Clive despite his rascally behavior on *The Senses*. Super excited, Clive had texted her that morning to see if she wanted to take a car over to the event together since they lived only blocks away from each other. But she'd declined, preferring to ride to Long Island City alone with Bo, his easygoing banter a balm.

Onstage, the bald, smiling podcaster who'd been hired by Hestia to interview their star said, "So, Clive, everyone knows you for your gritty dramas based on the real world. What drew you to this project?"

Clive flashed the grin that enraptured millions worldwide. "This may come as a surprise, but I'm actually a sorta kinda equestrian. It's more like a hobby. Can I say that?" He shrugged, face bashful. "Not Olympic level or anything, but back when I was growing up, I used to go to this summer camp where I busted my ass doing tricks..."

The actor could speak the King's English perfectly but often used the slightest hint of an around-the-way accent so he could claim his Jersey roots and pretend he hadn't received media training. Clive's ability to spout bullshit, unparalleled. He'd never sat astride a horse in his life until he started practicing for the series three months ago, his legs becoming so sore after a couple rides that he couldn't walk.

Gwendolyn scanned the crowd for anything suspicious. She was in spartan mode, clad in a ribbed black turtleneck and loose-fitting slacks with sample sneaker boots from another up-and-coming designer. Still professional, still city chic, but no-nonsense. She spotted a few undercover security specialists hired by the studio sitting among the crowd. All bases covered.

Guided by the podcaster, Clive and his showrunner jabbered away. Olga pointed out how the Carrigan novels focused on women in refreshingly nuanced ways. "I know," Clive replied. "I know. That's why I campaigned hard to be part of this project. It's an honor to work on this type of story with you, Olga, and Hestia. I know you're a feminist, and your dedication to taking care of your crew and cast, to maintaining a dignified set where everyone was treated equally..." He bowed his head as a smiling Olga placed her hand to her heart. The crowd burst into applause. The duo's performance, impeccable.

An onstage screen soon descended. Quiet fell over the lawn. A slight chill filled the air.

A perfect blue sky appeared, canyons and mountain peaks on-screen. The camera slowly zoomed closer and closer to a flurry of sandy dust. A bevy of horses ran by. A black mare with a streak of white from forehead to muzzle, a blond stallion with freckled sides...

The picture blinked out.

Olga jerked up in her chair, confused. So did Clive.

A new image appeared, a photo that filled the entire screen. A Black woman sporting a lime-green wig and barely-there brassiere and thong with high-heeled boots was crouched on all fours on a hotel bed, salivating. The bedsheets, crumpled, soiled. Her tongue impossibly long, lolling from her mouth, like something from a frog. Or demon.

Gwendolyn took in the whole image, a distorted screenshot from someone's social media account. The creator's handle floated above the image, *YaNeedaSarge*. And the caption read underneath the picture, "HOW U RIDE AAAAAALLLLLLLLL THEM HOs…"

The image flashed away, replaced by words that read "UR STAR RIDER" in jagged red letters that then began to bleed.

Gwendolyn's heart lurched.

The words flashed away only to be replaced by YaNeedaSarge's gaunt, pimpled face, which was then accompanied by Clive's latest headshot from IMDb, his skin smooth, cheeks round and full of color. One had to take a moment and stare at the pictures, but it was unmistakable. Two different photos, same person.

Gwendolyn dashed over to the stage technician stationed a dozen feet from where she stood with Zachensky. "Turn off the video!" she shouted.

"I…I already have," the technician said, right as she held up her hands and moved away from the console. Her teeth were chattering, the air arctic.

The image of the woman on the bed returned, only to rise and leave the screen, briefly covering the silver roof of the atrium before it soared high into the sky, where it stopped and hovered. Another screenshot from YaNeedaSarge popped up as well, a picture of a white sandy beach with two laughing men cavorting in Speedos, each of their packages humongous, distorted, almost spilling out of their trunks. The caption underneath: "WHY WE SHOULD BRING BACK ANTI-SODOMY LAWS…"

The men's faces elongated. Their eyes and noses and lips and shoulders and arms turned into a scarlet mess that melted from their bones, that turned white sand into striated sludge. The woman's face and back and hips and legs did the same, her flesh liquifying, her bones collapsing onto stained sheets.

Onlookers shouted, shrieked. A man leaned over from where he sat on the lawn and vomited into the grass.

Gwendolyn couldn't look away.

More screenshots attributed to YaNeedaSarge appeared. Some were innocent in origin and turned uncouth, all accompanied by misogynistic or homophobic or fatphobic or ableist captions. The images bled into the sky once again as more people screamed, as YaNeedaSarge's username floated overhead ominously. A record of Clive's past for all to see.

Four years ago, when Jessica and Gwendolyn had watched an off-off-Broadway revival of *Timbuktu!* at the behest of an associate, they weren't prepared for the acting tour de force that was Clive Sergeant. How charismatic and magnetizing he was amid the production's sparse set design. Nor were they prepared for the performer—offstage a strung-out mess—to beg the agency for representation. He said he needed Sublime to save his life.

Both women recognized his raw talent, Jessica particularly sensitive to his plight. Gwendolyn didn't trust Clive, was inclined to let the jittery actor tumble into the gutter of his choice, but she was obligated to follow her boss's lead. So they cleaned him up, got him into rehab, and bestowed on him a sparkling new image. Creating fresh personas, Gwendolyn's specialty. Per standard protocol for fledgling clients, Gwendolyn had requested Clive's passwords and scoured his social media only to be horrified by the bile she'd found. She'd spent hours going through his accounts, many long abandoned, deleting each and every one, clearing every history and cache she found until her eyes were blurry. Gwendolyn prayed that his old messages wouldn't come to light, that people would never connect the poison of YaNeedaSarge or YourHardSargeAF or GetStuffedbySarge to the celebrity god they now worshipped.

The audience on the Silvercup lawn continued to stare at the sky as more images appeared. The screenshots became mush and bled into clouds only to be replaced by smeared type in bright crimson.

TRAIDORA

MENTIROSA

BASURA

Gwendolyn took in the messages, whispered under her breath, "Blessed Lady." She ran over to Zachensky, noticing the band of cops stuck staring upward as well, everyone tinted red. "Your officers need to do something!" she yelled.

"I'm not sure there's anything we can do," Zachensky said. "Unless someone's trespassing or tampering with private property, this isn't technically illegal. Outside of stuff like porno, there's no law against sharing images in a public space... even stupid, crazy-as-hell images."

As the detective spoke, Gwendolyn noticed a pair of eyes trained on her from across the stage. Clive's. He was still seated, face furious.

Right. He was blaming her for this. Of course he was. Who else had access to his old accounts?

Gwendolyn ignored her client and bolted off the stage down a short flight of steps. She would find who was behind this and smash whatever equipment they were using with her bare fists if she had to, charges be damned. She made her way to one of the undercover security guys and grabbed him by the shoulder. "Have your people spread out, get whoever's doing this. Escort them off the premises immediately," Gwendolyn said.

She scanned the crowd as a chill seeped deep into her bones. The letters tinted the people and grass and pavement, the landscape transformed into a scene straight from hell. She looked across the street. To pull off a stunt like this, someone would need a large projector, not easily hidden.

She continued to scan, her eyes adjusting to the red. She wiped her runny nose and glanced downward.

And then she saw it.

A slim cable. Barely discernible in the grass.

Gwendolyn let the cable guide her line of sight. A rusted van was parked among a sea of Hondas and Toyotas and SUVs. An '80s model with a dent on its fender. She got closer and noticed horse stickers plastered on its window.

She'd found the culprit.

Gwendolyn charged over to the van, pulled open the door, and stopped.

There on the floor of the vehicle sat a thin young man, cross-legged, glasses and curly sawdust-colored hair partially covered by a baseball cap. His mouth formed a perfect *O*.

"You!" Gwendolyn said as she lunged forward and grabbed him by the collar.

"I'm sorry...sorry." The man held his hands in front of his face. "I wasn't able to get an invite to the event because I'm not legacy media even though my YouTube numbers are decent, so I had to figure out a way to get the scoop for my viewers about the show's launch because anything with Clive goes viral..."

Gwendolyn tuned out the gibberish, noticed that the van held plenty of books, mostly fantasy, including Erin Carrigan's full trilogy, *The Ride*, *The Saddle*, and *The Bit and the Bridle*. Again, she spotted the cable, which was hooked up to an open laptop. No projector in sight.

"You're...livestreaming," she said.

The man nodded. "Yep, I'm Skip. Skip Stewart." He held out his hand. "Run my own fantasy news platform. Ever heard of *Wear Your Pointy Ears on the Inside*?"

"No...no, I haven't," Gwendolyn said. "And why are you here?"

"Right. Look us up. And like I said, I didn't get a press invite but my fans expect inside intel on all the new shows, so I found a hidden spot close to the stage where I could place my phone and record...Um, don't mean to be pushy, but am I in trouble?"

Gwendolyn realized she was still holding on to Skip. She released his collar. "No, you're not in trouble," she grumbled. Fan-driven platforms were often key to a show's success, especially genre fare. "I'm sorry for...overreacting."

"Are you kidding? This is sooooooo rad," Skip said. "I mean, I wasn't expecting all that gross sky shit, but hey, all good. You should see my online numbers right now."

Gwendolyn nodded, seized by the thought that she should close the van door, renounce her chosen vocation, and order Skip of Pointy Ears to drive them away so she wouldn't have to face what was outside. Instead she managed a clipped "be well" and stepped back onto the studio lawn.

The screenshots were gone, the sky returned to its normal color, though the pall of clouds remained. Pandemonium reigned. Guests talked over each other, trying to figure out what just went down. Many were crouched over their phones uploading what they'd just witnessed to their feeds. The security guy she'd spoken to earlier walked over and shook his head. No need for words. His team had found nothing.

Another disastrous event.

She ran back to the stage. Clive was surrounded by his entourage while Olga stood far away from her star. The showrunner's face was flushed, filled with rage. Their world had changed in minutes. Gwendolyn hesitated. She needed a moment to figure out what she was going to say to Clive, how she could position this, spin it. Before she could open her mouth, the actor spotted her, jetted over, whispered in his Jersey accent, "You'll be fuckin' hearing from my lawyers," and stormed away, entourage in tow.

Gwendolyn closed her eyes, took a deep breath, and turned to the gaggle of creatives and execs still onstage.

This was no coincidence, another of her events so publicly sabotaged. What happened at the museum wasn't directed at LaMarque or Veronykah. This was a purposeful, vindictive message meant for Sublime. Or rather, her.

The bleeding image of TRAIDORA flashed in her mind. In the sky. On the wall.

Someone was coming after her. Someone wanted to ruin Gwendolyn.

CHAPTER SIX

# EL GRAN LIBRO NEGRO

Sitting at La Playa's register, Fonsi felt like his hands were awash in electricity as he traced the lines of Amede's red box. He'd placed the cube on a shelf beneath the register, out of his customers' sight, happy to be close to his ghost, or at least imagine they were close. After an intense morning run of customers, the shop had been empty most of the afternoon. So he perched himself on the tall oak stool and waited for Robyn to show up so he could head over to an art reception in Harlem.

Fonsi hadn't been able to bring himself to reveal to the Baileys that he was having intimacy with a ghost, not when the conversation had become so heavy with talk of a breach between realms. But Estelle was right. If he paid attention, something was different in the air. A slight pressure raking against flesh. A steady dreariness in the sky.

*The breach isn't my fault*, Fonsi had managed to convince himself by the end of the night. Still, he'd wondered, was a weakened barrier why he was able to connect with Amede in the first place? Was that what Amede meant in his last message on the bathroom mirror? So far, Fonsi hadn't been able to communicate with the ghost as he sleep-tripped, which was odd. Regardless of their tryst, what if the ghost was up to something and couldn't be trusted?

As questions swirled in Fonsi's brain, Estelle had moved into emergency mode, calling as many Guardianes as she could to try to figure out the cause of the breach. She and Tariq were going to head to Puerto Rico to find Humberto Ramos, the only other manipulator she knew, who just so happened to be living off the grid. Mr. Bailey would stay behind in New York, his knees not conducive to long treks through countryside.

Fonsi had promised Estelle that he would do his best to locate Giselda, though the prospect of tracking her down was beyond intimidating. He'd searched for "Giselda Rivera" online and found matches in New York, California, Florida, Texas, Panama, Dominica, even France. But none of these women were his cousin, all having the wrong age or skin color or family background.

And so Fonsi took a moment to do what he always did when he felt helpless and uncertain. He studied. In his lap he cradled El Gran Libro Negro, the big black book that held years of Guardián lore. The book he'd studied relentlessly as a teenager, when his true heritage was revealed. He imagined that centuries ago his order's mysticism had been preserved in gilded grimoires that sparkled, that magically opened at the slightest touch for purehearted seekers of knowledge. Instead, he peered at a thick binder with a peeling plastic cover holding a patchwork of punch-holed articles.

*Why does Guardián stuff always have to be so freakin' janky?* he wondered for the umpteenth time. Many of the book's pages were dog-eared or ripped. Others contained text covered with hot pink highlights and handwritten notes in the margins. Over the years, Fonsi had spent hours patching up Gran Libro with tape and hole reinforcements and page laminations. He'd made copies of the book for other Guardianes, but he always held on to the original. It was the least he deserved, Fonsi figured, after all the years he'd dedicated to their lore.

His eyes settled on a clause he'd read many times before about El Intermedio that he could practically recite by heart: "To initiate a breach, usually accompanied by extreme changes in temperature and weather, apparitions must work together and combine their spiritual powers. The rarest of phenomena."

It made sense. The last detected breach in the Bronx had occurred only because several ghosts had united to rip themselves from limbo. Teamwork was rare among spirits, considering how they siloed themselves away from each other, lost in individual obsessions. So what was happening now? Had another group of ghosts banded together to create chaos?

Once he was old enough to understand the nature of her gift, his mother, Ignacia, had regaled Fonsi with stories about how she and two other Guardianes had created a triad of power to resolve the Bronx breach. She'd positioned herself as the hero of the story, a hero in his eyes.

Fonsi set aside Gran Libro and looked at his phone and swiped. An image popped up, one he'd been staring at off and on all day, an old picture of him and his mother taken by Estelle with a digital camera when he was eleven. He and Ignacia were cheesing like no tomorrow, like they always did in photos they took together during his preteen years. Above them loomed Duarte, the bearded man his usual smug self. Ignacia's on-and-off piece who'd been a constant source of anxiety for her son.

✳ ✳ ✳

For years, Fonsi had indulged in a quiet sort of pride that by his thirties he was a legit business owner. A true accomplishment considering that one of the first adult role models he had for running a business was a shady gangster wannabe. Trevor Duarte was a neighborhood fixture

Fonsi occasionally spotted strutting into local restaurants or stores. After school, Fonsi would also run into Duarte and his boys when he stopped into a Te-Amo's to pick up comic books or satiate his cravings for Hostess Suzy Q's. (His mother warned him that the oversweet chemical-laced things would rot his teeth and put him into a diabetic coma, but he didn't care.) Duarte never acknowledged Fonsi, though one of his boys did chuckle and mutter "skinny little faggot" as he passed by one afternoon. One of many instances where Fonsi learned to bury his anxiety over being singled out for the way he moved through the world, the lilt of his voice and hands. It gradually dawned on him how Duarte and his crew never purchased anything, how they'd just linger briefly at a register or be led to the back by a worker. Weird, sure, but none of his business.

So it had come as a surprise when, on one fine Monday, ten-year-old Fonsi arrived home from school to find Duarte sitting on his couch, shades on, long black hair streaked with gray and pulled back in a ponytail. His mother, who had the day off after two double shifts, was in the kitchen making oxtail and dumpling soup, watching the telenovela *Yo soy Betty, la fea*. After Ignacia came out and made perfunctory introductions, Duarte said, "Yeah, I know little man. I've seen him around with his cómics tontos. ¿Qué pasa, papi?" Fonsi gave a quick wave and stayed silent, overcome with the feeling that a new era of life had begun.

Over the following months, Duarte would show up at his apartment for a few days at a time, mostly to eat Ignacia's food, lounge on the sofa, and watch football. Fonsi tried his darnedest to ignore the man as he sat at his kitchen table nibbling away at a Devil Dog, doing homework, or reading his prized millennium edition of the *Crisis on Infinite Earths* graphic novel for the umpteenth time. When Ignacia commandeered the remote in the days before Duarte, Fonsi had been forced to watch enough talk shows featuring single women looking for love to understand that his own mother might need somebody. So he tried to generate high-in-the-sky feelings, tried to tell himself that he should be happy because she finally had her own...special friend. And he was relieved that Duarte didn't find it odd how fervently Ignacia prayed in front of the home altar that contained figurines of orishas and photos of dead relatives. The few other visitors they'd had over the years found his mother's devotions strange and intense, but Duarte took it all in stride, even going so far as to take off his shades, sit down with Ignacia, and pray as he muttered, "Yeah, this voodoo shit is cool."

But no matter how hard Fonsi tried, he just didn't like the man. His gruffness. His condescension. How he never seemed to talk about ordinary things like his job or family. How he ordered Fonsi around to fetch him this or that even though he was technically a visitor and had two big smelly feet that worked perfectly fine. The way he sat in their living room, legs splayed on their old lumpy sofa as if he were reclining on a throne, his booming voice filling the apartment whenever he was on a call. Fonsi knew plenty of dudes who carried themselves around their neighborhood like this but never imagined he'd have to put up with Machismo Man on the regular after so many years of it being just him and his mom.

Duarte was far from a stable presence, disappearing for weeks at a time. Before each departure, he left wads of money on their kitchen table, more fifty- and hundred-dollar bills than Fonsi had ever seen in his life. For some reason it made him feel anxious and ashamed, the same feeling he got when Duarte and his mom disappeared into her bedroom for hours at a time. Cold hard cash on dull Formica, a silent flex, what allowed his mother's man to come and go as he pleased. Years later, after Duarte was permanently gone, Fonsi would come to better understand how certain things in the hood worked, like extortion and protection rackets and drug smuggling. Piles of cash on the table, no longer a mystery.

Duarte had been away for a while when Fonsi's mom, upon coming home from a cleaning job, sat cross-legged on the living room floor and chanted in front of her altar longer than usual. Much longer. She commanded her son to sit and watch what she was doing, to listen. Fonsi thought she'd lost it, the strain of a hard life finally causing Ignacia to snap. Or maybe she was really, *really* missing her dude—even worse. Such were Fonsi's ruminations until a halo of light appeared around his mother's head and her entire body emitted a faint glow. The living room began to feel like a sauna. She looked over at Fonsi, who was trying his darnedest not to be afraid. "Son, this is me," she'd whispered, "when I touch the other side." Her sweaty face was strained, tired.

Ignacia told him that she belonged to a mystical order called Los Guardianes that helped keep people safe from evil spirits. That the group had been tasked with monitoring a place they called El Intermedio, some sort of limbo where ghosts dwelled. That she could tap into the fabric of El Intermedio itself. A rare gift he'd just witnessed. "It was time for you to know," Ignacia added as she took the hand of her bug-eyed son. Unreal, all of it. Totally, completely wacky.

Fonsi said nothing during his mother's revelations. *Maybe I'm dreaming*, he thought as he lay in bed that night, unable to sleep. *Maybe I'm the one who's gone crazy.* The comic books and sci-fi/fantasy DVDs he kept obsessively alphabetized in his room provided no comfort, in fact seemed to taunt him, as if he'd become delusional because he'd spent far too much time in make-believe worlds.

The next day remained surreal, his mother taking him after school to Estelle's botanica, La Playa, to teach him about rituals and orishas when it came to Guardianes and their gifts. Fonsi tried to remain calm even though he felt like he'd been inducted into a coven of wizards. Or witches. He took in the store's candles and statuettes with fresh eyes, having once viewed the objects as gaudy trinkets held on to by hard-working, superstitious people who missed their native lands.

"What us Guardianes can do, some people call it working spells, some of us even use the term 'magic' occasionally, but most of us prefer to say that we practice art," Estelle confided in him. "And for real, this has to remain a secret, Fons." She spoke in the low, no-joke voice he sometimes heard her use with her kids. "You're old enough to know the truth...I told Ignacia it was overdue, that someone as smart as you would start noticing things and asking questions. What we've shared is only for us. For us to do what we were called upon to do, to serve, discretion is essential."

Fonsi nodded in bewilderment and mumbled, "I understand," even as he glimpsed the scowl on his mother's face.

Estelle encouraged him to visit La Playa as often as he liked. Days later, she gave him Gran Libro in all its raggedy splendor. "You're a reader," she said. "Sit with this, study it. It'll answer lots of the questions I see bubbling in your chest."

Fonsi held the dusty binder in his hands like he suddenly possessed the greatest of treasures. He knew he'd read the thing nonstop soon as he got home. "Does this mean...I'll have a gift one day, like Ma?" he asked Estelle. "Like you?"

"Baby, I hope so," she replied. "But there's no guarantee. Some Guardianes come from a long line of mystics, power running through their family for generations. Others... Well, for most of us, sweetie, becoming a Guardián, it's a calling. Some believe it's the orishas and saints guiding those with a certain mystical sensitivity to find others like them. My tías and tíos back in Puerto Rico were mediums, but your mother, no one in her family has that sort of power in their blood, not that we know of. She drifted to us as a teenager, when her gifts began to manifest." Estelle tugged Fonsi's cheek, a gesture of affection she'd had for him since he was a toddler. He thought he'd outgrown such things. "Regardless of whatever gifts are in store for you, little Fonseca, you're amazing," she continued. "So intelligent, with your books and illustrations and figurines. Destined to do your own thing."

That night, Fonsi read Gran Libro in bed until he was so tired that he keeled over into its pages, his mind barely able to absorb the binder's legion of secrets. The chapters on spirits in particular left him enraptured. The wonders revealed. That ghosts can manifest in our world only when tethered to specific items or property or land. That savvy ghosts can gradually build mystical power. That distressed ghosts who linger too long in El Intermedio often become loopy, deranged things. A whole new world at Fonsi's fingertips. Unbelievable.

More questions abounded. Was there some sort of ritual he should prepare himself for, as if he was going to be a santero? Would the orishas and saints grant him power if he prayed hard enough? Maybe Estelle was wrong. Maybe he could come into his gift if he wished hard enough. Maybe he could be a manipulator like his mom, though practicing art seemed to leave her wasted. And how she spoke about her power, with so much anger.

"I saved so many people," she said to Fonsi one evening as he sat on the living room couch, Gran Libro in his lap. He was in the middle of his third run-through, having already memorized a few passages. "What would've happened if those ghosts in the Bronx had run amok, messed with folks however they wanted. And look at how we have to live. How hard I have to work. I should be famous like Walter Mercado considering what I can do, what I know. Raking in the dough." She gestured at their tiny apartment, with its intermittent leaks and rickety plumbing and cracked ceiling over which they heard the pitter-patter of rodents. "If Duarte hadn't been helping us, we would've been fucked... and now he's not here." She clenched her fists.

*...look at how we have to live.* His mother's new mantra now that her son knew the truth. His mother, Ignacia, a powerful mystic who could never reveal to the world what she could really do, who had to earn money as an office cleaner. Who dropped out of her adult college courses once she was pregnant with Fonsi, her dream of becoming a physician's assistant abandoned. Her story a series of what-ifs.

Grief unexpectedly consumed the household during the fall of 2001 when Ignacia learned that Duarte had been killed. The circumstances were mysterious, just like everything else about him, but he'd apparently met his end in a parking-lot shootout between rival gangs that left two dead and four injured. Ignacia refused to tell Fonsi much about what went down, and news on the incident was limited. Shootings happened in the Bronx all the time, nothing to see there.

Ignacia cried for days, inconsolable to the Baileys, barely talking to Fonsi. The funeral itself was an embarrassing blur, his mother's keening drowning out the priest's benedictions as Duarte's mahogany coffin was lowered into a Woodlawn Cemetery plot. After the wake, she declared she needed time away, that she had to get out of the city, at least for a bit. She needed to go back home, to the beauty of Panama, to replenish her spirit. And so a sullen eleven-year-old Fonsi stayed with Estelle and Mr. Bailey while his mother went to heal her wounds.

Days later, while sitting on the beach of Isla Taboga reading *El Siglo*, Ignacia came across an article on the orphaned children of El Chorrillo, the neighborhood where she'd been born. A neighborhood partially destroyed during America's "Just Cause" invasion of Panama in 1989. The residents of Chorrillo were mostly poor, having always had it rough as the descendants of those who'd migrated from the West Indies to build the Panama Canal. During the attack that ousted General Manuel

Noriega from the presidency, hundreds of civilians had been killed or labeled as missing. Some of the surviving children were left to fend for themselves. His mother had stared at the *Siglo* orphanage group photo hard, her gaze landing on one particular child. The girl's face was the spitting image of her cousin's who'd died in the invasion.

"I had to go see her, mi Marianna poquita," Ignacia would say upon her return to America. "Had to see if that was actually Marianna's child." And so the next day Ignacia made her way north to the orphanage in the city of Colón, where she met Giselda, the only surviving daughter of Marianna, the cousin whom she hadn't seen since she'd left for America in the '70s. Giselda was initially distrustful of Ignacia, didn't say much outside of confirming that her parents and older sibling had been killed during the invasion. "I couldn't just abandon her," Ignacia would explain to Fonsi, feeling guilt for having left Giselda alone for so long. She'd presumed that Marianna's entire family had perished during the invasion. "Her father's side of the family still in Panama—hot drunken messes! And those of us on her mother's side, the few of us left, we were all in the states. Ah, Giselda, so pretty. So much energy, like Marianna. Seeing her in the paper was divine, was meant to be."

Somehow his mother finagled things so that she could bring Giselda to the U.S. in a matter of days. Fonsi was eventually able to suss out how things had gone down, that money had changed hands with Panamanian officials. The thousands of dollars his mom had squared away for a down payment on a house, much of the dough coming from Duarte? Gone. Fonsi got Giselda instead, who'd arrived at his apartment doorstep looking like she'd just gotten off the proverbial boat: T-shirt baggy and nondescript, acid-washed jeans off-style, hair dry and jacked up. For years he'd put up with his mom's sketchy boyfriend coming and going as he pleased, and now she'd brought a stranger to their home with no warning save for a brief phone call that a surprise was on its way.

The transition was rough, Fonsi informed right away that he'd be giving up his personal space in their two-bedroom apartment. From now on, he'd sleep in the living room. "As a girl, Giselda needs her privacy," Ignacia proclaimed. "She deserves her own room after all she's been through." But most importantly, like Estelle said, there'd be no discussion of his mother's mystical powers or Guardián affairs. They'd reveal their secrets to Giselda one day, when the time was right, when they were certain she could be trusted. Maybe.

Their first few mornings together were tense. Fonsi chomped through his bowl of Rice Krispies as he scowled at this girl who had him practically sleeping in the kitchen. Looking all kinds of feral, Giselda scowled right back, her eyes darting around the apartment like she was caged. Her gaze often settled on the family altar, which made Fonsi paranoid that his second cousin would soon figure out his mother's mystical background and flee in terror from la bruja diabla y su hijo maricón—the evil witch and her sissy son. Maybe his mother knew that was a real possibility, which was why during breakfast she poured Giselda's orange juice and buttered Giselda's toast and peppered Giselda with kisses and serenaded Giselda with Gloria Estefan's "Si Voy a Perderte." Or maybe his mother was simply overjoyed to have someone from back home in the house. The sweetness in her voice, something Fonsi hadn't heard since Duarte was alive.

Two months in, Giselda started to sit with Fonsi as he watched TV. She seemed only vaguely interested in the sci-fi/fantasy stuff and, when she had the remote, tended to put on talk shows or the news. She became absorbed, excitement growing in her eyes at the pretty newscasters or hosts, especially if they were Black. Didn't matter what the topic was, Giselda kept watching while Fonsi complained that they were missing the latest episode of *Xena: Warrior Princess* or *Voyager*. (He secretly thought it bizarre that his twelve-year-old cousin wasn't clamoring to watch the latest music videos so she could be in the know with other girls at school, though she did pay close attention whenever Destiny's Child came on BET.) She started to use her allowance to get fashion magazines, *Essence* and *Elle* her favorites, and Fonsi watched Giselda miraculously transform from the caged creature his mother brought home into a stylish teen with quiet swag.

The two grew closer. An odd couple, both outcasts, one by choice, the other by circumstance. Fonsi had resigned himself to a lonely life of academics, art, and fantastic stories once it became clear that he was considered too effeminate and sartorially challenged to fit in with other guys at school and on the streets. But Giselda, the stares she got everywhere, the effortless cool she wielded before aloof, Rihanna-type girls in the hood were a thing. How guys would approach her on the regular, some way too old. How other girls invited her to sit at their lunchroom table. His cousin mostly declined offers to hang, always polite, sometimes even demure.

Fonsi proudly shared with her his art and figurines he worked on when his head wasn't buried in Gran Libro, which his cousin regarded as some sort of dusty religious text that couldn't compete with her fashion mags. She eventually brought offerings to their altar, pieces of fruit and chocolate. "I did something like this back in Colón, at the church," she said in solid English. She gestured to the statuettes of the female orishas, like Yemaya and Oya and Oshun. "They remind me of what I used to see when I was little…in my dreams."

And then, the miracle. One night, as Fonsi pored over a Gran Libro passage about ghostly possession while Giselda studied an old *Cosmo* with Naomi Campbell on the cover, the temperature in the apartment plummeted. An odd occurrence considering it was June and they didn't have AC. The two cousins shivered under blankets on the sofa before

Giselda's hands began to radiate colorful light. The exact same way his mother's had.

"Un milagro!" Ignacia declared, rushing in from work to hug a crying, frightened Giselda, whose palms glowed a bright platinum embedded with specks of blue and gold and pink. "I knew there was a reason the orishas led me to you!" Fonsi sat on the sidelines as his mother explained Guardián lore in a way she'd never bothered to do with him. He soon understood why. Over time, he came to realize there was something truly extraordinary about his cousin. When his mother touched El Intermedio, the little bursts of energy she called forth would leave her drained. But for Giselda, power practically oozed from her pores. No incantations or chants necessary though they helped her focus. When her art filled the apartment, it was like they were being engulfed by a sea of sparkling light that revitalized the body and refreshed the soul.

Ignacia initially kept Giselda home from school for days out of fear that the girl would summon her gift in the middle of class. She patiently directed Giselda on how to rein in the energy, to look to the orishas for strength and calm. To look to herself. And all the time, Fonsi watched in their cramped apartment and wondered if he'd ever find his own mojo as his mother exclaimed, "Giselda, mi hermosa estrella." Her beautiful star.

Giselda, who by fourteen, as a former banana-boat girl with limited funds, had transformed herself into a supremely stylish kid, dubbed the Boogie Down's own Hilary Banks by a couple of neighbors. Who by fifteen had come into her manipulator gifts, one of the rarest powers ever found among the Guardianes. And who by seventeen, after a fire had destroyed their new North Bronx home and left his mother a charred corpse, had vanished.

A knot formed in Fonsi's stomach as he stared at the old image of his mother and Duarte. He clutched the phone hard, vision blurry from tears he refused to let fall. Fonsi had started to sleep-trip with ghosts just days after his mother's funeral, probably out of desperation to see her again. At least that's what Estelle theorized. He'd hoped his mother's spirit had managed to tether itself to an object even though everything she adored was destroyed in the fire. An empty hope he still clung to even though it had long outlived its usefulness.

As Fonsi sat in La Playa, mood shattered by old memories, heart full of yearning, he absentmindedly caressed the red box. A slight breeze entered the shop and ruffled the curls of his hair. An eerie tingling. A light pressure on his cheek.

Fonsi saw the shapes of lips, saw long, narrow features, faint and hovering. Flowy. As if he'd sent his soul to El Intermedio. A familiar image from his special night.

The spirit was here. Amede was in the shop.

Fonsi closed his eyes, arched his back. His head lolled to the side, his neck and arms and fingers and torso swaying. He lost all sense of time, was in and out of flesh, couldn't let the moment go. He needed this so very much, to drift away from the pain.

Fonsi emitted a low moan, as if his spirit were floating outside his body. The front-door chimes rang and he opened his eyes.

A statuesque, lean man appeared before him.

Amede, finally, manifested. What he craved above all.

Fonsi almost fell off his stool.

The man came closer. His red hair was short. Freckles dotted his light brown skin. Dark shades covered his eyes. He was clad in a beige sweater, plaid slacks, and boots. He cradled a thin glass vase that held a bouquet of roses.

"*Ohmigod*…you've gotta be kidding me. Raph, what are you doing here?"

Raphael placed the vase on the counter. He took off his shades and smiled. "Hey there, babes. How are you?" His tone was light, chipper, like everything was fine. Like he hadn't just strolled into the store of an ex he hadn't spoken to for weeks.

"No really, dude, what're you doing here?" Fonsi said. "This is where I work." The moment he was having with Amede, done.

"I remembered that afternoons in the shop are quiet sometimes, so I took a chance," Raphael said. "And wow, you haven't shaved…in quite some time. Everything okay?"

"Yeah…yeah, of course," Fonsi said.

"I know it's been hard. We've both been suffering."

"I'm not suffering. I'm doing great."

"You don't look great. You look like you haven't stepped inside a bathtub for a month."

"You know what? Get out and go to hell, Raph! You can't just come up in my shop and talk to me any old piece of way. I'm not putting up with your mess anymore."

Raphael held up his palms in surrender. "Okay, this isn't going the way I wanted. It's just, yeah, you look different. More gorgeous than ever. I just wasn't prepared for a granola, back-to-your-roots vibe. But you're wearing it like royalty."

"Oh shut up. You're full of shit."

"Ah, I see a smile there. A little one. You're happy to see me."

"I'm not happy to see you. I told you we're not doing this anymore."

"Via a phone call. A short, one-sided call, I might add. We should've had a conversation in person. Be responsible, emotionally mature grownups. You're my boyfriend, Fons, and…"

"I *was* your boyfriend. *Was.* It's done, Raph. And...and when did you start thinking of me as your man? You were the one who didn't want strict definitions."

"Right. Let's talk about that. I'd like to hear your side of things."

"You wanna hear my side of things? Now?!?" Fonsi felt heat in his cheeks, realized he was shouting. He almost never shouted, had come to believe from childhood that calling attention to himself was one of the worst things he could do. He thought of Tariq's observations about his stray outbursts.

Fonsi let the botanica's quiet engulf him and his ex for a moment. And then Raphael Murray uttered miraculous words.

"I made a mistake," he said. "With how I treated you. That housewarming...I should've warned you. I get why you're upset. I'm sorry."

"That wasn't a housewarming! I've never been so demeaned in my life. And...Wait, you're what?"

"I'm sorry. Okay, you know this sort of thing isn't easy for me...." At that, Fonsi rolled his eyes. "...but I've been thinking hard before coming here. I tried to write everything out in a long text to avoid violating your physical space, but my words kept reading like a sales pitch. I'm sorry, Fons. *Really* sorry. You're one of the brightest, most thoughtful guys I've ever met." He gestured to the shelves of the shop. "Your interests...how into Afro-Latine culture and spirituality you are. And art. And *food*. Gosh, I so miss your food, like when you'd make empanadas or arroz con pollo on Sundays. Or that yummy Panamanian corn drink your mother taught you how to make, chameche..."

"It's called chicheme, Raph..."

"Right, *chicheme*. Right. You're such a great cook. Masterful..."

"So you miss me being your servant..."

"No...noooooo, I miss your thoughtfulness, Fons. And your... understated worldliness. I miss how you'd take time to ask me real questions about my family back in the Bay Area, or about the real estate biz. And I miss how we'd sometimes cuddle and watch those sci-fi and fantasy shows of yours. I've even started to get into the X-Men because of you... Who'da thought? Me and mutants?!? It's just... I miss what we had is what I guess I'm saying." Raphael took a deep, short breath, words continuing to spill. "And I took it all for granted. I haven't met other guys who appreciate the simpler things in life. I don't think I really know how to appreciate the simpler things, and that's one of the reasons why I've started therapy. When we stopped talking..."

Fonsi tried to process what he heard, what he beheld, seeing Raphael for the first time with his shoulders slouched, eyes lowered. Vulnerable. Honest.

"You're telling me all this because..."

"Listen, I get it," Raphael said. "Maybe it'd be too much for us to jump back into things, but at the very least let's get a coffee. Just talk, you know? And be honest with each other. I'd like to hear more about what you want. You're right, our communication wasn't what it should've been."

More new language from Raphael. Disconcerting, overwhelming...

Fonsi inhaled, exhaled, picked up the vase, and handed it back to his ex. "I need some time. I appreciate you coming here..." *No, that was too nice, too charitable.* "I just think, for now, it's best if you left."

"Are you sure that's what you want, Fons?" Raphael stepped closer and took Fonsi's hand. "I'm not into begging, but for you..."

The sound of chimes filled the shop once again. Robyn walked in with a "Hola, Jefe!" They paused as their eyes scanned Raphael up and down. "Who's this?"

"Just someone who's about to go," Fonsi said, snatching his hand away from his ex. "Robyn, why don't you head to the back and..."

"Hey, you're Raphael, right?" Robyn said. "I remember you from a bunch of Fonsi's Insta pictures before he deleted them. OMG, don't you have nerve coming up in here. Tariq told me how you couldn't stop chasing ass, like you have some sort of *compulsion*."

"Robyn!"

"Firstly, I wasn't 'chasing ass,'" Raphael said, indignation in his voice. "It's called ethical nonmonogamy, not that it's any of your business. And second, I used to visit the store all the time to see Fonsi, so I have every right to visit..."

"*Firstly*," Robyn began, imitating Raphael's Cali accent, "I know all about how ethical nonmonogamy is *supposed* to work because I took Gender Studies 101, and I think you forgot the 'ethical' part when you were dating mi jefe. *Second*, even if you've been all up in La Playa before, our boy Tariq said you're a stingy mofo who'd never buy shit. Wasn't even tryin' to support your man's hustle. Least you could do is purchase something nice for the soul 'stead of coming up in here with tired-looking flowers... Wait, you're trying to make a comeback, aren't you?"

Raphael cleared his throat as he clutched the vase to his side. "I'll have you know I purchase spiritual wellness items all the time. And I would *never* buy something from Fonsi's shop simply because we're together. What a trite, condescending thing to do... and... and why am I even having this discussion? Who are you?"

Robyn puffed out their chest. "Me llamo Robyn Guerrera del Rivero, junior associate at La Playa Espiritu."

Fonsi rolled his eyes again. He'd never given Robyn an official title, even though he now realized he probably should. "Guys, I have somewhere I need to be. This place in Harlem," he said. "Raph, I think you should leave as well."

"No, no, I got this, boss, be on your way." Robyn waved their hand and swiveled back to Raphael. "So since you and Fonsi are kaput, you don't need to worry about being *trite* and *condescending* with your purchases."

They thrust a basket into Raphael's hands. "Take a look around, spend some money. Waaaaaaay overdue, especially if you're trying to make a comeback. La Playa, we need las platas, like yesterday. I told the boss we could increase our revenues easy if he would light more candles honoring Santo Antonio, but nooooooooooooooo, why listen to the newbie. Anyway, our My Little Orisha collection is on sale. It's a cheaper, more culturally affirming alternative to all those Black Ariels they sell at Target. You can get half a dozen easy now, save them for birthday gifts for the kids in your life. And then there's…"

Chimes marked Fonsi's exit from the shop. He felt a tinge of guilt for leaving an employee to deal with his ex, but if anyone could handle Raphael, it was Robyn Rivero.

## CHAPTER SEVEN
# SUBLIME CRUSH

Forty-five minutes later, Fonsi stepped into Faith's, regretting the promise he'd made to Arturo that he'd swing by. He looked down at the postcard flyer he'd been sent advertising the event, once again compelled by the beauty of his friend's work, the sunflowers and bees of the featured art so immaculately crafted that Fonsi wanted to walk into the image. His former schoolmate was stepping up his game.

The café was awash in swirling lights and sounds, the revelry doing nothing to sweeten a mood turned sour after thinking about mystical breaches and his dead mother and missing cousin. *I won't stay long*, he promised himself. He would go home in half an hour and try to reconnect with Estelle, try to come up with another contingency plan since there was no way he was going to find Giselda in time.

A trio of drummers was perched by the door. Patrons held their drinks as they swayed. A bulbous man sporting golden body glitter and a feather headdress zipped over as he called out Fonsi's name and leaned in for a hug. His arms were strong, solid.

Fonsi stepped back. The man's rich brown skin glistened, the smell of jasmine oil in the air. Besides the headdress, he wore nothing but a green thong. Recognition set in.

"Matteo? Wow. I mean, double wow. Er…I didn't realize it was you."

Matteo smiled and swirled. "I'm in an Afro-Brazilian dance troupe, just part-time when I'm not running the studio. Arturo asked me to perform, help entertain his guests."

Fonsi nodded, having met Matteo briefly when he'd visited La Playa some months ago with Arturo. Matteo, a chill yoga instructor who also hailed from Brazil and who'd raved about Fonsi's mini-sculptures perched on the botanica's shelves. Fonsi didn't know dude had been blessed with such…presence. *Of course I didn't*, Fonsi admitted to himself. *Not when I was up Raph's ass 24/7.*

Matteo leaned in again. "Arturo said you'd probably be here," he whispered. "I have to work the crowd, but maybe we can talk later, catch up? After things die down."

Before Fonsi could respond, another performer in a topaz headdress, red bikini, and high heels rushed over and started to samba in front of the two men, her arms undulating elegance. Matteo took Fonsi's hands as Arturo suddenly burst from the crowd, the four creating an impromptu circle dance in front of the musicians. Cheers filled the café even as Fonsi withered from embarrassment. He couldn't muster a coordinated two-step on the best of days.

The applause died down. Arturo embraced his friend. "Man, happy you're here," he said.

"Glad to be here," Fonsi lied as he looked down at his jacket. Dark mottled streaks covered the fabric. Oil from Matteo's hug. *And there goes my one good suit.*

The drumming died down, lights came on. Arturo glided to the center of the room.

"Everyone, thank you, thank you so much," he bellowed. His voice, a melodic lilt. "I wanted to welcome you with beautiful Bahia and Rio de Janeiro grooves courtesy of our dancers and drummers, but now you need to relax, check out the art. I have a few helpers floating around. We're happy to answer any questions."

Electronic bossa nova began to play from overhead speakers, a calm vibe descending upon the space. Matteo was besieged by a throng of admirers even as his eyes followed Fonsi's movements through the crowd. Fonsi felt like he was in the weirdest of dreams. In just a couple hours, his ex had shown up at his doorstep proclaiming he wanted him back followed by flirtation from a shiny, happy-go-lucky half-naked man who liked to shake his behind and do yoga. When had he become the sought-after prize?

Unable to process it all, he distracted himself by scanning the canvases on display. Arturo had indeed upped his collage game since they'd attended art school together. Out of the two, Fonsi had been far more devoted to his craft as a sculptor and illustrator. In contrast, Arturo had often found it hard to focus, not with the city's nightlife beckoning. Something had finally changed.

Fonsi's phone buzzed in his left pocket. A message from Robyn. *Yo, your ex spent dough like a motherfucka over here. See, Jefe, I always got you.* 😃😃😃🤑😃😃 *Let's talk about my commission…*

Fonsi couldn't help but smile, though he didn't want to think about his ex, who'd looked sharp as ever stepping into La Playa. The simple act of touching that man after so long…a delight, something he hated to admit. He wished Raphael was here, with him now. He would've certainly loved the art, especially Arturo's masterful use of color. But Raphael would've also loved Matteo's jiggly ass sticking out from a thong.

Almost an hour later, as the crowd trickled away, Arturo said goodbye to each of his guests until the only two people left up front were him and

Fonsi. Arturo grabbed a broom and started to sweep. Just like him, to be the one to clean up after his own event. Fonsi would've done the same.

Matteo rushed from the back, having changed into street clothes. "Hey, I'm sorry, Fonsi, it got so busy but I've gotta get out of here, have another gig at a club downtown." Matteo gave him a quick peck on the cheek and pressed a piece of paper in his hand. "Please, use this." Then he waved goodbye to Arturo and rushed out the door.

Fonsi opened up the crinkled piece of paper, saw Matteo's number next to a scraggly happy face and the words *Call me...*

He pushed the paper into his pocket and turned to Arturo.

"So, how are you feeling?" Fonsi asked, grateful that he'd hung around longer than he planned, preferring quiet time with his pal.

"Maaaaan, like this is just the beginning," Arturo replied. "I've barely been going out so I could get my work together, and I thought that would *kill* me. But I did it, just sold five pieces. *Five*, Fonsi! I can cover my rent for months."

"Major congratulations. Sky's the limit, Arturo. Don't stop."

"Yeah man, yeah. I'm off tomorrow. Gotta figure out how to celebrate. So what's going on with you?" Arturo hesitated. "You seem distracted tonight."

"Just, um, some old family stuff that's come up, nothing major," Fonsi said. There was no way he could go there about Giselda and his mom, not when Arturo knew nothing about the Guardianes. "Actually, Raph popped up at the shop, wanted to talk, see if we could fix things. I'm just in a weird space, dealing with his energy again." He shook his head, cheeks flushed. "You're right, I am kinda out of it. I'm sorry, I shouldn't be all stank and funky on your special night."

"Aw, sangue bom..." Arturo pulled Fonsi in for a hug. "You've gotta stop being so hard on yourself." What he always whispered to Fonsi back in art school. "Seems to me you really tried with that dude. I mean, no shade if you plan to give him a second chance, but I think you'll meet someone new, easy...when you're ready." Arturo's candor a kinder, gentler variety than Tariq's. He crossed his arms, wiggled his eyebrows. "Matteo sure was happy to see you."

Fonsi realized he was still holding on to the crumpled piece of paper in his pocket. "Yeah, he's...nice."

A big smile overtook Arturo's face. "He asked about you back when y'all first met, when you were still all about Raph. Time wasn't right back then but possibilities are in the air, brother. You gotta grab 'em. Maybe I'm being stupid, but *I* actually met someone new." Arturo demurely pushed his hair from his face like a bashful teenager. "A girl. I mean, a woman. Not like we've gone on a date, I'm just crushing on her hard. She's, like, so fuckin' cosmic and classsssyyyyyyyy." Arturo put his fingers to his lips, kissed the air.

"Um, cool," Fonsi said. "And you know this woman from...?"

"From here at the shop. She noticed my signature on the art and we started vibing on Friday. Super intelligent, energy like a goddess."

Fonsi shifted in his chair. He wasn't into hearing Arturo use that word for another one of his random crushes. "So, er, you're going to ask her out?"

"We'll see. I talked to a couple of regulars who live in the neighborhood, who've seen her around. They thought she was a corporate hotshot, but this one guy had the real intel. She's an entertainment publicist, been handling campaigns for his buddy Clive Sergeant."

"Wait, as in Clive Sergeant the actor?" Fonsi frowned. "I've been seeing trailers for his new series all over the place. They're trying to make it all prestige-y, but looks like trash."

"Yeah, I'm not surprised she's working on that level," Arturo said, Fonsi's screen snobbery ignored. "It's weird, like she gives off superstar vibes but she's also cool. Anyway, your boy did his research, got some info…"

"Okay, please tell me you're not being a stalker. Completely inappropriate. Do you know what women have to go through in this day and age to stay safe?"

"Nooooo, not stalking, Fons. C'mon, I'm not an idiot. Just curious, just doing my homework, like you always say I should. Found her profile online in this magazine, *Media Today*. She went to Wesleyan, graduated magna cum laude, worked her way up at an agency… I wanna ask her out but she's probably not trying to deal with broke-ass dudes."

"You never know," Fonsi said, though he pretty much agreed with Arturo's assessment. "And you're not broke. Of modest means, sure, slowly building resources…"

"Aw, Fons, too kind, too kind. Either way, seeing if she wants to hang, worth a try, right?" Arturo flipped open the laptop he'd placed on a countertop and scrolled down. He swiveled the screen. "That's her."

Fonsi stopped cold, breath gone.

He peered closely at the poised, professional woman in a cream suit lit by a digital glow. She was perched on a metal stool under the headline GWENDOLYN MONTGOMERY'S SUBLIME VISION.

The name was wrong, confusing really, and she was thinner than he remembered. But that face, there was just no mistaking it. That ethereal, gorgeous face, all grown up.

"She's baaaad, right?" Arturo said.

Fonsi moved closer to the screen, in a state of shock. "Arturo, what I'd mentioned about my family… that's who I'm supposed to be looking for. That's my cousin, Giselda!"

## CHAPTER EIGHT
# BRUJITA IN THE BRONX

For so many nights, she'd tried her best to escape the weight, the suffocating net that made eyelids leaden and limbs inert. That robbed her of so many days. Sleep, the best reprieve, better than disassociating from her body, which sometimes only made things worse. The weight had arrived many times before, though she thought she'd finally been rid of the horrid thing when she began working for Sublime. Supremely naïve and stupid.

She struggled to wake up. She was surrounded by blackness, dots floating in her line of sight. No…no, not dots. They were small butterflies. Glowing, with golden wings.

Something called to her. A buzzing. Persistent, unrelenting.

Gwendolyn opened her eyes.

Her cell was vibrating. She scooped it up from the nightstand, looked at the time.

10:18.

Gwendolyn shot out of bed. She'd overslept by three hours.

Jessica had left her several messages, the last one reading: *Not sure where you are but please call or text. Just want to make sure you're OK. Information leak, bigger than we thought…*

Information leak?

*Fuck.*

Since the Silvercup event, Gwendolyn had barely slept, food and drink an afterthought as she went into emergency management mode, emailing most of Sublime's clients, assuring them that everything was fine, that their planned events weren't in danger of being disrupted. They'd already received word from LaMarque's attorney that he would be ending his relationship with Sublime… *What a relief,* Gwendolyn thought…but even chill Veronykah had called and asked, "Gwen, sis, sorry to bother you, but should I be concerned?" It didn't take a rocket scientist to figure out that something screwy was going on with the agency. And in the midst of it all, James had texted, wanting to see how she was doing, having heard about the Hestia Studios fiasco on the news. She'd quickly written back that she would call him soon as she could, that she had to get everything under control.

Hestia had given no official statement about Clive's future with *The Ride*, though most pop culture pundits predicted that the star was about to be unceremoniously dropped from the show. Several media outlets verified that the screenshots floating above the Silvercup lawn were indeed from his old social accounts, with the caveat that the images were grotesquely distorted, someone's idea of a sick joke. But the core elements of the screenshots, real enough. Clive issued a public video statement apologizing for his youthful ignorance and explaining that his messages posted pre-sobriety didn't represent who he was today. Didn't matter. His followers were pissed. It was one thing to sell yourself on roguish charm and sparkling eyes during interviews, another to degrade huge segments of your fanbase who yearned for an alternative to male toxicity. All Gwendolyn and Jessica could do was wait for the inevitable call from his lawyers with accusations that the agency was responsible for the debacle that torpedoed his career.

Gwendolyn gargled mouthwash as she tried to get her brain to wake up. Jessica's text about an information leak meant that another emergency had just landed smack-dab at Sublime's doorstep. She put on a denim jumpsuit, grabbed a jacket, stuffed her hair into a beret, and ran out of the apartment. Her first thought as she reached the elevator... *Bo*.

A few minutes later, a black sedan pulled up outside of her building.

Bo jumped out. "Got here fast as I could once I saw your text. Kicked out my passenger."

"Waitaminit, what? Bo, I would've gotten someone else."

"Don't worry about it. But... you okay? You look..."

*Like someone who ran outside without washing her ass or brushing her teeth, I know.* "Can't go there. Sorry. Just need to get to work."

Bo opened the door. "My bad, Ms. Montgomery. Let's hit it."

As the car pulled off, skies still overcast, Gwendolyn scrolled through her messages. Jessica had sent a flurry of short texts earlier in the morning. *Someone hacked into Sublime server, leaked private emails to the press,* she wrote. *Call me.*

Gwendolyn tried to process what a hack could mean for the agency. Contract logistics for Sublime's clients, probably exposed even with extra security measures. And though Gwendolyn was careful with what she wrote in her emails, the junior associates weren't. There were sure to be snarky chains about some numbskull celeb riding their asses. And what if the hackers had gotten access to the agency's banking system? Sublime was already barely holding on.

Then Gwendolyn saw the text from Jessica that made her jump: *Couple of emails leaked about Clive. Media's aware we knew about his behavior. Want official statements, I'll handle.*

Gwendolyn massaged her temple. What was the point of someone doing something like this? Sublime didn't have any major beef with clients or other companies. Who'd ever heard of a PR feud?

So many people were counting on her. Jessica, the junior associates, clients. The agency would go down...because of her. She allowed it all to sink into her bones as the world she'd created as Gwendolyn Montgomery unraveled. Out of all the places she could've chosen to live, why in the world had she returned to New York? Had she not been careful enough? Did someone track her down because of the *Media Today* profile? (Agreeing to do the profile, so very stupid.) Were one of the Guardianes after her, maybe trying to teach her a lesson? But that didn't make much sense considering how much time had passed since she'd walked away from being Giselda Angelica Rivera.

One of Giselda's earliest memories was of sitting amid the ruins of El Chorrillo after she'd managed to claw her way out of the ruins of her family home. *Necesito a Helena,* she thought. She had to dig herself free so she could reach her big sister, who always looked out for her when Mami and Papi weren't around. She would reach Helena and be swept up in her arms and covered in kisses, and things would be fine.

But her sister was nowhere to be found. The explosions and fires and screams had frightened Giselda so much that she thought it best to scurry into a little nook. Men in green uniforms and painted green faces saying words she didn't understand soon found her and brought her to a building that belonged to la policía, a building Giselda vaguely remembered being pointed out by Mami and Papi.

The green uniforms left la policía and she sat with Black and brown men who felt more familiar, who sang her lullabies and gave her huevitos de leche. They soon brought over a nice older woman with curly white hair who spoke to her in a gentle voice. When the woman asked what her name was, the little girl chirped, "Me llamo Giselda..." But when the woman pressed her to share her family name, she didn't understand. Her parents and siblings and people in the neighborhood had called her the name she'd shared, Giselda. She was barely three, too young to understand the concept of surnames.

Over the years, her recollection of that time was sparse. Giselda did remember being driven to a hospital and then a big school where many others stayed. The woman from the police station carried her around, asked adults if they knew the girl's family. Giselda wasn't sure how much time passed before she was driven far away and carried into a plain brown building with a large cross above its entrance. At the orphanage, the staff were nice enough, though she eventually began to understand that they mostly kept their distance, especially after the incident. At five years old, she got into a fight with another girl, Irma, who'd tried to steal a one-legged doll Giselda had been given by a kind caregiver. A wailing Irma walked away with burns on her arms where Giselda had grabbed her. That's when Giselda earned the nickname from other kids that stuck. Brujita...little witch. Hardly anyone messed with her after that, not when they saw Irma's scars.

Over the years, Giselda liked to sit for stretches of time by herself in the chapel, sometimes entranced by an old, chipped statue of the Virgin Mary, a statue that for some weird reason reminded her of the faceless lady who occasionally haunted her dreams. The silence of the space was good. It helped her to concentrate, to remember Helena's cocoa butter smell and Mami's tinkling laughter and Papi's tendency to swivel his hips and break into reggaeton moves when he got home. Silence helped her hold on, helped her find the joy within. All that mattered.

Even with the loneliness, Giselda became a top-notch student who picked up smidgens of English from the American shows she watched on the orphanage's cracked TV screen. It was her chance to see Black and brown people who looked like her but who weren't poor and forgotten, who walked and talked and pranced like "gente gigante"...so big, so special and spectacular. "Americanos Negros bonitos," staff sometimes exclaimed when the television was on. Beautiful Black Americans. African Americans. Black people who didn't have high-heeled rabiblancas sneer at them in stores in Panama City and mutter, "Negrita fea." *Ugly Black girl.*

Deep down in her heart, that was where Giselda thought she needed to be, among these people where she could walk and talk and prance like a superstar, too, to be closer to the pretty Black and brown ladies with money. So the arrival of Madrina when Giselda was twelve years old had seemed like a miracle. This boisterous woman in a floral caftan and hoop earrings had swooped into the orphanage out of nowhere, claiming she and Giselda's mother were cousins, that she would never have left Giselda to suffer had she realized the girl was still alive.

The first question Giselda asked her supposed cousin as tears streaked down the older woman's face: "¿Cuál es mi apellido?" *What's my last name?*

"Rivera," Madrina had said. Giselda's family surname was Rivera. And her mother's maiden name was Harewood. "Técnicamente somos primas, pero llámame Madrina, por favor." *Technically we're cousins, but please call me Godmother.* Giselda nodded, letting the discoveries about her name and new connections sink into her bones. She was a little more complete, finally.

On the fourth consecutive day of her visits, Madrina declared to Giselda, "Mi amor, prepárate. Nos vamos a América!" They were leaving for the states, immediately. Which seemed impossible, like magic. (Giselda would eventually understand enough about the world to deduce that Madrina had bribed orphanage administrators with large wads of cash to send the girl on her merry way with appropriate paperwork. No magic there.) Leaving Panama was a blur. Giselda needed only thirty minutes to pack up her scant belongings. A day later, after a night sleeping side by side with Madrina in a hotel bed—the softest, plushest bed Giselda had ever lain on—she was shocked to be on a plane for the first time. There were plenty of Panamanians onboard, their familiarity a comfort, but also lots of people speaking English so fast she couldn't keep up. The air in the main cabin had a sour smell and the turbulence made her stomach churn, but she persevered until they landed in JFK. By the time she'd reached the South Bronx and met Madrina's moody but tolerable son Fonseca, she was relieved. She'd made it.

Having someone like Madrina who lavished attention on her, who took her to the hairdresser, who bought her a full two weeks of new clothes during Macy's one-day sales—no words. Giselda almost fainted when she got off the 2 train at Thirty-Fourth Street and saw all the people on the street rushing to and fro, their arms laden with bags. Giselda sensed what it must be like to be a princess who could now sport pastel-colored blouses and crisp blue jeans and textured miniskirts at school. Who could buy fashion magazines and try to put herself together like the gorgeous Black models and actresses she stared at for hours. Giselda held on to the idea she was royalty as she settled among Bronx brown tenements, as she coped with constant noise from overhead trains and sidewalks littered with trash and leering men who reeked of liquor at bodegas. Giselda was no fool. It took her no time to understand this new home of hers wasn't totally safe, that there were plenty of people living here who were also poor and forgotten. So much of what she'd devoured on that cracked screen back in the orphanage, an incomplete truth.

Much later, when she had come into the gift that she suspected might be her birthright, when Madrina was treating Giselda less like a fashionista and more like an indentured servant, Giselda would recall her childhood yearnings to be one of the beautiful Black people of America. Right before Madrina's death, she was accepted to Wesleyan on a full scholarship, still seventeen, having had no choice but to use her birth name. She immediately filed the paperwork to have her name changed the day she turned eighteen, enduring multiple visits to the Panamanian consulate and U.S. Citizenship and Immigration Services. She'd applied to Wesleyan as Giselda Angelica Rivera but entered as Gwendolyn Sims Montgomery, a name cobbled together from a hodgepodge of African American heroes. The surname she'd once been so grateful to discover, abandoned. After what she'd endured with Madrina, the terrible things she'd done, she was determined to finally create her American dream on her own terms, fresh, glistening identity included.

And now the dream was over.

※ ※ ※

"Ms. Montgomery…"

Gwendolyn saw Sublime's building looming above. She grabbed her bag and dragged herself out the car. Bo stepped out the car, too. She took in her driver, saw the concern in his eyes, the empathy. Bo was thoughtful, like James in some ways, but also very different. More of a Joe Schmoe who balanced toughness with calm, earnest vibes. And so down-to-earth. Why hadn't she appreciated that before? Gwendolyn felt the urge to fall into his massive arms and give up, just let him take care of her and drive her away somewhere.

She muttered "goodbye" and ran into the building. The doorknob to Sublime's entrance was warm, as if it were a sweltering summer day. She pushed open the door, scanned the space. Several employees were hunched over their desks. Phones rang incessantly.

Gwendolyn headed toward Jessica's office. Her boss had her headset on, sweating bricks as she talked and texted. A message popped up on Gwendolyn's phone. *On call w/ Variety re Clive*, Jessica wrote. *Done soon.*

She gave Jessica a thumbs-up through the glass wall. One of the IT people, Samantha, sat at a nearby desktop with Amir, a new associate.

"Hey, Gwen," he said, and straightened up as if she were his commanding officer in a platoon.

"Hi, you figured out who's behind the hack?" Gwendolyn asked them. There was zero time to waste.

"No. This is so screwy," Samantha said. "I checked our servers, did multiple scans for viruses and other types of malware. Nothing. I'm sitting with everyone's individual stations to see if I can find anything. And on top of that our climate control has gone bonkers. I've adjusted our thermostat so it should feel frosty in here, but the heat's still raging. Fuckin' bonkers."

Samantha wiped her brow with her forearm just as the terminal made an eerie screech. Gwendolyn and Amir jumped at the sound right before the screen went blank. Two seconds later, the word *TRAIDORA* appeared in bright red, blinking on the screen, followed by *GISELDA RIVERA*.

"What in the—" Samantha recoiled from the keyboard, hands in the air. "Don't know what this is. Wasn't me."

*Of course*, Gwendolyn thought, rigid, numb. Final confirmation that someone was after her, not that she needed it at this point. Her sweater clung to her back, slick with sweat.

"*Traidora*, that's...that's the same word that appeared in the sky at Clive's event. Saw it on social," Amir said. "And who's Giselda?"

More computers made the same grating sound. Gwendolyn turned around to see several other screens go black and light up with the word *TRAIDORA* in bright red.

"Yo," an associate yelled as he tapped one of the buttons on his keyboard. "What's this?" His face, lit up by the screen, took on a hellish hue.

"Gwen, I need to sit down," Amir said. "Not feeling so good."

"Ohmigosh," she said, realizing he must be overheating. Sweat poured down his face. "Let's get you out of here." She turned to the room, shouting. "Everyone, we need to leave. Take the stairs, not the elevators. It's not safe, this heat'll make us sick."

People hesitated for a moment, confused. "I mean it," she bellowed. "Everybody out…*Now*!!!" With that, they all started running to the exit. Gwendolyn turned to Samantha, who was right beside her. "Call 911 when we get downstairs. Tell them someone hacked our climate control and to send an ambulance, that an employee might be suffering heat stroke."

Rushing out with anxious associates, Gwendolyn guided Amir down a few flights of steps to a small metal bench right outside the building. He sat down, looking like he was about to pass out. Then she did a headcount, ignoring the gawking pedestrians. Gwendolyn tried to remember whom she'd spotted upstairs, if they'd all made it outside.

Someone was missing.

*Shit.*

She beckoned to Samantha, just a few feet away and texting like there was no tomorrow. "Stay with Amir," Gwendolyn said. "I gotta go back up and get Jessica. Her asthma…"

"Jessica's still up there?" Samantha's eyes widened. "Jeez, Gwen, wait for help to arrive—I called 911, like you said."

Gwendolyn ignored her and bounded through the building's entrance yet again, racing up the stairs. She gingerly touched the office's doorknob with her finger and drew back. The metal, burning hot. She bunched the fabric of her jacket around her hand and opened the door. A surge of heat enveloped Gwendolyn's body, raking her flesh, singeing her nostrils. Shimmering air warped the desks and computers and artwork on the walls. She glanced over at the portrait of Jessica in her leopard print, the woman's face melting, her makeup streaming. Her body was lopsided, folding into itself. Heat distorting light, warping the image, or something else?

Gwendolyn tried to concentrate. There *was* something else in the office. A subtle tingle. An energy bubbling against her skin that she remembered from long ago.

The computers had gone dark except those that had *TRAIDORA* blazing on their screens. The machines no longer shrieked but emitted low, breathy sounds that hissed and shushed and crawled against her skull. Words...she heard words. Her birth name. *Giselda.*

Jessica was still sitting at her desk, head lolled over. Gwendolyn ran over and shook her boss, shouting for her to wake up. She would heft the woman up on her shoulders and carry her out of the office if she had to. She screamed her name again. Jessica jolted up in her chair, dazed. "Gwen," she muttered. Her voice was small, tentative. As if she were a frightened girl.

Outside, the computers continued to whisper.

"We've gotta move," Gwendolyn said. "Do you need your inhaler? I know it's hot, but if you can stand, I'll help you to the stairs..."

"I hear her," Jessica said. She clutched Gwendolyn's sweater. "Can't stop hearing her in my head. I see her face, her bones. Jesus...she's calling me. Saying she's coming."

"Who?" Gwendolyn asked.

"Mama..." Jessica whimpered as her eyes filled with tears, as she put her hands to her ears. "She's on her way. My dead mama, she's coming back."

CHAPTER NINE

# FEATHERS

Fonsi slowly opened his eyes. His right hand was cramped, his head heavy. He was on his back, on his bed, the studio dim. He pushed aside his duvet and clutched the café receipt he'd asked Arturo to print out for him last night.

"I need a memento, something, *anything* associated with my cousin," he explained as they sat inside Faith's, Fonsi reeling that Arturo had actually met Giselda. "You have her receipt, right?"

Arturo let out a huge puff, clearly skeptical that this *Media Today* woman was his pal's long-lost relative from the Bronx. He turned to the register. "I'll do this because it's you, Fons, but you have a nerve calling me a stalker," he said. "This is weird."

With Guardián edicts floating in his head, Fonsi couldn't reveal to his buddy what he could do as a medium. He also knew receipts didn't have any personal intel that would be useful in locating someone. And he couldn't stop wondering why Giselda was going by the name Gwendolyn. "Congrats again on your exhibit," Fonsi had said and dashed out the café before Arturo could ask him any more questions.

Fonsi sat up in his bed and studied the crumpled piece of paper that detailed Giselda's Friday morning purchase. It was a long shot, a dumb one, really, that he could make contact with a spirit connected to his cousin. The odds of a random ghost fastening themselves to a newly printed receipt? Ridiculously low. And the odds of said spirit knowing his cousin? Even lower. There'd been no hum to the paper, no ringing that sparked his intuition. Fonsi scooched out of bed and threw the receipt into the trash. Exactly where it belonged. A reminder of his limitations.

An hour and a half later, Fonsi stood outside Faith's after having purchased an English breakfast tea that warmed his fingers. Arturo had the day off, so there was no chance he'd run into his friend and contend with more awkwardness. It was a reasonable enough assumption that Giselda lived close by if she was a regular at the café, and so he figured his search should begin here. Fonsi gathered his courage and told himself that sometimes it was okay to do utterly ridiculous things.

"Have you seen this woman?" he asked a man on the street. Fonsi held up his phone and waved Giselda's picture in his face. He did this with more than two dozen people on the corner like he was a broke mofo selling ass. Most pedestrians ignored him or looked askance—not surprising in New York. After Fonsi had approached a suited-up, auburn-wigged woman with a rhinestone purse and stern Maxine Waters–auntie vibes who proclaimed, "This is *extremely* inappropriate," he knew it was time to change tactics.

Fonsi went all around the neighborhood from building to building, lobby to lobby, praying he would find his cousin, that he would spot her name. He started at 125th Street and Frederick Douglass Boulevard and moved south. He walked one avenue east, checked properties with even numbers, and then walked back west, checking properties with odd numbers. Methodical, diligent.

*This is ridiculous*, Fonsi thought after noticing plenty of buildings didn't list resident names in their lobbies. But something pushed him on, told him to persevere as his eyes scanned for *Gwendolyn Montgomery* or *Giselda* or *G. Montgomery*.

Fonsi eventually stood on the corner of 119th and Adam Clayton Powell. A slim gray-and-black tower loomed above him one street over, the building a stark contrast to the squat red- and brown-brick structures that occupied the rest of the block. According to the plan he'd crafted for himself, he should have started walking west, but in the distance something caught his eye, a moving truck parked outside the tower. Two workers hefted a sofa into the back of the vehicle, followed by another worker who awkwardly carried a humongous terra cotta floor vase, the piece of furniture almost half the size of the man's body. The vase held a cluster of peacock feathers with colors that shone, their blues and turquoises and golds so bright that he couldn't turn away. A slight breeze appeared, carrying a sweet aroma.

He stopped, felt something present, ineffable, and abruptly changed his plan. Fonsi walked a block over and into the small lobby right as the movers strolled back inside. Its walls were silver, shiny. The smell of roasted pumpkin and honey permeated the space, what he'd smelled outside. He wondered if someone was cooking on the first floor.

Fonsi scrolled the list of digital names highlighted on the intercom panel. *...Ingalls...Jonas...Lloyd...Matthews...Montgomery...*

He held his breath, read the entire name.

*Montgomery, Gwendolyn, 6G...*

His world went still. He heard the ping of an elevator. Seconds later, a bespeckled white man frowned as he dashed by and left the building.

Fonsi's fingers shook. He dialed the numbers that appeared next to Gwendolyn's name. 6182...

A shrill ring echoed through the lobby. No answer. He swallowed, redialed the numbers. The ringing began again, and then...

*"Hello? Who is it?"*

The voice was scratchy. Distorted by the speaker maybe. A woman's voice, he suspected, though he couldn't tell if she was Giselda.

"Um...hello..." He paused, not having thought through what he would say, even after all the time spent searching for her. "Hi...this is Fonseca Harewood."

Silence.

*"Fonseca Harewood...as in Fonsi, from the Bronx?"*

And then he knew.

"Yes, Giselda...yes, it's me," he said.

A pause.

"Sixth floor," the voice said, and buzzed him in.

Fonsi took the elevator up, hands in his pockets. This had suddenly become easy. Too easy, perhaps, Giselda letting him up just like that. Maybe she'd already sensed that something was off with El Intermedio, that she was needed.

Questions flooded his mind. Did she still practice her art? She was already powerful when they were kids, almost without trying. Did any of her colleagues know she was a Guardián? Seemed unlikely.

The elevator doors opened to a hallway that was bare save for a nondescript wooden table with a garish azalea floral arrangement. Fonsi spied the door marked *6G* to his right but hesitated, unsure once again. Anxiety added lead to his feet, the manic energy he possessed bouncing from building to building nowhere to be found. Before he could knock, the door flew open. Giselda, after all this time, clad in a bright pink bonnet and furry cream robe with matching slippers.

"You're here," she said.

Fonsi awkwardly leaned forward. A reflex—they'd been raised to greet family with hugs and kisses no matter the circumstances—but his cousin stepped back. Still, she beckoned him inside.

"Come in," she said. Her voice was raspy, as if she had a cold, or had been speaking nonstop. "Leave your shoes in the foyer. Sorry the place is a mess."

Fonsi scanned the living room. With the exception of Chinese food cartons flanking metal chopsticks, a half-empty bottle of water, a few scattered papers, and two open laptops, everything was in perfect order.

"Sit," Giselda said. She gestured to the couch and rubbed her eyes. "Can I get you something to drink? Water or juice?"

"Er, yes, sure. Whatever's convenient."

Fonsi sat down and continued to check out the place without looking like he was looking. Neo-Nordic decor with minimal ornamentation. A slim black-and-white kitchen photo with roses. A painting of a sandy beach with clear blue waters above the couch. Jute off-white carpet underfoot. Overall, the space was upscale, serene and cozy to some, Fonsi supposed. But to his Caribbean American eyes, far too sterile and bland. His once stylish cousin, imprisoned in a West Elm catalog.

"Uh, nice place here," he called out to Giselda. She had the television on MCURY, muted with captions on. His Spirit Sense tingled, just a bit. Was there a presence in the apartment?

"Thank you. Work in progress," she said, and returned from the kitchen with a glass. "Fresh mango juice. Added water to cut down on the sugar."

"Appreciate the hospitality," Fonsi said. Giselda had definitely changed, which was to be expected considering she was older and they hadn't seen each other in years. The way she enunciated her words, tone crisp. Her Spanish-inflected accent, once so thick, gone. The Bronx accent she'd also developed, gone. And how she'd taken a seat across from him, back straight, legs crossed, hands clasped on knee like an international dignitary running a meeting in fluffy robe and bonnet.

She leveled him again with her eyes. "So, I presume you're here to explain what's been going on. And you look…different."

"Yes, I'm here to explain," he said, ignoring her comment about his appearance. "But, Giselda, just to be clear, you're going by Gwendolyn now?"

"I'm not *going by* anything. My legal name is Gwendolyn. *I'm* Gwendolyn." She crossed her arms. "So, explain how you're involved with what's been happening."

Fonsi shook his head, opened his arms wide. "Uh, well, I'm happy to try…" His cousin looked haggard despite her beauty. She was staring him down, superior host to an uninvited guest. "But first I think it makes more sense to find out what's been going on with you."

She grabbed the bottle of water on the table. "I've been up all night trying to do damage control for the agency I work for. There was a prank someone pulled at the office with our computers, and the temperature… Bizarre. My boss is asthmatic, had to be taken to the hospital." Her gaze remained on Fonsi, unwavering, accusing, as she explained what happened at the Brooklyn Museum and Silvercup.

"With what went down at the office, especially when I heard my birth name," she continued, "that's when I knew, it was something supernatural. The blaring heat, and before, at my events…the cold, exactly what used to happen when anyone messed with El Intermedio. Could feel it in my bones, didn't want to admit it. And then, not even twenty-four hours later, you're here at my doorstep. Final confirmation that this is Guardián bullshit."

Fonsi had in fact heard about the bizarre incident at the Brooklyn Museum on the news, though he hadn't had the slightest idea his cousin was involved. "Okay," he said. "Okay…I don't mean to be presumptuous, but everything you've described, sounds to me like you're being haunted. Like spirits are doing their thing."

"Spirits?" His cousin leaned forward. "Really?"

"Think about what you shared about your events and the office,

Gisel...er, Gwendolyn. I mean, it would take an incredible amount of power for ghosts to pull off hauntings like that, but it's possible. Unlikely, sure... Almost all entities I've encountered get their spook on in really limited ways. Pushing phones off counters. Late night whispering. Walking through walls, that sort of thing. And it usually takes tons of juice for them to do even that." He pushed aside the thought of his liaisons with Amede once again. "I'm just not sure why someone would be targeting you."

His cousin pursed her lips. "Right," she said. "My boss, she claimed that she heard her dead mother's voice. Saw her mom's bones. Right... ghosts."

Fonsi recounted what he'd learned about the breach and its connection to the seasonal equinox. "The barrier between our world and El Intermedio is breaking down," he said. "Estelle thinks spirits are finding it easier to do their thing in our realm, which could explain how they were able to more easily wreak havoc at your events. The breach, that's why I'm here, to ask for your help."

His cousin blinked, unmoved. He was beginning to understand she'd worked hard to distance herself from Guardián affairs, and here he was bringing the order's business back to her doorstep as she sat in her very beige, very vanilla home.

"You described super hot or cold temperatures during each incident," Fonsi continued. "Obvious signs that portions of El Intermedio were leaking into our world. Honestly, I'm surprised you didn't figure that out immediately. Always happens when you use your gift."

Gwendolyn clasped her hands on her lap. "I don't practice anymore, Fonsi. Haven't used my gift in years."

"Um, I see." *Wasn't expecting that.* "Well, even if you stopped using your abilities," he continued, "you can't have forgotten what it felt like. You and Ma used to practice all the time. It was like second nature—"

Fonsi stopped himself, deciding it was best not to revisit the past. At least not yet. "This breach with El Intermedio, it can be repaired only by someone with your gift. A manipulator. Which is why I'm here."

"You want me to use my power... as a manipulator?" She looked stricken. "I left that part of my life behind long ago."

"But your gift is a blessing from the divine," Fonsi said. "How could you..."

"My so-called gift led to nothing but grief and pain. I wanted a new life. I deserved a new life after all the shit I put up with."

"What *you* put up with? Okay... whatever, *Gwendolyn*. It doesn't really matter what you want right now. We need you." Estelle's words floated in his head. "You can't hide from who you are, how special you are."

"You're sounding just like Madrina. About how grand our talents were. *My* talent. And look where it got her."

Fonsi took a deep, deep breath. He wasn't ready to talk about his mother, even as he yearned for answers about her death. "Ma may have been a bit over the top..." Gwendolyn glared at him as if to say *Understatement of the year*. "...but she always encouraged you to exult in who you are. I mean, look at your place, Gwendolyn. You're a Guardián... supposedly... I guess. Where's your altar? How are you honoring the orishas?"

"I have an altar," Gwendolyn said. "In the closet."

"In the *closet*?" Fonsi yelled. "You were bestowed with magnificence... and you put your altar in a closet?!?"

"It's a really big, nice closet."

"Geez, how could—"

"Fonsi, our ancestors had to hide our connection to the orishas for centuries to survive. You know that, so quit your sanctimonious nonsense. I show reverence in my quiet way. I haven't forgotten."

"Our ancestors had to make tough choices, code our traditions for safety because they could be *murdered*. And you, of all people, what you were given…" He waved his hand around the living room. "You're ashamed of who you are, your heritage. No wonder this apartment is so dead and dry."

"Fonseca Harewood, how dare you? You have no right to come up in *my place* looking like a stoner, talking crap…"

Gwendolyn's phone buzzed. She glanced down, mumbled, "I have to take this," and put on a headset as she walked into another room.

Fonsi didn't mean to raise his voice. But this person, Giselda or Gwendolyn or whoever, she was crazy. She was one of the most powerful mystics in the city…maybe on the planet…and she'd let it all go. His stomach churned. What if she'd lost her power? What if his efforts were for nothing?

He glanced over at the television and saw yet another story about the weather on the screen, this one focusing on online chatter. Some conspiracy theorists believed the strange cloudiness had been created by foreign governments to camouflage weapons testing while others proclaimed the climate crisis to be further along than experts realized. The sky, a reminder.

Fonsi stood up, ready to get back to business. He needed to focus on the breach, try to convince his cousin to practice her art. Differences could be hashed out later.

Gwendolyn came back into the living room, face perplexed. "My boss's wife called, said she's much better, about to be released from the hospital. But I just got a message from, er…a friend thanking me for sending him a gift. But I didn't send him anything."

Fonsi tried to read his cousin, saw her physical discomfort over mentioning her "friend." Someone she was seeing? Or someone she had beef with?

"I don't mean to pry," he said, once again trusting his intuition, "but can I take a look at the message?"

Gwendolyn frowned and thrust the phone over to Fonsi. He looked at the selfie of a man who he imagined had developed a litany of self-care rituals over the years, his skin aglow, his teeth white. But his eyes were what stood out. Disarmingly kind. He was smiling big time, holding up a snow globe centering a petite Black doll in a fluffy platinum gown. Her dimensions were asymmetrical, crudely crafted. Amateur shit Fonsi could've made when he was nine years old.

The doll stood in front of a sparkling silver pattern. Diamonds.

Fonsi stared at the globe, his Spirit Sense on high alert. Something was there.

*Gwen, thank you for sending this*, the message from James W read. *You're Superwoman squared, considering everything you're dealing with. Call me, or I'll call you, whenever.*

Fonsi scrolled to the next photo and saw the tiny card that had been sent with the globe. The note read, *So you'll think of me...* To which James had replied with ten eye-heart emojis.

"I...I wouldn't send him a snow globe," Gwendolyn said. "I mean, he likes that sort of thing, I guess, but it's not my style."

Fonsi focused on the image, déjà vu smacking him hard upside the head, like Gwendolyn was a backroom client at La Playa. His Spirit Sense screamed.

He said, voice low, "Something about this is off. Connected to what you've been telling me."

Gwendolyn's face fell. "You don't mean..."

Fonsi nodded. "I think a spirit has tethered themself to the globe," he said. "This guy, James, something's coming for him."

CHAPTER TEN

# SHATTERED MIRROR

As she sat in the back of Bo's sedan, Gwendolyn tried to calm herself. It had been so long since she'd dealt with Guardianes bullshit, but she remembered basic mystic principles, including how spirits can anchor themselves to physical objects that hold sentimental value. She prayed Fonsi was being paranoid, that someone wasn't bringing James into this, but after all that had gone down...

The drive south to Chelsea was quick, tense. Bo withheld his usual banter, glaring at Fonsi instead. Gwendolyn didn't bother to explain that the mangy man sitting next to her who smelled like potpourri was a long-lost cousin. Per Fonsi's instructions back at her place, she'd texted James that she hadn't sent him the globe, that he should leave his apartment. *Get as far away from that thing as possible!!!!* she wrote, as if the ornament were poisonous or embedded with an explosive. She'd called James a dozen times. No answer. No reply to her texts.

"We're almost there," Gwendolyn whispered to Fonsi twenty-three minutes after they'd left her place. She refused to think about what might be happening, refused to ask what could be happening. As soon as they arrived at James's building, the cousins ran from the car and into the lobby right as a giggling couple was leaving. Gwendolyn grabbed the main door before it closed, not bothering to buzz James's apartment.

She pressed 18. In less than a minute, they reached his floor. The elevator doors opened and frigid air filled the car, as if a February day had descended into the hallway.

"Oh no," Gwendolyn said, bolting straight to James's apartment, understanding what the cold meant. The door was cracked open. She and Fonsi slowly stepped inside, their breath misting. Glass was everywhere, the large mirror in the foyer shattered. Small crunching sounds echoed through the space as they crept forward. She heard a small buzz.

The apartment was enveloped in a deep purplish blue, specks of light breaking up shadow. Books splayed and overturned. James's desk upside down. G.I. Joes strewn on the floor. A faint metallic scent permeated the air. Gwendolyn looked back up, to her left.

"No...no, no, no," she whispered, overcome by what she saw, barely aware that Fonsi was by her side. The crunching sound, relentless, in her ears, her head.

There was James, propped up high against a wall. Shards of glass pierced his body—his arms, legs, chest. Glass in his thighs and torso and shoulders and...God...his neck. His limbs twisted, akimbo.

*No.*

On the wall next to him, written in streaking, jagged blood once again, *BASURA*.

The crunching grew louder. Something else crashed in the apartment. From the bedroom.

James opened his eyes, saw Gwendolyn. He groaned and jerked forward.

"Don't move," she said. "You could hurt yourself. We're going to..."

"*Get down!*"

Fonsi pushed Gwendolyn aside. Shards of glass flew straight above her head, like daggers thrown from an assassin's hand. She screamed as she fell to the floor atop pieces of the broken mirror. Fonsi pulled her behind a steel cabinet. Sharp pain coursed through her knees and palms. Blood gushed from her left hand.

She felt something tugging at her flesh, trying to get at her, as if it wanted to slam her up against the wall with James. Gwendolyn pressed her body down and grabbed a handle on the cabinet to anchor herself, ignoring the pain in her palms. The metal, bitingly cold. She heard another crash. A pot tumbling to the floor.

"There's a presence here," Fonsi whispered. "It's a spirit doing this, obviously. A powerful one. We have to find the globe, destroy it. Break the ghost's anchor."

Gwendolyn nodded, trembling. She and Fonsi surveyed the room from behind the cabinet, trying to be as still as possible, though Gwendolyn felt ridiculous. She had no idea how hauntings worked. Could the spirit see them where they crouched? Attack them at will? This feeble, tired attempt they were making to hide, did it even matter?

Another crash rang out, close behind them.

Fonsi pointed to something on the floor not far from James. The globe, barely discernible in the shadows save for its diamond pattern throwing pinpricks of light around the living room.

Gwendolyn heard the sharp crinkling noise, saw another mound of shards from the far-right corner of the apartment rise. The spear of glass shot forth as Fonsi ran to where James hung suspended.

"*Fonsi!*" she yelled, energy stirring within. He turned around and leapt, landing on the couch right as a spear of glass crashed into a bookshelf, missing him by a few inches.

The shards re-formed for another strike. Fonsi scooted off the couch and onto his knees, preparing to make another grab for the globe. He was shivering, his clattering teeth echoing through the room.

The large spear shot toward him.

"*No!*" Gwendolyn shouted.

A massive blast of heat exploded from her hands, blazing through shadow, shattering the spear of glass. Shrapnel flew everywhere. Gwendolyn recoiled, stunned. Fonsi crouched down and shielded his eyes. James shrieked and shrieked as shrapnel pierced his flesh.

Fonsi grabbed a coffee table book lying on the floor and brought it down on the globe.

A glacial wail filled the apartment, rattling the walls and ceiling. The eerie purplish blue vanished, replaced by dim grayness coming from the windows.

Gwendolyn ran over as James slid down. She could see how badly hurt he was. His face was swollen, bruised. His body, covered in cuts. God, so much blood…

"Hey, Gwendolyn," he croaked out. "Sorry about this." He reached for her, took her hand.

"Please don't talk, sweetie, okay?" she said, crying. She tried to remember James's face from when she last saw him at the museum, gallant, unhurt. As if she could somehow will him to appear that way now.

"I promise I'll fix this," she whispered, cradling his palm against her face. "I promise. Fonsi, call 911. Please."

## CHAPTER ELEVEN
# IN HER BODY

Gwendolyn sat in the waiting room of Chelsea Medical Center, numb, surrounded by peeling pea-green wallpaper with a light sparkle pattern. A faded watercolor still life of lavender flowers sat above a cluster of couches. The faint smell of urine and ammonia lingered in the air. Eyes closed, she wrapped her arms around her torso and cradled her body. She began to rock. Gwendolyn imagined she was in James's arms, his flesh fresh and soft as she returned to the night she'd allowed herself to lie in his arms. She wanted to conjure up his smell and smooth skin, not the jagged, mutilated mess she'd discovered in his apartment.

*I won't remember him that way. I refuse to remember him that way.* The man she was still getting to know. When she hurt like this, Gwendolyn usually disassociated and left her body. Drifted above the world with no sense of time until she found it safe to fully return to bones and heartbeat. She wasn't about to do that now. She would stay in flesh, endure the queasiness and fatigue, the jaggedness in her throat, the pressure in her head. She would endure all this and more. Penance.

Gwendolyn and Fonsi had ridden with James in the ambulance before he was wheeled into the ER on a stretcher as medical staff shouted in rapid fire, "Level 1… Trauma bay… Resuscitation…" Soon after their arrival, a triage nurse introduced himself to Gwendolyn and said, "Why don't you let us take a look at you?" She stared down at herself. Her clothing, covered in gunk. Her left hand and knees, still bleeding.

The medical staff removed splinters of glass from flesh and treated her cuts as she sat down. Her wounds inconsequential compared to what James was going through. Gwendolyn remained outside of the ICU for over an hour before the doctor approached her with an update. James had just finished surgery and was on a respirator, in critical condition, no guarantee he'd pull through.

"I need a moment," she said to Fonsi before dashing away and finding a quiet corner to sit by herself. She thought about the last time she'd seen James before the attack, how she'd treated him at the fashion event. How she'd practically kicked him out of the museum after things had gone wild. Her rudeness, uncalled for. He hadn't deserved that, didn't deserve any of this.

Gwendolyn kept ending up back at the dream she'd had just days ago of James being swallowed by shadow. Could she have prevented this if she'd been smarter? If she'd admitted to herself that supernatural forces might be at play? Her instincts had warned her that danger was coming, her dreams such a fertile place when she was younger, and yet she'd done nothing.

She leaned over and clutched her stomach, trying her best not to heave, not to fall down and wail and scream and make a fool out of herself right there on the ICU floor. Her face started to burn, but she kept it all inside, breathing, breathing.

"Ms. Montgomery…"

Gwendolyn looked up, unsure how much time had passed. Detective Zachensky stood across from her. She straightened up and wiped her face with her sleeve. An array of emotions surged...surprise, confusion, resentment. Gwendolyn was once again about to speak to this man looking a disheveled mess, her sweater and jeans torn and stained.

"What are you doing here?" she said. She knew she sounded dismissive. Good.

Zachensky sat beside her. He wore the same vinyl jacket from the first time they met. "Different precincts have been talking about what happened, some poor joe skewered in his apartment. And then when I heard that you and your cousin had called it in, that you'd discovered the victim..." Zachensky hesitated. "I thought I should check in." He glanced over at Gwendolyn, eyes locked on her bandaged hand and clothes covered in James's blood.

She remained silent, tried her best to stay calm and resist telling Zachensky to get lost. Pissing off a cop was not in her best interests.

"I'm very sorry about what happened with your...um, friend." Zachensky cleared his throat. "Your boyfriend?"

"We were starting to see each other," Gwendolyn said, nauseous. She was finally able to admit she and James were a couple. *This is what it took.*

"Again, I'm sorry." He paused. "Um, well, the scene, it's...it's strange." The detective stumbled over his words, trying to change the subject. "Looks like there was a blast that caused the mirror in Mr. Watson's apartment to shatter, and that shards from the mirror caused multiple wounds. But the issue with that theory is an explosion should've caused more damage. A lamp and a few pictures were overturned, a smashed snow globe, that sorta thing...but nowhere near the type of destruction we'd expect. And even the trajectory of the debris is off."

Gwendolyn kept her eyes down. She had nothing to say, had no words to describe what happened, refusing to go into the workings of ghosts. Let the cop think she was withdrawn, in shock.

"Someone sabotages two of your events and then comes after the person you're seeing," he continued. "On top of the emergency called in at Sublime yesterday. That's a lot, don't you think? You have any enemies, Ms. Montgomery?"

She shook her head in response. "None that I know of," she replied. "Our business can be petty and competitive, but no one would go to such lengths for revenge."

Zachensky stared at Gwendolyn. Hard. "I really don't know what else to tell you, Detective," she said.

He pointed to her hand. "You okay?"

Gwendolyn glanced down at her bandage. "I...fell into the glass," she replied. "I freaked out, when I saw that James had been hurt."

"Of course." Zachensky spoke slowly. "Of course. Anyone would be upset to find someone they cared about like that. Considering what happened at the museum, Silvercup... If you don't have any enemies, then seems like you've been having a string of really, really bad luck." He rose from his seat. "For your sake, I hope your luck starts to improve soon. But if it doesn't, maybe we'll need to have another conversation. I hope that won't be the case, but people are getting hurt. Seriously hurt. Try to stay out of trouble, Ms. Montgomery." And then the detective turned and left.

Fonsi walked over with two cups of coffee. "I saw you two talking," he said. "Figured I should wait until he left before coming over. How'd that go?"

Gwendolyn shook her head. "Not good," she whispered. "Zachensky, he's fine. Actually helped us out at the museum and Silvercup. But I can tell, he knows something's off. That I'm not telling him everything."

Fonsi passed his cousin her drink. "When you deal with spirits on the regular, you get used to coming up with excuses for the bizarre. I've never had to deal with cops, but I guess it was inevitable. After all these years of keeping ghost shit quiet." He gripped his cup tightly. His wrist was shaking. "Whatever that thing was back there was a beast. I think it was using tons of whatever power it had to hurt James, otherwise we would've been kaput." He took a moment, as if mentioning what had just happened was insensitive. "I've never experienced an entity with that kind of juice. Has to be connected to the breach."

"I don't give a flying *fuck* about the breach," Gwendolyn whispered through clenched teeth. "I just want James to be okay. This isn't his world. He shouldn't have been involved in any of this."

She felt her phone vibrate in her pocket. How many times had the blasted thing buzzed over the past few hours? She couldn't care less about work, her surroundings a stark reminder of what mattered, of who mattered. Gwendolyn turned to her cousin abruptly. "Fonsi, thank you, for what you did…at James's place," she said. "For stopping that…that thing. You saved us."

"And you saved me," he said. "Pretty badass moves back there for someone who hasn't used her gift for years."

Gwendolyn gazed down at her bandaged hand again, the same hand through which she'd channeled her power. What she could do almost effortlessly as a teenager, bringing bits of El Intermedio to the real world as waves of light, or blasts of heat or cold, among other feats she'd barely discovered. Gwendolyn had wondered at times if her gift had abandoned her after being inactive for so long. A paranoid thought.

"I think sometimes I've felt it, you know, over the years," she said. "When I was tired or…or depressed, or just high on insane energy at work. I could feel something bubbling under, like it wanted to be released."

"Maybe your art's always been with you," Fonsi replied. "I read that magazine profile about you, how your events have an 'unearthly quality no one else can top.' Maybe you were adding extra pizzazz without realizing it. You're blessed. That specialness, that gift, it's something you can't run from." Fonsi paused. "Or keep in a closet."

"Ms. Montgomery…" The two were interrupted by a woman approaching them in a long navy raincoat, lavender sweater, and black boots, her resemblance to James striking. She carried a large bag, a stuffed animal peeking out from its left corner.

"Hi. Don't mean to interrupt, but I'm Anita," the woman said. Her eyes were puffy. She'd been crying. "I'm James's big sister. I'm sorry it took me so long to get here, but I live all the way up in White Plains. Had to find someone to watch the kids."

Gwendolyn sprang up and introduced herself and Fonsi. Anita pulled her into a hug. Gwendolyn was taken aback.

"I'm about to go see James in a minute," Anita said, her words nervous, rushed. She absentmindedly ran her fingers through her hair. "Doctor's with him now. Our parents are on the way from PG County, should arrive tonight. And our baby sister, Diana, she's over in Houston, will try to get here by tomorrow."

Gwendolyn nodded. "I remember you from one of his photos…at his place," she said. "We found his phone, and I asked the police to reach out, that I knew he has sisters. I know this is awful."

"I'm just happy you came across him when you did. And thank God you weren't hurt. I…I just don't understand who'd want to do this."

Gwendolyn gestured to the stuffed animal. She needed to switch topics before she started to bawl. "You brought him a gift?" And that's when she noticed the toy—that it was, of all things, a rat?!? She focused again, took a closer look. No, an otter. An old, beaten-up otter, with one of its button eyes missing and a small chewed-up ear dangling precariously from the side of its head.

"This was his favorite stuffed animal when he was a kid. I mean, the boy looooooooved ole Otto." Anita chuckled, sad. "Only gave it up when he was, like, eight or nine after other boys on the block kept making fun of him when they came over. But he refused to throw Otto away, just put it in the family attic and gave it to my daughter years later. She wanted me to bring it over for him, for him to have something that he loved so he'll get better soon."

Gwendolyn heard the words and looked at the raggedy toy. Tears erupted.

"I'm so very, very sorry," she said. "I… It's all my fault. If I hadn't…"

"Excuse me," Fonsi said, and grabbed his cousin. "I don't mean to be rude, Anita, but I think we need some air."

Fonsi guided Gwendolyn from the ICU to the hospital lobby and out onto the street. Gwendolyn hadn't cried in years and suddenly she couldn't stop, as if tears from long ago had found her, just like her art. She was thankful for the fresh air, such as it was in downtown Manhattan, with the fumes from rush hour traffic and odors emanating from overflowing trash bins. A steady stream of pedestrians went by. A few stared at her bedraggled appearance. She didn't care.

"All of this shouldn't have happened," she cried. "I…I didn't want to have anything serious with James…with *anyone*…because of my past. He's too good for all of this."

"Someone's trying to rattle you, using people around you," Fonsi said. "You can't blame yourself. I've studied Guardián history a million times in Gran Libro, and yeah, sometimes we've had beef, but never anything like this, at least not in modern times. This is something else. But we'll figure it out. We're not alone." He hesitated. "To be honest, I'm not the best at working with other Guardianes, but doesn't matter. There are folks who'll help us."

Fonsi's words made sense, but Gwendolyn still felt like she was on her own, so used to handling things by herself outside of Jessica having her back. Someone, or something, had been watching her, following her, knew everything about her work life and personal life. Jessica hurt, James hurt... *badly*... because of her. Because she was a target.

A tense silence fell between the cousins. There was another issue they had to contend with, something Gwendolyn had been putting off.

"I'm sorry about Madrina," she said. There, she'd said it. What she knew Fonsi had been aching to discuss since the moment he stepped into her place. She'd always been better at difficult talks when they were kids. Some things didn't change. "And I know you have questions."

"Yeah, I do, sure, but maybe this isn't the best time," Fonsi said. "You're dealing with a lot."

Gwen looked up at the sky, fresh tears falling down the sides of her face. She would push through. After all this time, her cousin deserved an explanation. "That night, the fire, I didn't mean for what happened with your mom... to happen. Wasn't my idea. Madrina wanted us to be in ritual, form a dyad and call forth El Intermedio, to practice like we always did, to hone my power for the umpteenth time. But for some reason, that night I couldn't control the energy coming forth. Something, way, way off. I swear to you, Fonsi, what went down, I had no control."

"Then why'd you leave?" Fonsi said. "Why didn't you explain yourself? When the firefighters put out the flames and inspected the house, they found Ma's corpse almost burned to the bone. Me and Estelle tried to put two and two together to figure out what happened. No help from you, obviously."

"I couldn't stay, Fonsi!" Gwendolyn said. A couple of pedestrians jumped at the sound of her voice. "It was too fuckin' much. With the fire, with my history, I couldn't stay. I'd had enough."

"But *me*? What about me? After Mom was gone and you left, I had nobody. Just like that, in one night. I mean, if it wasn't for the Baileys taking me in... All those years together, hanging nonstop, I thought we had each other's backs, Giselda."

Gwendolyn ignored the urge to correct him yet again about her name. "I wanted to be there," she said instead. "I thought of you every day..."

"Yeah, until you didn't and moved on. How long that take?" Fonsi said, his voice cracking. His face was shaded by the neon pink sign of a bar. "Why didn't you call? Just let me know you were okay? And *explain*? A few Guardianes thought you jetted because you'd taken Mom out with your power, that y'all had gotten into a nasty fight. Estelle and I came to your defense, said there was no way you'd do anything like that. How you and Mom loved each other."

Gwendolyn had to stop herself from laughing in his face. Fonsi still didn't know the full story, was still clueless about the true nature of her relationship with his mother. About the horrendous things they'd done. Still stuck in his head and mystical obsessions, oblivious to the harshness of the world.

"Fonsi," she said, trying to keep her voice level, "how do you think Madrina was able to afford that house we moved into in the North Bronx? All the furniture she bought, paying for your art classes, stuff like that? How life got easy quick... Where do you think she got the money?"

"What? I...I don't know. I just thought maybe she'd been saving, after all those double shifts. Why are you bringing that up?"

Gwendolyn's phone buzzed again. "Shit," she said under her breath, and finally pulled it out. There were missed calls and several unread messages, the most recent one from a Nurse Lancaster at the hospital.

*Ms. Montgomery, so very sorry to bother you during a difficult time, but we have news about Mr. Watson.*

"Fuck," Gwendolyn mumbled before she and Fonsi sprinted back to the hospital. When she got to the waiting area outside James's room, everything slowed down. A couple nurses wore stricken faces. Anita was bent over in a chair, crying into her fist.

Gwendolyn knew. She just knew.

"He's gone," Anita said. "Lost too much blood, the doctor said, too much of a shock to his system." She clutched Gwendolyn's sleeves. "I haven't... I can't even call our parents. This'll kill them. Oh my God..."

Anita crumpled forward and wept in Gwendolyn's arms. She made her body strong, hard like titanium once again. She wouldn't dare fall apart, not when she was responsible for this. Gwendolyn willed numbness into her bones, refused to let tears fall. She looked over Anita's shoulder and spotted James's frayed otter on the floor under a chair. The old toy, keeled over.

Gwendolyn closed her eyes and let Anita's sobs fill the room. Fortifying herself wasn't working, not in the face of such abject pain. She gave up the ghost, finally losing the fight to stay in her body, and floated away. She imagined herself hovering high above the ICU, watching the others with their crestfallen faces, and thought it better to return to James's apartment. She remembered them having breakfast. The aroma of fresh bread. The touch of his hands. The plushness of his robe. His goofy baritone-to-tenor laugh.

Right. Far too much. She was about to break.

She opened her eyes, looked over at her cousin.

Fonsi had turned a deeper shade of red. The same shade of red from the Silvercup Studios lawn.

"Gwendolyn?" he said.

She swiveled around. The nurses stared out a large window at the end of the hallway.

Gwendolyn peered out the window as well. The twilight gray of the past few evenings was gone. The clouds now a deep, rusty crimson.

The entire waiting area was tinted. Behind her, a metallic clang. Someone had dropped a tray. She let go of Anita, who was completely still. Gwendolyn drifted to the large window, Fonsi beside her. She reached out for him, grabbed his hand.

The clouds that had lingered for days now were gone. For as far as she could see, there was nothing but blood-red sky.

## CHAPTER TWELVE
# BLESSED SWEET LADY

Officials are doing everything in their power to figure out the cause behind the strange atmospheric disturbance blanketing New York," said the MCURY reporter. "The governor has called an emergency meeting of top meteorologists from around the country to determine why city skies have turned scarlet. The disturbance, which appears to be spreading, is currently covering all five boroughs, most of Long Island, and parts of New Jersey and Pennsylvania. The governor and mayor of New York will appear together shortly at a press conference…"

A little after seven in the morning, Fonsi stared at the flashing news captions on his small TV, barely able to come to grips with how reality had transformed in hours. His entire studio apartment, shaded red. Early yesterday evening, once the skies had turned crimson over Manhattan, Giselda—or rather Gwendolyn—had turned to him in the hospital, terror in her eyes, and muttered, "I'll try and handle the breach. Come to my place tomorrow morning, around ten. I'll have everything prepared." Fonsi nodded, the skies a clear sign that time was slipping through their fingers with the equinox less than a day away. He felt for his cousin, sensed how awkward it was for her to leave the hospital even though

Anita was a mess. He understood why Gwendolyn had left without seeing James's body. She would have fallen completely apart when there was so much to do.

Fonsi headed back to La Playa that evening to gather supplies...candles, incense, totems...but most importantly, Gran Libro. He'd put all that he needed into his denim knapsack, which sat on a chair by the door, ready to go.

He grabbed his phone and made a video call. In seconds, Tariq's face popped up on his screen. He'd texted his best friend the night before asking if they could talk in the morning, preferring to speak with a clear head.

"Me and Mami take our asses all the way to Puerto Rico for an ancient-ass manipulator in the bush, and all you had to do was take the Number 2 downtown and...*bam*, Giselda!" Tariq said. "But on the real, sorry to hear about what happened with her dude."

"It was horrible," Fonsi said, shuddering at the image of James impaled on a wall. He couldn't go there, couldn't let what he'd witnessed creep back into his head. "How are you and Estelle?"

"Mami and I found Humberto last night. He's living like a hermit in Loíza, in the forest. He refuses to leave Puerto Rico, doesn't care how red the skies are in New York. Mami brought him to our hotel, been talking to the mofo nonstop trying to convince him. No deal. To be honest, Fons, I'm not sure I want to get on a flight with ole boy. I mean, he has conversations with coquis y bananaquits *on the regular.*"

Fonsi shook his head. "Maybe y'all should stay where you are. I think...it's getting crazy here. Estelle's keeping her cool?"

"You know Mami. Once she sets her mind to something, Energizer Bunny. She's making me stay on the phone 24/7 with other Guardianes to try and locate another manipulator if we can't get El Rey de los Bosques here over to New York. And she's telling Pops how to create a ward around the house if shit hits the fan. But if you already found Giselda...then we're good. Y'all got this, right?"

"We'll see," Fonsi said, unable to bring himself to tell Tariq the full truth, that Giselda hadn't used her gift in years, that he wasn't sure what type of control she had at this point.

He soon hung up and then remembered to text Robyn, kicking himself for not thinking to check in on his employee the previous night, just in case they were freaking out about the red skies. *Don't go in to work*, Fonsi messaged. *Take a paid day off. Having emergency. Stay home, be safe, and place the saints and orishas around your apartment.*

Fonsi summoned a rideshare, put in his phone's earbuds, and left his building to wait outside. He glanced up at the crimson sky. The air clawed at his eyes, his scalp, his arms. People on the streets were agitated, uncertain, as if they could discern something dreadful was on its way. He spotted a caravan of people rolling their shopping carts down the block, bags brimming with food, probably coming from the Key Food supermarket around the corner. Something he hadn't seen since the blizzard of 2021. One woman with brown twists gathered in a floral headband spoke loudly into her phone: "Rojelio, no basketball with the boys today. Make sure to take your behind straight home after ninth period!"

He stepped into the car as he listened to an online news stream. Reports said the Air Quality Index was fine, so there was no reason for parents to keep kids home from school or for people with respiratory issues to stay inside. But some folks were doing just that, refusing to take their chances with strange skies. Others were already making bigger moves. All routes leading out of the city...jammed. Fonsi figured people with loot could afford to hightail it out of town to vacation homes or friends or relatives or hotels. But what about the poor who couldn't afford to leave, or those who were elderly or infirm? Or the people, like Fonsi, native to the city and with nowhere else to go?

Another news clip reported that scientists at NASA and the Pentagon were speculating that a mirror on an errant satellite might be somehow reflecting solar energy from the sun onto New York streets. Videos were going viral with people in fear that city dwellers were being slowly fried or radiation poisoned to lessen the population of the Big Apple and make room for the elite. Zealots were all over the sidewalks praying and proclaiming the apocalypse had finally arrived, brandishing signs that read REVELATIONS IS UPON US and REPENT FOR YOUR SINS!!!! As Fonsi grew closer to his destination and turned off his earbuds, he realized his driver was speaking in rapid-fire Spanish, shouting words like *diablo* and *demonios* and *infierno*. Fonsi didn't have the heart to tell the poor fella he wasn't far from the truth.

He jumped out the cab as soon as it reached Gwendolyn's building, giving his driver a big tip as if it might be his last. He went up to Gwendolyn's place and she opened the door in a white tee and canary-yellow blazer with matching pants covered in a daffodil print. Her feet in cream slippers with bronze buckles.

"Whoa, you look…uh…" *Like walking grace*, he wanted to say. *Not like someone who's just watched her man be slaughtered by a spirit.* Fonsi was instantly transported back to Bronx days with his cousin. Beautiful Giselda, who served awe-inspiring presence for days.

"Come in. I've almost finished setting up," Gwendolyn said, and pointed to the center of the apartment. "I just need to run to my bedroom for a moment." Her voice was soft, tired. Her eyes bloodshot.

Fonsi stood in front of the altar. Her coffee table was covered in a gilded cloth that swept much of the floor. Atop lay a small mirror with a golden frame and a bowl full of lemons, oranges, coconuts, squash, and pineapples in front of a large light turquoise vase with bronze filigree. The vase held five peacock feathers, the green, teal, and brown plumage a perfect match. On the floor surrounding the display were five bowls of honey, which were in turn surrounded by a perfect semicircle of five frosted cupcakes. All of this flanked by two bouquets, five sunflowers in each vase.

Fonsi stared at the food and shining feathers and remembered what had drawn him to his cousin's building in the first place.

Gwendolyn brought out a two-foot-tall statue to the living room and set the figure down on the coffee table in front of the golden-framed mirror. Fonsi was startled by the immaculateness of the statue, the shimmering textures of her crown of hair, the glittering, deeply grooved fabric of her dress. The folds of her topaz gown flowed, as if she'd been caught flying through the air. Or rather, he realized, floating through water.

"Oshun," Fonsi whispered. "Blessed lady…"

"I had a sculptor create this for me years ago," Gwendolyn said. She bowed her head, her face lined with reverence. "This really talented artist, Jenny Akinyeme. She lives not that far from here in Sugar Hill. I didn't say anything about who the statue was meant to represent, just gave specifications. What she should look like, the colors she should be wearing… When I'd finished my description, Jenny said, 'Sounds like you're describing one of the orishas, Oshun.' I thought it was a sign she was the person for the job."

Gwendolyn gave a slight, sad smile and wiped her eyes. "For years growing up, I would have visions of a regal woman, her face blurry. It wasn't until I came into my gift, after you and I weren't speaking so much anymore, that I realized she was Oshun, that she'd been with me all my life. I know Guardianes don't have to favor one deity, that we're supposed to honor all the orishas for our art, but she's always been special to me… even after I walked away from the order. I'm not sure if I would've survived what happened in Chorrillo if it wasn't for her." Gwendolyn gestured to the rest of the altar. "I think she's somehow connected to my gift. I mean, lately her symbols have been popping up in my dreams constantly. This is such a modest offering, but I tried to make everything beautiful."

"It *is* beautiful," Fonsi said, nodding to the honey and cupcakes. Layers of sweetness for their sweet orisha. He stared at his cousin: she wielded beauty and elegance like a second skin even during miserable times. Of course she would favor Oshun, the most resplendent of goddesses. "And I see that ring you wear, the sunflower. Her favorite flower."

Gwendolyn caressed the petals of the ring she wore on her right index finger. "My little way of always having her with me. I've had this since we were kids, remember? Got it from a street vendor. I know folks gravitate toward other orishas for strength, like Shango and Yemaya or Oya, but there's something about Oshun that makes me feel like myself, like I can be both strong and beautiful. Like there doesn't need to be a choice. It's why...it's why I try so hard with my work, to give it a certain something, because of her. Before I returned to New York, I worked for years at this corporate events place in Connecticut. Really nondescript, out of the way. Made myself safe, small. When Jessica found me at this random party she'd been invited to, when she gave me the chance to work with her, to be part of something grand, I couldn't pass it up. To share what was in my heart through the agency. And then I felt so stupid, like I'd made such a mistake coming back here when things started going crazy. Like I should've been smarter." She wrung her hands. "I don't mean to go on like this, Fonsi. It feels good to talk about this stuff with somebody... after so much time. To talk to you."

"Yeah, it does feel good," Fonsi said. And it was the truth: to be reunited with his cousin, his closest friend growing up. He wanted to be furious about how she'd left, had every right to be furious, but he missed her. An essential part of who he was, returned.

Gwendolyn nestled herself on the cushions on the floor. The room darkened as she used a remote to draw the shades and turn on a lamp in the corner, which emitted a low light. Fonsi glanced at the altar again and realized what was missing.

"Candles!" he said. "I brought a few from the botanica. We should light candles."

"Absolutely not," Gwendolyn said. "No fire. And Fonsi, for real, interacting with El Intermedio, you know the weather goes nuts. Us being in ritual together, it bolsters my gift, sure, but if it gets too hot or too cold or some other crazy shit happens I can't control, leave me, run like hell. I can't have you being hurt."

Fonsi nodded, a tightness filling his chest. Gwendolyn... actually had his back. Which he hadn't been expecting. Why was he surprised? "I understand," he said. "I think we'll be fine. Sunset isn't until a little after seven, signaling the end of the equinox. We have plenty of time to fix this. I...er...I'll start." Even though he'd emailed her passages to study last night, he knew he was far more familiar with Gran Libro than Gwendolyn. He'd memorized a passage meant specifically to create connection with El Intermedio. "Please join in whenever you like."

He began a prayer.

*Orishas, saints, ancestors of the sky*
*We seek your wisdom and power*
*We seek connection to the place*
*Where spirits dwell on high...*

Fonsi felt a lightness, a sensation he hadn't experienced in so many years, not since his mother allowed him to sit with her and Giselda during their rituals. The apartment became warm. He opened his eyes. Gwendolyn's fingertips were sparkling with colors. A faint amber halo pulsed around her head. He hadn't seen her work her art in so long. It was frightening, and magnificent.

She joined him in the chant, Fonsi enveloped by floral scents, the smell so intense, so cloying, he could barely breathe. His spirit was pulled from his body, his soul swimming and tumbling with Gwendolyn's, the entire apartment turned upside down. They went higher and higher, floated through the living-room window, instinctively reaching for red sky. Sleep-tripping without slumber. Surreal. Something he only experienced the few times he'd been in ritual with the Baileys.

A white glistening rupture appeared, a huge, swirling nucleus in the red light. The breach, he was sure. The cousins grew closer to the rupture, alternating waves of heat and cold striking Fonsi's soul. Lines of yellow light emanated from Gwendolyn, her power shimmering, streaming from her hair and eyes and fingertips. It was as if she knew instinctively what to do, didn't need Fonsi's guidance at all. But then he noticed her spirit form start to wobble, unsteady in its arc.

Gwendolyn jerked and recoiled from the fissure of light. She screamed. *No.*

Her spirit was shredded, bits of her soul self sucked into the slim fissure. Fonsi pushed himself toward her. An invisible force grabbed him and hurled his spirit backward into flesh.

He gasped, clutched the sides of the cushion on which he sat. He was back in the apartment. Kaleidoscopic colors pulsed throughout the living room. Gwendolyn thrashed about on the floor, groaning.

There was a flash. A boom. The vase holding peacock feathers shattered, bowls of honey and water overturned. The statue of Oshun crashed into the mirror.

"Ohmigod..." Fonsi, half-blinded, jumped up and collided with the coffee table. The light subsided. Gwendolyn gave a strangled cry and lay still. Fonsi ran over to her, his vision obscured by flashing black spots.

He shook her. "Gwendolyn," he said. "Wake up."

But she wasn't moving.

CLARENCE A. HAYNES

# AN ANGRY GODDESS OF LOVE

*For eons, she'd shared the story of her creation. For eons, she'd shared the story of how she almost died. People refused to listen.*

*When Oshun came into being, the youngest of orishas, oh, how glorious it was, the brooks and rivers and waterfalls she called forth. The greenery and flowers and wildlife she summoned. The spaces she created for stillness and contemplation, to unburden the soul and laugh from the belly and enjoy the pleasures of one's own body. To unburden the soul and laugh from the belly and enjoy the body of another.*

*She expected celebration. But the other orishas were too busy tending to the sky and oceans and land, consumed by the tasks for which they'd been born. They couldn't be bothered to shower her with the honors she deserved. Oshun, a fragile, trifling being whose gifts to the world were unimportant. Beauty ignored. There were other things to do.*

*Oshun began to wither and perish, only to be revived by the all-seeing creator and her own desires once the other orishas realized their mistake and begged for forgiveness. Once the rivers dried up and the earth was on the verge of becoming a bleak, crusty thing where no one exulted in flesh and spirit. She could serve beauty for days, but beauty must be honored to thrive.*

*She'd almost died, and people ignored the lesson.*

*Among the orishas, Oshun became the favorite of her creator, loyal and true. She watched civilizations rise and fall. Saw her image honored and exalted in festivals and fashion. Saw her image distorted and trivialized as a skin-deep thing to be sold. As something that wasn't sacred, intrinsically connected to love.*

*The consequences were dire. The creation of the in-between place. El Intermedio, many called it... Il Purgatorio to others... An abomination. Murk created by anguish, the collective anguish of those who died in turmoil, who hadn't been sufficiently loved. Whose inner beauty had never been honored, who held on as restless phantoms. Oshun knew the truth. That if one's beauty was ignored, wasn't cherished by the world, pain and destruction ensued.*

*She'd almost died, a goddess...a goddess!...and they buried the lesson.*

*She was loving Oshun, the mighty, the resplendent. She was loving Oshun, the limited, the shunned.*

*Oshun saw tragedy on the horizon. A breach through which restless souls would flee. She'd shared symbols and signs and positioned her followers around the world as best she could. They would fuel her power so she could share power when called upon. Bestow her blessings to her beautiful champion. Finally. Before it was too late.*

*She'd almost died, and yet the lesson was hidden.*

## CHAPTER THIRTEEN
# EL CHORRILLO

Gwendolyn was on the ground, flanked by smoking ruins. She blinked and pushed herself up, tried to make sense of her surroundings. She was having a dream, had to be. She'd been in her apartment, had formed a dyad with Fonsi, had begun to reach out to the barrier between worlds with her gift. How much time had passed?

Just as she'd been about to seal the breach, something pulled at her, grabbed her, tore into her spirit. She'd been cut into pieces, lost all focus, and then…

Gwendolyn took in the caved-in building in front of her. The first place she'd ever lived.

She was back in Panama. In Chorrillo. Where she'd been born.

Gwendolyn stilled herself. She wouldn't succumb to terror…no, not yet. She had to think, be rational. Was she dead? Had she been sent to some sort of hell? Why had she been brought here?

It had taken her hours to climb through the rubble when she was a small girl. She'd been half-asleep in her bed with Helena when she'd heard noise, lots of it, her parents rushing over to wake her and her big sister up, to put on clothes. "Muévete!" her mother yelled at the top of her lungs. "Tenemos que irnos, ahora!" They needed to leave immediately, run. They lived too close to the military barracks, which were being attacked.

She had no idea what was happening. Giselda could barely comprehend her mother's words before the gigantic boom, which was followed by shrieks of terror and their walls collapsing. In the darkness she heard a ripping sound before she plummeted, before something heavy pressed upon her body.

"*Mami!*" she screeched. Giselda lay there for she didn't know how long, hoping her father would find her. Dig her out. Hours might have passed before she saw slivers of light breaking through the darkness, barely discernible at first but then increasingly bright. She had to push her way through, get to the light, even as she could barely breathe. Rubble tore at her skin, her hands were on fire. Didn't matter. Mami and Papi and Helena could be on the other side. Helena might be looking for her, calling her name. She had to get out.

Gwendolyn peered down at her body. She was no longer little Giselda. Of course she wasn't. A silly, desperate thought. She glanced up, saw a convoy of soldiers in a camouflage jeep approaching. A flag with stars and stripes jutted from the rear. Americans.

"Hey," Gwendolyn called out. "Hey!" The soldiers paid her no mind. Could they hear her? Was she beneath their notice? She vaguely remembered this moment, how as a child she'd sat amid the rubble after she clawed her way out, buried her head in her hands, and wept until infantrymen approached her.

She tried to pass through the terror that threatened to grip her body, to think through what she was seeing. She needed to breathe, to center herself. But her body felt... odd. Light. As if she couldn't find her center.

Something wasn't right.

She once again scanned her surroundings, took in the mounds of broken concrete and scorched, twisted metal. The wood and glass and random items from homes destroyed. The scorched slipper and broken stirring spoon and cracked picture of a long-haired Jesus with pale skin. The shimmer that glossed over all the objects, making them fluid, flowing. The edges blurry.

Gwendolyn peered down at her palms. The tips of her fingers shimmered as well, wispy. Like smoke, or little rivers.

*This isn't real.*

She replayed in her mind what had happened. She'd touched the breach with her soul self and been pulled in.

*I think I know where I am.*

Another jeep full of soldiers went by. A stout brown woman crossed the street, followed by a bearded man with long hair and tattooed arms.

The person she'd last gazed upon as a smoldering corpse in the Bronx wore a grin on her face.

"Mi amor, hello," Madrina said. "Giselda, so good to see you again. Welcome to your death."

CHAPTER FOURTEEN

# I CAN MAKE YOU FEEL GOOD

"Gwendolyn, get up," Fonsi whispered, crouched over her body. "Please...please wake up." Ten minutes had passed and she still hadn't moved, though...*thank the orishas*...she was breathing.

*This isn't happening*, he thought. After all this time, he'd found his cousin, gotten to spend time with her after he'd long accepted he'd never see her again. They'd barely had time to talk before all the craziness, and now she was gone.

He leaned back onto a cushion on the floor and bit at his nails, anxious as he took in the disheveled altar. His reflection in the cracked mirror...haggard, ugly. Broken. He looked back at Gwendolyn. He'd fucked up, hadn't been able to measure up, again. Like when they were kids. Everything a mess.

*No...stop...you can figure this out...*

Fonsi moved closer, tilted his cousin's body into a position he hoped was comfortable, and then started to pace the living room, resisting the urge to run to his knapsack and open Gran Libro to search for a passage on what to do if someone collapses during ritual. He needed to calm himself, take a moment, think things through. Calling an ambulance was probably the best solution, though heaven knew what he'd say to the paramedics to explain why his cousin was knocked out and her apartment wrecked.

Something had attacked Gwendolyn, had sucked her soul self into the breach, into El Intermedio. Which meant he had to find her, get to the other side.

Fonsi stood up, breathed deeply, tried to focus. To reach the in-between place he'd need to do what he always did as a medium, look for a spirit that he could connect and commune with and get answers. Should he run outside? Use his Spirit Sense to scout a random ghost on the street?

Or was there a simpler solution? When he'd first stepped into the apartment, there was a slight ringing, a buzz, even before he'd detected that something was up with the globe that had been sent to James. Could it be Oshun? He stared at her statue, which he'd stood back up after it fell over.

No.

There was a presence besides the orisha. Small, but there nonetheless. He felt the tug, a pull. He needed to follow it. Try to listen.

Fonsi stopped pacing and slowly walked to his cousin's bedroom. The buzz in his head grew louder. His jaw dropped when he walked into the closet, half the size of his entire studio apartment. *Geez, how much is Gwendolyn's rent? Or does she own?* Both sides of the walk-in were covered in clothes, almost as if he were in a fashion showroom, or what he imagined a fashion showroom to be. Fonsi moved along the hangers and garments. He breathed, and breathed, and listened.

Fonsi followed the tiny sound only he could hear. There, underneath a rack of silk blouses, lay a large black box on a slender mahogany dresser.

The box was filled with accessories...earrings, bracelets, rings. In the midst of it all sat a brooch in the shape of a sunflower, its petals an assortment of colors, hot pink and royal blue and topaz.

He picked up the brooch. The craftmanship was impressive, as if whoever had made the thing had spent hours working on each metallic petal to get its grooves and textures just so. The hum in Fonsi's head now drowned everything else out. This was it.

He strode into the living room and reclined. He had to fall asleep with the brooch, had to move past the stress of what was at stake as his cousin lay unconscious on the floor. Embrace a meditative state and sleep-trip. He'd done it before, connecting with all those ghosts for his clients. He had to do this now for himself, for Gwendolyn.

*Don't fight it*, he told himself. *Let go.*

Fonsi walked into a humongous, slightly tilted room. He tried to right himself, to find his balance.

Exposed brick walls were covered by black posters foregrounded with colors so bright they hurt his eyes. On one of the posters, a woman and man lay entwined under twinkling stars, their afros perfect in their roundness. Another poster featured cascading waterfalls surrounded by a lush swaying forest of green, and yet another offered a portrait of a man with a high-top fade and glasses, a plump purple crown in his lap. In one corner of the room, a pair of floor-to-ceiling windows flanked a winding wooden staircase that led to a red sky. A dude with locs grooved to synth-y soul by one of the windows, hips in motion. The music had a slow grind, something from the '80s or early '90s.

The dredloc turned around to face Fonsi. "Oh," he said. "Hey." The spirit opened his arms wide, a bejeweled, bare-chested prince welcoming a guest to his private gallery. "Welcome, dawg. I'm Jamar."

"What's up from the other side. I'm Fonsi." He made sure to use his standard greeting when sleep-tripping. He had to keep his tone calm, modulated, aware that ghosts were desperate to connect with those who still possessed breath. *Be easy*, Fonsi reminded himself. *Give him a chance to have his say before asking about Gwendolyn.*

"Oh, I'm *real* good, now that you're here," Jamar replied. "You a fuckin' snack." He sized Fonsi up with his eyes. The spirit wore his dreds half up in a bun. Blue and black strands flowed down his back, past his behind, brushing purple pants that were loose, supple, reaching his ankles. The hem of his slacks blurred at bare feet. Lovely, manicured feet.

Jamar's body—neck and chest and arms and torso and toes—was covered in tattoos, their colors relatively muted compared to the posters' neon hues. A stream flowed across his stomach. Crows fluttered on his shoulders. On his wrist rested a thick platinum bracelet embedded with a pharaoh in a sapphire headdress. Fonsi ignored the opulence, zeroed in on the more modest necklace the ghost wore, a pendant at its center. A flower. An exact replica of the brooch he'd discovered in Gwendolyn's closet.

The amount of power Jamar must've been using to pull off such a display—off the damn charts. Fonsi had a hunch. "Was this what you used to do?" he asked. "Selling jewelry, or art? Or...working in entertainment? A musician?" Fonsi stared hard at the ghost, who could've easily been a rapper.

Jamar smiled, flashing teeth capped with diamonds. "Yeah, dude, I *create* jewelry." He touched the pendant resting against his chest. "And these posters, what I grew up with. My pops used to hang them up in our place when we lived over here in Harlem."

"The posters..." Fonsi murmured. He peered at the art again. The stars were in fact flashing gold nuggets. The forest flanking the waterfalls held a sea of emerald rings. The crown perched in the man's lap was full of rubies that complemented the garnet gems lining the frames of his glasses.

Jamar parted his lips. His teeth shone brighter. A snake tattoo moved across his chest and nipples. The contours of his muscles grew more defined as he drew closer.

"There's someone I'm looking for," Fonsi said, struggling to keep his focus as a forgotten ache bloomed. This ghost reminded him of around-the-way dudes he used to hook up with shortly after coming out. Super sexy dudes. Swag off the damn charts but somewhat lost. "My cousin. Maybe you, uh, might have seen her back on the other side." He gestured to the brooch on the ghost's neck. "She's in possession of jewelry I think you made?"

"Yeah, Gwendolyn… Man, one of a kind. Like a supermodel. She bought one of my pieces at a shop in Strivers Row that my brother owns. Shit wasn't cheap, dawg. I was like *oh damn* when I peeped the purchase price. Word. New Harlem." Jamar touched the flower. "Here in limbo, I wear the brooch like a necklace."

"So you've seen Gwendolyn?" Fonsi said, relieved. "I mean, on the other side…"

"Yeah, Gwendolyn, so dope how she took care my shit. My brother LJ didn't have a clue how to handle my pieces. He hired a jeweler for his store who told him he could make real dough selling my stuff, which he kept in a suitcase for years, dawg. My treasures, the hotness you see here, in a smelly *suitcase*. Wanted to slap dumbass LJ upside his head. Never understood how hard I worked."

"Just to be clear, you're saying… you're saying you were angry because your work wasn't appreciated. You weren't appreciated." Fonsi had to show Jamar he was listening.

"Damn right I was angry. If my fam actually had my back…" Jamar's muscles deflated. His body became transparent. "I made mistakes, man.

It was hard in the '80s, with that junk everywhere on the street. I ain't know people could overdose. I ain't know folks could die…"

Jamar started to ramble, his words coming a mile a minute as he spoke about Harlem's crack epidemic and how he could've been somebody if he hadn't gotten in with a young and dumb crowd and how drugs fucked everything up and how if his family had been there for him, *really* been there for him, things might've turned out differently, he might still be breathing. The avalanche of memory, typical for the dead.

The ghost was heading down a lane Fonsi wasn't trying to walk, even though he empathized. Still, he'd gotten some important information. If Jamar had passed away in the 1980s, then he would now have been stuck in El Intermedio for decades. A significant amount of time for a spirit. Too long, in Fonsi's experience. Jamar's grasp on things might be very off, warped by his years in limbo.

He had to steer their talk back to his cousin.

"Your work, Jamar…your jewelry…I can tell, you took pride in what you did…in what you do. My cousin's the same way."

"Yeah…yeah, man." Jamar's eyes bulged with intensity. "Could do all sorts of costume jewelry. Didn't even realize that's what it was called. Costume jewelry, like I was doing some Wonder Woman shit. Necklaces, medallions, bracelets, all of that…my jam, dawg. I also did upgrades for people with dough. I could take real gold and platinum pieces and then weave my stuff into what was already there. Unique, one of a kind. Even had some rappers reach out. Big Daddy Kane, Slick Rick, Salt-N-Pepa. One of them ladies from the group, she was like, 'Yeah, we want that type of elegance for our shows.'"

"Right." Fonsi gestured around the loft. He began to speak quickly. "I can see that's important to you, Jamar, just like it is for Gwendolyn. For me as well, with my sculptures. The three of us, we're kindred spirits. Creatives. Artists. That's why I want to reconnect with my cousin, because of how special she is to me. Do you know if she's here, in the in-between place? Have you seen her?"

Jamar peered down at his glowing toenails. "Right, man. You, um, you said Gwendolyn's your fam. She seems like good peeps."

Fonsi noticed how the ghost's face was morphing, becoming gaunt. His tattoos no longer moving.

Jamar clasped his palms together. "I'm sorry, man. Real sorry. I had to do it. They told me to watch your cuz, report back on her and get my reward."

"Wait...what? Who said this?" Fonsi asked.

"They promised me freedom." Jamar's face sagged even more, becoming corpse-like. "Freedom for all us ghosts. That getting Gwendolyn here is how to maintain the breach. You know how much I went through? I just wanted to be free. You get it, right? After all I've been through... I died too fuckin' young, man. I deserve to be free."

"So you know about the breach," Fonsi said. He balled his fists at his sides. "And why would you need to bring my cousin to El Intermedio? I need to know..."

"You're powerful." Jamar's voice deepened as he floated closer. "I can tell. Help us. Leave your body behind. Join us. We're gonna be free."

Jamar's athletic form returned, muscles pumped. His bulging crotch grazed Fonsi's, blended into Fonsi's, their spirit selves merged. Fonsi gasped, couldn't move. A spirit had never touched him like this before, not in limbo.

"I can make you feel good," Jamar whispered. "We can get down and shape our bodies and fuck whenever you like, dawg, as often as you like." The ghost breathed hard into his ear, grazed Fonsi's neck with his lips. "I've messed with nice dudes like you on the other side, all sensitive and soft. I know motherfuckas out there ain't treating you right. I can. I will."

An ache blossomed in Fonsi's chest again as Jamar's hands moved up and down his shoulders and torso and thighs. An electric sensation cascading through his form, a thousand fingertips making themselves known.

"No... No!" He pushed himself away. He didn't want to stop. "Where's Gwendolyn? You said she's in limbo. Where's my cousin?"

The ghost recoiled, scorn on his face. The type of scorn manifested by men dumb enough to presume someone else's body is their own. "I ain't telling you shit!" Jamar yelled. "You just like the rest of them, not having my back...like my fuckin' fam." Mounds of flesh melted and fell from his body. His teeth became long and yellow and jagged. "Imma get back...I *deserve* a second chance."

The loft vanished, brick walls and windows gone. Posters dissolved, swept away by the spirit's deep, contemptible voice. Fonsi was engulfed by crimson fog. The true nature of El Intermedio revealed.

Jamar sprang upon Fonsi in the murk and clutched his wrists. His flesh melded with Fonsi's again, the sensation now revolting, bee stings laced with poison.

"You ain't gonna stop us, motherfucka!" Jamar shouted, his breath fetid. Tarry blackness oozed from his mouth and nostrils and eyes. "I ain't that powerful, not like others up in here. It's taken all I got to keep this itty-bitty space, to hold on to my shit, make my shit hot. But when the barrier's broken..."

Fonsi shoved the spirit off him as hard as he could, clawed at the gunk that had latched on to his face. He could barely see.

"You won't stop us!" Jamar yelled. He crouched in the mist, a cat ready to pounce. "I'll get that crazy bitch, the manipulator. She'll take care of you. She'll fuck'n destroy you!"

Jamar sprang forward.

"*No!*"

\* \* \*

Fonsi stumbled from the couch and emptied his guts all over his cousin's pristine jute carpet. He told himself to breathe, that it was okay, that he was back in his body. That he was okay, which wasn't true.

He picked the flower brooch up and threw it down, the thing hot to the touch, scalding his fingers. Jamar was still tethered to the object, had been spying on Gwendolyn, on him. Who knew what else he might try.

Fonsi ran to the kitchen, bent down, and rummaged through his cousin's lower cabinets. He needed something heavy, solid. And then he saw it. A hammer.

Something covered his mouth. Like thick slime, or tar. Stinky, horrible… what he'd just experienced in El Intermedio.

He couldn't breathe. Jamar, exerting whatever pieces of power he had left.

Fonsi tried to keep his head clear, tried not to panic as the pressure increased. He raced across the living room and tripped over one of the cushions on the floor, almost falling onto Gwendolyn. He righted himself, took several steps forward, raised the hammer, and brought it down on the brooch.

A roar filled the apartment. Fonsi dropped the hammer and covered his ears as he was enveloped by Jamar's head, with all its drooping skin and rotting teeth and wild locs.

And then the ghost was gone.

CHAPTER FIFTEEN

# MUSH

Gwendolyn tried to focus on the woman who'd raised her since she was twelve. Madrina was draped in a long emerald-green caftan, the one she favored when they engaged in ritual. The same one she wore the night of her death.

Madrina's skin shimmered. Her gold hoop earrings danced with light. Her eyes, blood red. Like a demon's. "Giselda," she sang. Her voice echoed throughout the landscape, tone way too sweet. Behind her, Chorrillo continued to smolder.

"We've waited so long to get you here. So many years."

"Here. Where's here?" Gwendolyn already knew the answer.

"You've reached El Intermedio, amor."

El Intermedio, the limbo that was the current source of all her problems. Right. Gwendolyn tried to take in her godmother, how the edges of the woman's body blurred if she focused just so. The way Madrina said *amor*, the word laced with both sugar and arsenic.

Gwendolyn gathered her thoughts, tried to be brave. "Madrina, if we're here together… What you just said a moment ago, does that mean… Am I really dead?"

Madrina smiled, the curl of her lips exaggerated and clownish, made from rubber. Gwendolyn suddenly wished that Fonsi were here. The in-between place was his domain, his specialty, though she'd never wish for him to see his mother like *this*.

The man next to Madrina stood motionless, expressionless. He was rugged in a black tee and pants, tattoos in motion on his arms. No, not tattoos. Sigils of some kind. His jet-black hair and beard were speckled with gray. His face familiar.

"You're still holding on to life," Madrina responded. "But the longer your spirit is out of your body… Well, you'll be dead soon enough. We'll be reunited, together again. As it should be."

"How'd I get here?" Gwendolyn searched her memory, returned to when her soul self touched the fissure between realms. When she'd been fully immersed in her art after so long. Even with the fear and uncertainty over what she needed to do, the feeling had been exquisite. "That was you, wasn't it? The energy that grabbed me, that tore into me…"

"Guilty," Madrina said. "Though Duarte helped with the incantation." She gestured to the man standing behind her. "He's learned so much over the years, about how to build his power as a spirit."

*Duarte.* Gwendolyn's eyes locked with his. The man in the large framed photo grouped among the ancestors on Madrina's altar when they lived in the Bronx. Duarte, whose name always made Fonsi roll his eyes. His death, the reason Madrina had returned to Panama in the first place.

*Why in the world did they pull me here?* Gwendolyn needed to keep Madrina talking. Ghosts were ridiculously chatty, or at least that's what she remembered from Gran Libro, dying to converse with the living in whatever way they could. A side effect of years of isolation.

"You needed me to make contact with El Intermedio," Gwendolyn said, praying her godmother would confirm her suspicions. "You needed me to...touch El Intermedio, so you could grab me, before the equinox ends."

And that's when the truth of it all really hit her. This woman had messed with the people she loved. James, Jessica... Even put her own son in danger.

Fury erupted within.

"You...you planned all of this," Gwendolyn said.

Madrina nodded, head bobbing up and down maniacally, features blurred, blending into surrounding smoke. "We had ghosts watch you. Gathered as many as we could, a legion really. Called upon spirits to build up their power, sabotage your events to get your ass here. To divert your attention away from the work you obsess over. We needed you to investigate, yes, to have you 'touch El Intermedio,' as you say. Easy to take your soul from your body once you were in ritual."

"James... He's dead. Because of you."

Madrina looked squarely at her goddaughter and shook out the sleeves of her dress. A trademark gesture when she was among the living to rid herself of negative vibes. "Wasn't our intention. The spirit tethered to the globe was a maniac who went too far. Souls who stay too long here in limbo, they lose themselves. We wanted to get your attention, not butcher him. But sometimes sacrifices need to be made."

"Why would you do this? You had no right!" Gwendolyn yelled.

"Oh, I have every damn right to do what I want when it comes to my freedom," Madrina said. "All of our freedom."

"Ghosts can't just roam around unchecked!" Gwendolyn sputtered. Seeing Ignacia again in the afterlife was not on the agenda, the woman a weird, jittery phantom whose attitude *clearly* hadn't improved with time. Gwendolyn was starting to get it, what her being brought here meant. If she didn't figure out a way to seal the breach before the end of the equinox...

Duarte stood silently beside Madrina, disconcertingly still.

*Enough of this*, Gwendolyn thought. She silently summoned her gift and probed as she tried to find the breach, mindful she was a disembodied entity in El Intermedio, mindful she was surrounded by illusion, the rules of engagement more nebulous.

Something was off. She glared down at her hands, which emitted a meager glow.

"Your art—weak and mushy, right?" Madrina said. "Things are different here in limbo. As a ghost, you won't be able to seal the breach... at least not for a while. Much harder to generate your power in El Intermedio. Do you know how long it took me to build up enough juice to create a breach between our worlds? To make sure I didn't magic myself into oblivion while setting spirits free?"

An overwhelming terror coursed through Gwendolyn's spirit. Her power was indeed off, as if stuffed with cotton. Inert, unable to build momentum and lift off. She couldn't feel her real body, hadn't the slightest idea how to navigate limbo. "You can't do this," Gwendolyn said, trying to stall and quell her panic. "You're a Guardián. You're meant to maintain balance between our worlds, not unleash spirits on innocent people. Think about who you are. Think about Fonsi, what he's dedicated his life to."

"Oh, I'll see my son soon enough when the barrier's gone. And you'll be able to roam the world freely, too. Much better than what I had to deal with after you abandoned me, leaving me to fester in this godforsaken place. You might've been the one who was hot shit when I passed, but I've nurtured my art, made it strong again best I could, like when I was young. No distractions."

"I didn't know you were here," Gwendolyn said. "After the fire..."

"After the fucking fire you left me," Madrina shouted, her mouth transforming into an abyss that swallowed the air and earth and debris around her. A grotesque, impossible sight. Gwendolyn gasped, stifling a scream. "Thousands of souls are in El Intermedio. You didn't try to find me, didn't care if I'd delayed true death."

"I'm sorry," Gwendolyn said. Her words a misplaced politeness she wanted to swallow back up right as they fell from her mouth. She owed Madrina nothing. Not after the shit she'd put her through. Madrina was a symbol of all that was ugly and cruel in Gwendolyn's past life, all that she'd worked so hard to leave behind. Family, blood, no longer important.

Madrina's eyes were enlarged, crazed. Maniacal. "Do you know what *we* endured to make all of this work?" the woman said. "How long it takes to corral ghosts, to get them to give up their fuckin' obsessions just for a moment and stop and listen...actually think and *listen*...and figure out how to escape this place? The amount of energy needed...? The years it took?!" Madrina's head zoomed from her body, almost colliding with her goddaughter's face.

Gwendolyn instinctively recoiled. Her ghostly form floated backward, as if underwater. The simplest of motions, a mystery to her senses. Years had passed since she'd read Gran Libro and studied how El Intermedio worked. She could barely remember something as basic as how ghosts moved. The feeling unnerved her.

The ruins of Chorrillo turned misty. Gwendolyn noticed several other spirits hovering nearby, slinky, shadowy figures who started to surround her. Their limbs, impossibly long and loose. They no longer looked human.

Madrina gestured, and they were at a beach, the smell of sand overpowering. Light turquoise waters lapped at Gwendolyn's feet, a thick canopy of trees to her right and left. Giddy shrieks. Gwendolyn looked around. She knew this place. They were still in Panama, at La Playa

Blanca, one of her favorite places to visit as a child. The orphanage had occasionally taken her and the other kids on field trips there.

"A saving grace of El Intermedio is that you can shape it to whatever you need it to be, to your needs," Madrina said. "Something even the most basic, fragile ghosts manage to do. What you did to me? The fire destroyed everything. I had nothing of value left, nothing to tether myself to on the other side. I would've surely entered true death or gone fuckin' insane in this place if Duarte hadn't found me. If *he* hadn't managed to hold on."

"You're a badass mystic, Ignacia. Always will be," Duarte said, finally speaking. His voice, a no-nonsense Bronx baritone.

Like the ruins of Chorrillo, the beach began to go misty as well, replaced by a thick, soupy redness. Gwendolyn tried to regain her bearings, to orient herself. She suddenly had no sense of up or down, no sense of perspective or a horizon as the shadowy figures crept closer.

One streaked forward, grabbed at Gwendolyn's forearm. She shifted away from the ghoul, from the vileness of its touch. The sensation beyond nauseating, as if her stomach were being pulled through her throat.

Gwendolyn had put up with enough. At the end of the day, the very source of her power came from El Intermedio. And if that was the case, she could manipulate this place at will, didn't matter how weak her art was as a spirit.

Another shadowy figure came close. Lean, athletically built. Parts of his body badly scarred.

She released a wave of energy, shoved Madrina and Duarte and the ghoulish thing away. The scarred ghost returned in a swift motion and clasped Gwendolyn's hand. Disgust spread through her limbs and chest. These things wanted to hurt her, wanted to torture her. She had to get away.

With all her might, she envisioned a burst of bright light. Thick crimson burned away as Madrina screeched at the top of her lungs, "Stop it!" Gwendolyn began to run, exhausted from the little mystical feat that would've been child's play on the other side. Her movements were awkward, sluggish. She tumbled forward and fell, braced herself for pain. There was no impact. She simply hovered, suspended in thick red fog.

*This isn't real*, she told herself. *This isn't my real body. These aren't real legs. I don't have to run.*

Gwendolyn had to think like a spirit.

She focused on her form, tried to imagine it as a solid thing to maneuver, and pushed herself away from the scene, the sensation akin to swimming. Madrina and Duarte, right behind her.

A league of ghosts began to follow, their apparitions on Gwendolyn's tail. She concentrated again, shaped the ether around her, and emitted more pulses of light, the strain excruciating. Crimson fog was replaced with a kaleidoscope of colors. The apparitions shrieked and retreated in terror. Still, a long shadowy arm managed to reach for her through the ether, just like before.

"No!" Gwendolyn screamed, her form aglow as she heaved herself forward and swam through the murk as fast as she could.

## CHAPTER SIXTEEN
# SO LONG, GOODBYE

"Breathe, baby, breathe. It's gonna be okay."

Estelle was calm and composed as she FaceTimed with Fonsi from the boarding area of Luis Muñoz Marín International Airport. But she was wrong. It wasn't going to be okay. Fonsi could barely get out what had happened. He'd been bawling nonstop since his encounter with Jamar, the waterworks finally stanched by Estelle's steady vibes.

"I should call an ambulance," he said, wiping his eyes. "She's been out too long."

"You can get Giselda to a hospital, but they'll only be able to keep her body alive," Estelle replied. "They can't do a thing for her spirit, hon. She'll be good as dead. You need to get her soul back to flesh."

"Which I don't know how to do," Fonsi said. "I can't feel her anywhere. I don't think she's tethered herself to something, at least not in the apartment. And maybe she can't. From what that nutty ghost said, it sounds like something purposely attacked her to drag her into limbo. I think that's what I saw, when we were in ritual. Maybe she's totally lost."

"No, she's not," Estelle said. "Fonsi, no other Guardián alive understands spirits as well as you do, has studied Gran Libro as closely as you have. Wherever your cousin is, create a tether for her. Tap in to her gift. Help her find her way back by surrounding her body with what she loves. That girl has been strong since ya'll were kids, survived so much back in Panama, ain't no one going to hold her back against her will. You know that. You know *her*. Create a beacon with ritual, with people you can count on. You got this, baby."

Fonsi nodded, but he didn't think he could do it. His cousin, good as dead.

"Tariq and I are on our way to New York with Humberto. But…" Estelle hesitated. "I don't think we're going to arrive before the end of the equinox. And Humberto's control of his gift at this point is… It's spotty. He tried to seal the breach over here in Puerto Rico—didn't work. But at least we got him to come to New York, to see what he can do there." Estelle's face got closer to the screen. "Like I said, our best bet is getting Giselda back to her body, making sure she repairs the fissure before sunset."

"Right," Fonsi said. "Right." *We're doomed.*

"Hold on. Mijo wants to wave goodbye before I hang up." Fonsi's screen blurred. In a second he saw Tariq with a scowl gesturing at the snoring withered man resting on his shoulder. Had to be Humberto. Crumbs of food were encrusted in the old manipulator's beard. Tariq tapped his fist to his chest, pointed at the screen, and mouthed the words *we love you.*

Fonsi limply waved goodbye as the call ended. He glanced over at his cousin on the floor. She looked peaceful, though only the orishas knew what her spirit faced.

To create a beacon for Gwendolyn's ghost, he had to surround her with what she loved, or at least what he imagined she loved, considering their years apart. To create an altar around her body that would speak to her art. A fundamental part of being a Guardián: connecting with objects that sparked your soul, that enlivened your power. At the end of the day, perhaps his order wasn't so different from ghosts and their obsessions.

He looked around the apartment. Even the most mundane items could hold sentimental value for those who'd crossed. He ran into her bedroom, grabbed the bonnet and robe she'd worn when he'd first visited. He spotted the suit she wore for the *Media Today* profile hanging in a corner and grabbed that as well, along with a fistful of necklaces and bracelets from her jewelry box. His Spirit Sense was quiet. The items were ghost-free, no more deranged, dredhead apparitions waiting to entice with their moving tattoos and diamond-studded teeth and emerald-encrusted art.

Fonsi ran back into the living room and gently placed the items all around Gwendolyn. Something felt off, the objects too random, not informed by any real knowledge of his cousin's current life. He started to pace again, and glanced over at the statuette of Oshun. Fonsi kicked himself for ignoring the blessed lady.

He muttered a quick prayer and placed the orisha by Gwendolyn's side. Estelle said he needed to create a beacon. Oshun would be the beacon for Gwendolyn, so obvious. She'd felt the goddess permeating her dreams through her life. He could create a beacon for Gwendolyn by re-creating an altar for Oshun.

He picked up the sunflowers from the floor and placed them back into a vase, making sure that the flowers were bunched in a group of five. He grabbed a couple of chocolate bars from the fridge and broke them up into chunks on a plate in front of the statue. He carefully repositioned the mirror in front of the goddess and replaced the honey. And he rolled up the ruined carpet and placed it in a closet.

Fonsi surveyed the living room, a tad hopeful. And now, to complete the ritual, he needed people. There were no other Guardianes in this section of Harlem, at least none that he knew of. He didn't need a mystic immersed in the ways of his order, or some sort of devout spiritual practitioner. He just needed someone who believed in him, who would willingly share their energy. Someone he could trust, like a brother.

He pulled out his phone and dialed Arturo, praying that he'd turned up for his shift at Faith's, that he hadn't been freaked out by the hellish skies. His pal's face popped up on the screen. "Fonsi, OMG, *telepatiaaaaaa*! Was just going to call you. Guess who showed up over here."

Arturo swiveled the phone to his left. There on-screen, standing in front of a painting... *You've got to be fucking kidding me...*

"Raph, you're at Faith's?!?!" Was the guy stalking him? Just two days ago at La Playa, and now at the café?

His ex shrugged. "So, back at your shop, dealing with that annoying employee of yours, their words got to me. I realized maybe I've been coming across as a cheapskate creep. I can do better. I got myself over here. Thought I'd purchase a couple of pieces for my home office. I totally believe in dopamine decor, as you know."

"You're shopping for art, now?" Fonsi asked. "Can't you see what's happening with the skies?"

Raphael waved an N95 mask in front of the screen. "Used this during the pandemic and I'll use it for bad air. Climate change is something we all have to grapple with. We've had red skies before."

"This isn't climate change!" Fonsi yelled.

Raphael frowned, clearly not understanding what the fuss was all about. Fonsi took a deep, deep breath and tried to find the silver lining. Maybe Raphael's presence had solved his dilemma. He needed as many people as possible to form the ritual for Giselda. Maybe his prayers had been answered.

"Arturo, I'm sorry to ask this," Fonsi said, "but I'm at my cousin's place a few blocks away. Can you clock out, come over?" He paused, not quite believing what he was about to say. "And, Raph, can you come over too?"

"Fonsi, I'm still on my shift," Arturo said. "I mean, we have a couple of people here to fill in, but technically I can't…"

"Please," Fonsi interrupted. "Please, I need you to come over. I wouldn't ask under any other circumstances. Please…"

Arturo hesitated, wearing the same skeptical look he had when Fonsi revealed that he had a long-lost cousin repping celebs. "Okay," he said after a moment. "Okay. I'll stop by."

"Me too," Raphael said, his voice way too cheerful.

Fonsi hung up and texted Arturo the address. He tried his best to straighten up even more, though he knew Gwendolyn's knack for perfection was beyond him. *What if they think I did this?* he thought. *What if they think I hurt her?*

In less than ten minutes, the two men buzzed from the lobby. "What is *this*?" Raphael said upon entering the apartment, sensing something was off. He stopped cold when his eyes landed on Gwendolyn. "Whoa. Who's she?"

"What happened?" Arturo asked, running to Gwendolyn's side. He fell to his knees, arms spread open.

"Please, you two, I know this looks nuts. *Beyond* nuts, but I need you to listen. You can sit… or stand, but I have something to explain to you." And with that, Fonsi unburdened himself, telling his friend and ex that he could commune with ghosts through his dreams, that he belonged to a hidden order of mystics, that he'd sought out his cousin to repair a breach between the realms of the living and dead. He told them all of this and more as fast as he could, urging them to trust him to create a ritual that would bring Gwendolyn back home. Fonsi knew he sounded insane, like a one-way trip to a nice quiet room with cushioned walls was in order, but he had no choice, no time to waste.

Raphael stared at his ex as if he'd gone completely bonkers, while Arturo's expression was more complex. A mix of confusion and, if Fonsi was reading his friend correctly, betrayal?

"So let me get this straight," Raphael said. "You're a psychic who can talk to dead people in your dreams. And you basically need us to save the soul of this comatose woman through some sort of séance. And we have to do this before sunset, or ghosts will take over the city?" He fake chuckled. "I mean, what am I supposed to say, Fons? You're doing mushrooms now?"

"There are so many things in our world that can't be easily explained. I swear to you, Raph, I swear, I'm not bullshitting." He pointed to the window, to the sky. "The truth of what's happening is just above our heads."

"Really, Fons, even with the type of silly woo-woo stuff you're into, I thought you were better than that," Raphael said. "I thought..."

"Okay, enough." Arturo held up his hands. He rose from where he'd been kneeling by Gwendolyn, face twisted as if he was trying to figure out several puzzles at the same time. "So that's why you wanted a receipt of Gwendolyn's transaction? Almost like you were trying to do a reading?" Arturo glared at his friend. "It isn't that crazy, Fons, if you'd been straight up with me. I mean this is weird," he said, waving around at the apartment. "Being up in someone's place while they're knocked out. But you being a medium, okay. I have family back in Brazil who've practiced Candomblé for generations. And they're cool." Arturo drew closer to him. "What you are...what you're saying you are, why didn't you tell me? You're special."

"I'm not supposed to share who I am, what my order can do," Fonsi replied. "Guardianes, we're sworn to secrecy. Our entire purpose is about keeping things in balance, not causing a whole bunch of people to freak out over what's actually out there. Nothing I've spoken about here can leave this room. But under the circumstances—"

"I don't like this," Raphael said. "I'm sorry, but whatever game you're playing isn't funny." His words were tight, grating. Typical Raphael. "We need to call 911 and get her to a hospital." He waved his hand dismissively at Gwendolyn. "This looks bad, three brown men in an unconscious woman's apartment. We could get in trouble. *Major* trouble."

Fonsi was on the verge of dropping down to his knees and begging if he had to. "*Please.* If what I propose doesn't work, we'll take her to the hospital right away, I promise." *It has to work*, Fonsi thought, aware that doctors would have no chance of reviving his cousin.

"No," Raphael said, and took out his phone. "I'm calling the police. This isn't right. And to think I wanted to give us another try. All the money I've spent trying to win you back. That hocus-pocus bullshit with the botanica has messed you up."

Fonsi felt hit by a ton of bricks, seeing how Raphael looked at him, a complete about-face from the tenderness he'd shown at La Playa two days ago. The outright irritation and condescension in his gaze. The blatant air of *Why do I even bother with you?* This kooky artist with strange ideas whom people merely tolerated. Rage erupted. Having Raphael here, a mistake.

Fonsi no longer cared if he held his tongue, wishing he had Gwendolyn's power to blow up Raphael's phone in his damn hand.

"Fuck you!" he screamed. "If you don't wanna help, then get the fuck out! Call the cops then."

Raphael backed away. "Yeah, I'm getting the fuck out all right," he said. "So long, Fons. You've totally lost it. Good riddance."

Arturo walked toward the living-room window, his body engulfed in red, faint streaks of light reflected in his glasses. "Um, guys?"

Fonsi peered out the window as well, a slight buzzing in his head.

A huge white fissure had appeared in the red sky. Bursts of pulsing light shot forth from the breach, some heading straight down to the street. Others crisscrossed through the sky and zigzagged around buildings, piercing windows.

The ringing in Fonsi's head skyrocketed, the noise overwhelming. His Spirit Sense went haywire.

A car overturned as manhole covers burst from the street. Glass from another apartment building exploded onto the sidewalk.

Fonsi backed away from the window, heard muffled shrieks from outside. And then he really felt it, the buzzing, a clarion call of when his intuition was alerted to ghosts. They were all around him, everywhere. Piercing sirens layered on top of each other that crashed into his skull.

He fell to his knees. Something wet and salty streamed down his lips.

"Your nose," Arturo said as he crouched down beside his friend. Fonsi touched his face, drew his hand away. His fingertips, covered with blood.

"It's okay," Fonsi murmured, but that was a lie. He could barely keep his eyes open, though he was able to make out Raphael standing at the window, frozen.

"What's happening?" Arturo whispered.

"They're...they're here, all around us," Fonsi whispered. "The spirits, they're escaping. They're leaving El Intermedio."

## CHAPTER SEVENTEEN
# DIABLA

As she lay floating in crimson ether, drained, spent, Gwendolyn realized that everything Madrina had explained to her seemed to be true. Her powers were obviously dampened within El Intermedio. She hadn't used her gift in years but knew what she was capable of. Projecting bursts of light like she just had? Once an easy feat, something she did with minimal effort. But now the very same act had left her burnt-out and half-dead.

She was in trouble, her knowledge too rusty. She had no idea how things worked in this realm, hadn't the slightest clue how to locate the breach and finish what she'd started with Fonsi. Gwendolyn gazed upon herself. The edges of her body were transparent, misty, blending in to surrounding red mush. Was this what Madrina had warned about, that you had to pace yourself? That if you used too much juice too fast here, your spirit would fade away? Didn't matter. She needed to stay alert in case one of those shadowy ghosts returned. *As if I could put up any sort of fight.*

It was interesting, to have a moment to pay attention to the sensations she experienced as a spirit. Her form airy, ephemeral. Not so different from when she disassociated from her body on the other side. As if she could take her consciousness and move it through the world without being burdened by flesh that endured too much. Gwendolyn finally noticed what she was wearing as a spirit, the LaMarque linen suit she so cherished that was now part of a trash heap. She didn't understand why this was what she manifested. Wasn't important. She was exhausted, had to rest, recharge. She closed her eyes, just for a moment, just for a bit, to regain her strength.

She woke to the sound of people yelling and pivoted toward the noise. Her movement was slow, painful. Something burned her throat. Smoke, thick, blinding. Smoke and flames, her destiny.

Several people were fleeing from a one-story building that occupied the corner of a city block. E. 141st Street and Third Avenue in the Bronx, a corner full of meaning and memory. A site of shame. The Latin fusion restaurant Presente was burning, the flames and black smoke entrancing in how they undulated and flowed, consuming the building's colorful entrance. A facade she'd adored, doors flanked by muralized depictions of brown folks draped in white who danced among vines interlaced with Latin American flags.

Gwendolyn was beginning to understand. El Intermedio was responding to her memories. Her traumas. What she saw was actually coming from *her*, from when she was still Giselda.

The fire that consumed Presente, the culmination of Madrina's big plan not long after Giselda turned seventeen. For weeks, Madrina had started going around to shops and restaurants in their South Bronx neighborhood wearing a black bob wig and gaudy shades, demanding that they each pay her thousands of dollars in cash for "protection." A similarly disguised Giselda accompanied her godmother on several runs when she should have been in school, but Madrina insisted on her presence, including a morning visit to the drab, twenty-five-year-old laundromat Sudsy Heaven on Willis Avenue.

"Work with us and your business will stay afloat," Madrina decreed to the elderly Cuban couple who ran the establishment as they stood around a crooked plastic folding table, the place empty of customers. Giselda suspected they'd owned the place for a long, long time. "Turn away, do your own thing, our 'people' will have no choice but to get involved. Do *not* go to the police. They won't be able to protect you."

The old Sudsy Heaven man seemed perplexed by Madrina's words and attitude. But his wife, who sported a fuchsia mohawk and several gold chains atop iguana neck tattoos, made the sign of the cross, called Madrina "una perra diabla," and jabbed a bony finger into Giselda's chest. "We're not scared of your kind!" she shouted. "God will protect us." Giselda lurched away, feeling unexpectedly seen by Caribbean punk abuela. She remembered her nickname as a child back in Colón. *Brujita.*

The impromptu meetings Madrina demanded were laced with mortification for Giselda's teenage heart. Most of the business owners, mainly men, dismissed Ignacia's threats as ridiculous and laughed in her face. "You're really not going to like what'll happen," she warned. Their cavalier attitudes, transformed in days.

Madrina decided to make a lesson out of the laundromat, followed by a drycleaner on 147th Street. She instructed Giselda to work her power after midnight, when the streets were deserted and businesses were closed outside of random bodegas. And thus a compliant, reluctant Giselda buried her emotions deep as she stood in front of Sudsy Heaven, summoned El Intermedio, and sent it forth as fire. She watched the laundromat's steel gates melt and its windows shatter and roof cave in. Once she heard sirens, she fled the scene, the old woman's bony jabbing finger floating in her head.

Rumors spread among South Bronx businesses about the mysterious bruja who could have your business blown up if you didn't pay up. Physical evidence of how she did it? Nonexistent, nothing left behind that indicated whom she was working with. Properties simply went up in smoke, as if something had descended from the heavens and swept them away in a fiery conflagration. Madrina became notorious, and business owners met her demands to be paid in large wads of cash. Within months, she'd accumulated enough dough to escape their South Bronx apartment, she and Fonsi and Giselda able to move into a new home near Co-op City. Fonsi oblivious to how his mother earned her money.

"I won't do it," Giselda declared when Madrina had initially presented the plan. "It's my gift, my art. You can't make me."

"Then I'll throw you out," the older woman replied. "If it wasn't for me, where would you be? Viviendo sin plata en el barrio, en Colón o Chorrillo? Walking the streets, getting dick for dough like a puta? We're doing what we need to do, what Duarte would've wanted. What you *owe* me. I could've bought a house with his money if I hadn't had to bribe folks to get your ass to the states."

Giselda didn't know what to say to Madrina, didn't know much about Duarte outside of Fonsi describing him as a gangster type his mother hooked up with. The doting, sweet Madrina who'd rescued Giselda from the orphanage had become a fond memory. Maybe that woman had never existed, was a lie. Over time, bitterness had permeated Madrina's words, her walk, even her talent. Despite her defiant words, Giselda knew why she was the one being made to destroy businesses. Her godmother's gift had slowly become this weak, deflated thing that lacked juice. She didn't know if Madrina would've been able to call forth fires in ritual with others, much less by herself.

Giselda had little choice but to obey. The thought of not having a home or being sent back to Panama to God knew what, even with her gift... terrifying. And so she'd resigned herself to doing Madrina's dirty work, performing repulsive acts as she pushed aside her conscience, as she realized that her supposed savior, who once sang to her sweetly in Spanish, saw her as nothing but a work mule to be exploited. She'd made a terrible mistake, putting her trust in someone who claimed they wanted to take care of her. Other Guardianes would think Giselda a wicked, evil thing if they ever found out that she was skulking around destroying property owned by folks who worked nonstop for their little piece of something. Most of the world would think her a wicked, evil thing. And they were right.

Most business owners got Madrina's message. But one spot held out, the restaurant Presente. The place was known in the neighborhood for its ceviche and rotisserie chicken with green sauce at affordable prices. The owner, a loud man with a curly toupee, had cursed Madrina out after she made her threats. He'd run toward her, fists pumping, about to strike her down. "Touch me, you're dead," Madrina spat on her way out the door, Giselda scurrying behind her. For his dumb arrogance, he needed to be made an example of.

Giselda would have preferred to follow protocol, to wait until after midnight, when the eatery would have been long shut down, before she did her thing. But Madrina was clear: Giselda needed to strike at 10 p.m., right when the business was closing, when the workers and owner were still inside. To teach a lesson.

That night, crouched in a nearby alleyway with a heavy heart, Giselda called forth flames with a short chant. Fire engulfed the dancing figures and flags among the vines. Employees fled outside, screaming. The owner ran back inside multiple times, making sure all his workers got out safely, eventually becoming covered in so much soot that Giselda could no longer discern the color of his clothes from where she hid.

He collapsed right as fire trucks arrived. EMS workers hurriedly placed an oxygen mask on his face while his staff huddled around, inconsolable. Giselda watched it all. She muffled her cries in her sleeves as tears streamed down her face and smoke burned her throat and flames consumed the building.

For weeks, Giselda had nightmares about Presente burning. She never found out what happened to the restaurant owner, if he'd survived. The restaurant never reopened. She purposely walked past the site for days on end, morbidly obsessed with the ghost of a place that reminded her of what she'd done. Other people in the neighborhood gradually moved on and started going to the hip new soul food spot up the street. But Giselda's days became awash in anxiety and guilt. She withdrew from school, having already earned more than enough credits to graduate with honors and earn a full scholarship to Wesleyan. She and Fonsi grew distant, their silence reminiscent of when she'd moved to the states.

One afternoon, the *Daily News* frontpage that asked IS THE BRONX BURNING AGAIN? stopped Giselda in her tracks as she approached a newsstand. The headline appeared above an image of the charred Presente juxtaposed with the ruins of a South Bronx tenement from the '70s. Giselda wanted to burst into tears. It kept coming back, the hurt and pain, never-ending. She should've died in Chorrillo. Madrina had saved her, only to punish her, use her. Take her down a path for which she'd never be forgiven.

And so when the ritual with Madrina went totally wrong just two weeks after she'd burned Presente down, when Giselda endured another night of flame, she was shocked to find she was still alive. That it was her godmother who'd been killed by the mysterious explosion that overturned candles and set the den ablaze. As Giselda ran out of the burning house, she couldn't help but wonder if the orishas and saints had listened to her prayers and provided an opening. The fear of being by herself and out on the streets, gone. She would make her way, figure out how to survive with her wits alone. She never wanted to use her art again. The cost of it all, too much.

The night her last home in the Bronx burned, Giselda Rivera died.

* * *

*I deserve to suffer like this for what I did*, she thought again as she floated with Presente ablaze before her. For years, Gwendolyn had chosen freedom without feeling like she deserved it. The decision a dreadful weight that brought her low so many times without warning.

Her form was now translucent. She'd used too much power too fast, had nothing left to keep herself together. She was going to enter true death.

A shadowy figure swam toward Gwendolyn through the red murk. She kept her gaze on the approaching ghost, tried to stamp down terror. She needed to resign herself to her fate.

The ghost drew closer, the same entity whose body was covered in scars. He took Gwendolyn's wrist. This time there was no pain.

The spirit pulled her away and Presente receded into mist.

## CHAPTER EIGHTEEN
# GRAPHIC MATERIAL

"It's okay, man. We've got you."

Fonsi hadn't realized he'd collapsed, barely felt Arturo guiding him away from the window. Gwendolyn was still on the ground. He leaned over to check on her. She was still breathing.

Raphael stood by the apartment window, mesmerized, streaks of white light reflected against his face. "What is *this*?" His words a whisper.

"It's happening," Fonsi said as Arturo led him to a chair. "Spirits are leaving limbo." Fonsi saw a news anchor speaking animatedly on the TV. He grabbed the remote, turned up the volume.

"...reports are coming from all over the city of strange happenings as orbs of light fall from the sky. There's panic in the streets, several explosions reported. We have no idea if this is some sort of terrorist attack, foreign or domestic." The MCURY reporter spoke fast even though his demeanor was poised. "The mayor and governor have declared a state of emergency, with the governor also announcing she's calling in the National Guard. We'll continue to bring you up-to-date news on what's happening."

Fonsi could feel ghosts everywhere. They filled up ether, spilled onto streets. Arturo pressed a paper towel against Fonsi's nose. "What should we do?" he murmured.

"Some of the spirits, most of them I think...they're pretty much benign, aren't interested in going after people," he replied. "Or at least they don't mean to. But there'll be some, way too many, they'll want revenge. They'll want to hurt others. Inhabit random objects or even other people. Destroy us. Because of how they've suffered."

He pushed himself up. "We have to get my cousin back. I have no idea if she's capable of sealing the breach within El Intermedio itself, if she even has any idea what's happened to her, but we can't take that chance. We have to try to get her back into her body so she can work her gift."

Arturo nodded. "Whatever you need, I'll do it."

Raphael drew closer. The look on his face one of complete shock. "I'm so sorry for not believing you, Fons. I didn't know. I couldn't—"

Fonsi held up his hand. "All good. This is a lot to take in. I get it, Raph. Really."

The anchorman continued to read the news, rigid, unblinking, like a robot. "We're receiving reports of strange disturbances from residents throughout the city. People are loading clips onto social media. Please be warned, some of this material is graphic..."

Fonsi's eyes locked onto the screen as he watched his worst nightmares come to life. A woman was lifted and slammed repeatedly by an invisible force into a brick wall, her body going limp, neck twisted. Inside a pastry shop, a scarf coiled itself around someone's head as they clawed desperately at the fabric. At a hospital, staff ran for their lives as an orderly in scrubs lying prone on the floor was sliced and diced by flying scissors.

"What...is this?" Raphael whispered again. He began to tremble.

Fonsi turned off the TV, a surge of protectiveness blossoming in his chest. Like Raphael was a befuddled backroom client overwhelmed by mystical realities. "We have to do this quickly," he said, and lowered himself to the floor. "Us Guardianes, when we form our circles of power, we focus on our devotion to our deities or each other, channeling lines of energy based on emotion and intention. Arturo, you met Gwendolyn at Faith's, you know what she's like. And…" Fonsi hesitated. "…I know you're really into her. Focus on that feeling. Focus on drawing her back to us."

He turned to his ex. "And, Raph, you've never met her. You don't know her. Focus your energy on me. On believing in me, as much as you can. Or if that's too much to ask, you can focus on her, this orisha. A goddess." He gestured to the statuette of Oshun. "On her majestic presence. You've always been into that, right? Beauty, presentation. If that's what you need to guide you, fine."

"Whatever you need," Arturo repeated.

Raphael was silent, eyes like saucers. He managed a nod. In that moment, despite their beef, Fonsi wanted to take his irritatingly clueless, shallow ex into his arms and tell him that everything would be okay. That they could fix this.

He gestured to the cushions on the floor. "I'm going to start a chant. I haven't done many higher rituals before, and to create a beacon for my cousin, I'm gonna have to improvise. So bear with me." He paused. "And also, please, if you want, join in."

Arturo plopped down on a cushion, solemn, back straight, as if he was about to embark on the most important mission of his life. Raphael sat down on another cushion, his movements slow, tentative. He looked toward the door and then returned his gaze to Fonsi, who closed his eyes.

A loud noise boomed outside, coming from the hallway. Maybe from another apartment. Then came a shout, a high-pitched scream. Fonsi's eyes flashed open.

"What was that?" Raph jumped up. "Ohmigod…"

"Ignore it," Fonsi heard himself say. Firm and focused, a surprise.

*You can do this.*

He took deep breaths, again and again. He imagined the pain in his head was inconsequential, something that held no power over him. To create a tether for Gwendolyn, he conjured the chants and incantations he'd memorized from Gran Libro years ago.

He began to sing. His voice cracked.

*O orishas on high, hear our plea*
*We ask for your favor*
*O Oshun, blessed with love and glee*
*Your sweetness we savor…*

He asked Oshun to have mercy, to guide Gwendolyn home. To bring her back. Another voice joined him in song. Strong and tender. Arturo's.

Fonsi looked upon Gwendolyn once again.

*Please come back, cousin. Please…*

## CHAPTER NINETEEN
# THE SUN BURNS

Gwendolyn drifted as she was pulled by the silent ghost. Visions manifested around her, cascading around her body. The ruins of Chorrillo smoldered. Her parents embraced and moved their hips to Spanish reggae from Renato. Helena read her a picture book about talking trucks that drove off the page. Madrina and Fonsi sat before their altar surrounded by flames. Fonsi worked on a ten-foot sculpture in the middle of their living room. Vines overran Presente's ruins. Her Harlem tower rose like a beanstalk high into the clouds. James came back to bed naked, dripping blood. Jessica posed in leopard print, dripping blood. LaMarque's couture runway keeled over, dripping blood.

The vision of Fonsi returned. He was sitting in their South Bronx apartment the day before he turned seventeen, working on yet another of the statuettes that were becoming his trademark. He was on his third incarnation of Yemaya, the revered mother orisha of oceans, whom so many West Africans upon being enslaved would worship under the guise of the Virgin Mary, passing the tradition on to their descendants.

The evening of Fonsi's birthday Madrina had to work a double, but she'd promised she'd take the kids out to dinner at Presente over the weekend, only a few months before Giselda would burn the place down. Giselda had no knowledge of the trauma her future would hold when she ran up on Fonsi at their place, bellowed a hearty "Feliz Cumpleaños," and thrust a leatherbound scrapbook into his hand. She'd worked for weeks, gathering as many print photos as she could, snooping into his things when he wasn't home, taking her own pictures of his favorite comics and action figures that inspired his art. Fonsi was completely stunned as he accepted the gift. The two danced to Missy and Aaliyah and Ne-Yo CDs, ate red velvet B-day cake before dinner, and did dramatic ghetto-fab poses in front of the mirror. Fonsi rocking a green polo shirt with a thin chain, faded jeans, and white kicks. Giselda in all denim with oblong silver hoops, relieved her cousin had taken her advice to lean into his urban boy-next-door look. To embrace that he, too, could be fly.

After they fell on the sofa in their pajamas that night, giggling like hyenas about super fine (and super ugly) guys, Fonsi got serious and revealed how much he envied Madrina's love for her. For a moment, Giselda hadn't known how to respond. She'd never been a particularly mushy person when it came to sharing her feelings, but she knew this moment of gravitas required *something*. And so she pulled her cousin close and whispered, "Well, *I* love you, hermano. Always, always, forever." The words felt odd coming from her lips, the unease a visceral thing that she felt in the pit of her stomach for the rest of the evening. But what she'd said was true, the discomfort worth it.

Fonsi carving a white-robed Virgin Mary floated into Gwendolyn's line of sight, that maternal energy he'd craved most of his life. The statuette twirled in front of the two cousins on the couch, the sculpture growing so large it swallowed them whole. And then Mary vanished, replaced by El Intermedio's ether and silence.

Amid the murk, an exhausted Gwendolyn spotted a brilliant, shining orb on the horizon. Soupy scarlet limbo transformed into a warm, celestial orange. The scarred spirit who'd pulled her along peered over at her with concern. Her spirit self was almost invisible. She was thankful that in her final moments there was no pain, that whatever this ghost was doing didn't hurt.

The spirit peered at Gwendolyn for a moment and let go, swimming away. She drifted in the ether toward the shining orb. How good it felt, how wonderful. Her body, receiving energy. *Maybe it can restore me, restore my art.* An intriguing idea among a sea of random thoughts.

She remembered her last vision of Fonsi. Of James, Jessica…of who she was. Who she still wanted to be.

The glow grew brighter.

Gwendolyn pushed herself toward the light. The small exertion, excruciating. Her body faded more. It hurt, but she couldn't stop, drawn toward the orb. She'd channel whatever she had.

She wanted to close her eyes once again. The light overtook her vision, replacing El Intermedio's murky crimson. The sparkling, shimmering hues were familiar, like her dreams as a child.

*Blessed lady, Oshun.*

She heard a voice.

Yellow light surrounded Gwendolyn, filled her eyes. This was what it felt like to move through the sun, a sun that didn't burn, but energized. That healed.

She continued to move, to swim. Her spirit light and airy, her form something she could no longer see. The light grew brighter, warmer, began to burn through Gwendolyn's soul self. Platinum heat and fire that seared, transformed. Took everything away.

She was no longer comfortable, no longer welcomed this. It hurt too much. She wanted to send herself back to scarlet nothingness, hitch herself back on to the silent spirit. Gwendolyn wanted to live. Needed to live.

She could've found another way to survive, with her gifts and smarts. But she lacked the strength.

The yellow became a cornucopia of color, her consciousness scattered. Was this it then? True death, what all spirits inevitably experience? Joining the ancestors? She hoped she would see her parents, and Helena, after so much time.

The burning took Gwendolyn, eradicated her.

Then pain.

An explosion.

And then...

## CHAPTER TWENTY
# PYNK POSSESSION

"Hey. Gwendolyn, hey."

She blinked. Three blurry faces hovered above her, dark, shaded in deep red. She jerked forward.

The faces came into focus. The person closest to her. Her cousin.

"Fonsi?" she said. Her voice a scratchy, ragged thing. "Is that you?"

"Gwendolyn!" Fonsi swept her up in his arms. "Thank the orishas."

She inhaled and savored the feeling of air in her lungs. She clutched Fonsi's T-shirt and drew back, looking at her hands to make sure the edges of her fingers weren't blurred or wispy. She sank into her hips, tried to trust what she was feeling. Real gravity. A heaviness. Bones and skin.

She was back in the world of flesh, of blood. Alive. Gloriously alive.

Gwendolyn hugged her cousin hard.

"It worked," he said, and clutched her more tightly. His body was drenched in sweat. "I wasn't sure. Thought I'd lost you again. You don't know…"

"I heard her voice," Gwendolyn whispered, looking at the statue of Oshun. "She came to me. I thought I was about to die. At first I saw scenes of Chorrillo, and other scenes from my past. *Our* past. But then eventually it was her, bringing me home."

"Of course," Fonsi said. "The ether of El Intermedio, it's literally shaped by the obsessions of spirits, what they haven't let go of. If Chorrillo was still in your heart, if there's unresolved stuff, it would show up."

"Right." Gwendolyn grasped the corner of the cushion on which she sat, rubbed soft cotton between her fingers. She smelled the oils Fonsi used for his afro, some sort of basil and coconut mix. "I'm alive," she muttered more to herself than her cousin, beset by the urge to scream the words out loud, to shout to the rooftops and beyond…

…*I'm alive!*

Crouched next to Fonsi was that handsome collagist she'd met at Faith's. And above them all stood a freckled, redheaded man who couldn't stop fidgeting. Fonsi quickly explained how Arturo and Raphael had helped bring her back.

She slowly rose, testing her legs, and uttered the most profuse words of gratitude she could muster. Arturo clasped his hands in front of his face and bowed. "You're welcome, Gwendolyn," he said. Raphael only nodded, his eyes distant, his face a mask of terror.

"Fonsi, I…I know who's behind the barrier breaking down." She took a deep breath. "It's Madrina, and Duarte. They orchestrated everything. Got ghosts to sabotage me, my events—knowing I'd have no choice but to investigate the in-between place."

Gwendolyn explained everything, though she wished she could've lied. Fonsi's stricken face broke her heart. "So it's Ma," he mumbled. "That's what this ghost was talking about, when I sleep-tripped into El Intermedio and tried to find you. He'd mentioned…this other manipulator." Fonsi nodded in quick bursts, as if he needed to convince himself. "Right. Ma and Duarte. Even as a dead man, fuckin' ruining my life."

A loud crash filled the apartment. Noise rose from the streets, followed by shouts and sirens.

"I need to see what's going down," Raphael stammered. He clawed for the remote lying on the coffee table and turned on the television. A quivering reporter with big curly tresses spoke into her microphone, right in the middle of what appeared to be a blizzard. Jamilah Martinez in Hell's Kitchen gestured to people running, turning back and forth between the street and camera as if she wanted to make a break for it herself. A humongous figure made from a patchwork of cardboard boxes roared and stomped down the sidewalk. The box thing moved through the crowd, grabbed a fleeing man, and crushed him into the snow.

Raphael screamed and clasped his hands over his mouth.

"Blessed Lady," Gwendolyn mumbled.

The image returned to a harried anchor introducing what seemed to be someone's social feed showing a flushed, weeping woman in a baseball cap and thick parka recording a video. For the past half hour she'd been unable to leave her kitchen. Something had been holding the door closed while the cabinets behind her slammed open and shut, open and shut. "I'm freezing, but I can smell gas, I think from my oven," she said. She rattled off her address. "Please, someone, anyone, I need help! I don't want to die!"

The feed switched to a man screaming repeatedly as he was held down on his bed while sheets wrapped themselves around his neck. "Someone actually recorded this instead of trying to save the poor guy?" Arturo muttered.

The feed switched again to someone standing in an attic, their arms hugging air as photos and teddy bears and toy racecars floated around their body. An oasis of peace.

*It's already happened*, Gwendolyn realized. *Spirits have crossed...*

"We have no idea whether these images might be some sort of publicity stunt or terrorist deepfakes," the news anchor said, "but please know our team on the streets say they're seeing some of these acts with their own eyes. We know this is remarkable, unfathomable, but we ask you to stay with us. 911 has been inundated with calls. Area hospitals report that their emergency rooms are overwhelmed. We have reports of casualties…."

There was a crash. "Good lord!" the anchor screamed. He ducked as something flew over his head and crashed into the MCURY logo hanging in the background. The flying object, a camera, its lens shattered, began to move and reshape itself, becoming something jagged and sharp with long teeth that gleamed. Its legs squeaked and herky-jerked as it approached the news desk, sprang forward, and sank metallic fangs into the anchor's neck. Blood gushed forth as people shouted and wailed. A woman jumped on-screen and tried to drag the camera away. Her colleague moaned, "Please…please…"

The screen went blank, replaced by vertical color lines and an emergency siren. Silence rang through Gwendolyn's apartment.

"Spirits," Fonsi said, "their powers have built up after so much time on the other side. Ghosts who've remained in El Intermedio for too long, it drives 'em nuts. To be cut off from the real world, unable to accept true death, join the ancestors. If they haven't made peace, all they want to do is…"

He cried out and placed his head between his fists.

"Fonsi," Gwendolyn said. "What's happening?" Was he having a breakdown? Was the news about his mother too much?

"It's my sensitivity," he said through clenched teeth. "I can barely think right now. Ghosts are everywhere."

"Then we need to stop this, repair the barrier," Gwendolyn said. She propped her cousin up by his forearms, as if she could will strength into his body. "How much time do we have? Before sunset. You said we need to seal the breach before the end of the equinox, right?"

"It's 6:15," Raphael said, holding up his phone. His voice, tiny and meek. "Not even an hour."

"Then we need to perform another ritual. I need to reconnect with El Intermedio. This can't become permanent. I know what…"

A loud boom echoed outside the apartment, coming from the hallway, followed by another shriek. "Shit!" Arturo yelled. "Someone needs our help."

"No, we have to help Gwendolyn." Fonsi frowned hard at his friend. "We have to stay here and—"

"I saw what was going on outside when we were doing that ceremony to bring her back. People are hurting out there, man. Being killed. I'm not going to stay here while folks are being fucked up."

"Arturo, listen," Fonsi said, his voice a warning. "I know how you are, but—"

More banging filled the space. Someone shouted for help outside, in the hallway. Arturo glared at Fonsi and ran into the foyer. Gwendolyn followed him and left the apartment, her cousin right behind. The table close to the elevator had been overturned. Gwendolyn heard a low rumble, saw a large figure hunched over someone on the floor. Two women, a young couple who lived a few doors down whose names escaped her. Both perennially polite, content to offer a smile. The woman standing up was in a tattered fleece sweatshirt emblazoned with felines and the slogan *Pynk Pussay Paradise*. She clawed at the other woman, in torn athleisure wear, who was defending herself with a large metal tray covered in scratches. The woman in pink, her body was distorted. Massive. One arm much longer than the other, the knuckles grazing the carpet. An eerie sound…growling…filled the hallway.

"Step away," Arturo said.

The larger woman turned around, salivating. Her eyes were wild, irises black. Her growl morphed into a hawk's cry laced with metal, a sound Gwendolyn had never heard in her life. Arturo held up his fists and planted his legs.

"Don't!" Fonsi shouted. "You can't handle this. She's possessed."

With a rattling screech, the woman jumped onto Arturo. Her fetid, rank breath overwhelmed Gwendolyn even from where she stood.

Fonsi jumped on the pink woman's back, tried to pry her hands from around Arturo's neck. Raphael peeped his head outside the apartment and darted back inside. Gwendolyn remained calm, steadied herself. She had to parse through what she was witnessing. This woman, her neighbor, was possessed by a spirit from El Intermedio. And Gwendolyn, as a manipulator, controlled everything that was *of* El Intermedio.

She reached out with her power, touched the energy that resided inside the ravenous woman, an energy that was an insane, raging ghost. Gwendolyn reached deep into her neighbor's body, grasped the spirit, and tugged with all her might.

The pink woman shrieked and trounced Arturo into the floor. She pivoted and squinted her eyes, as if noticing Gwendolyn for the first time. She screeched again and leapt forward, swiping at Gwendolyn's face.

Gwendolyn stumbled backward as the woman grabbed her neck with both hands. She couldn't breathe, was starting to black out as she clutched her neighbor's arms. Heat pulsed through her fingers. There was a smell, singed fleece. She didn't want to burn her neighbor, but Gwendolyn refused to die…she *wouldn't* die…not after she'd made it back, survived the in-between place…

"Hey!"

A familiar voice. Louder, gruffer than she remembered.

Gwendolyn dropped to the floor as a huge man picked up her equally huge neighbor and threw her several feet into the hallway mirror. Bo turned around and ran up to Gwendolyn, who shouted a warning as the woman in pink leapt several feet onto Bo's back, shredding his skin with her claws. Gwendolyn once again focused her energies on the apparition that had nestled itself within flesh, that wanted only to lash out and hurt others. She grabbed the spirit and, balling it up into a tiny sphere, pitched it through the ceiling as high as she could imagine, way up into the heavens.

The woman in pink fell to the carpet coughing violently. Her body shrank, muscles disappearing as she vomited a tarry bile, the stench unbearable.

The other neighbor, whom Gwendolyn had forgotten, rose from her hiding spot next to the overturned table. "Yvette, are you...?"

The woman in pink touched herself like she was waking from a dream. She took in the group of people now surrounding her. Bo and Arturo were still erect, ready for a fight. "I was by the window and something entered my body," she said. "And that light...I don't know what happened, I just felt...like, sick. I saw my father..."

"Your father?!?" Yvette's partner glared at her. "What are you talking about? You don't talk to that drunk."

"Molly, yeah, I know, haven't seen him since he kicked me out the night I came out. That was twenty years ago—"

"This must seem crazy, for both of you, but I can explain," Gwendolyn interrupted. Yvette probably had no idea her apparently estranged father was dead, much less a miserable spirit who'd escaped from limbo. "Maybe you should come with us. Come to my place, where you might be safer, at least for a moment."

"I'm not staying anywhere with you fuckin' people," Raphael shouted. He stood outside the door to Gwendolyn's apartment clutching the wall. "I didn't sign up for any of this Ghostbusters crap. This is nuts."

"Raph," Fonsi said, his voice measured.

"No." Raphael waved his finger. "No more from you." He bolted down the hallway. Fonsi ran after him with no hesitation. Raphael yelled like a maniac, overcome as he swung a right hook before disappearing through the stairwell exit. Fonsi dodged the punch by a mile and came to an abrupt stop. He placed his hands on his knees.

Gwendolyn dashed over to her wheezing cousin. His face, a sunken, gaunt landscape drained of color.

"Sorry, cuz," Fonsi said. "So sorry, but I don't think I'm going to get through this."

And then he collapsed.

## CHAPTER TWENTY-ONE
# FAMILY

Fonsi, no longer able to block out the noise from the hordes of ghosts, crumpled to the ground right after Raphael took off like a bat out of hell. He chuckled, though it hurt to laugh. He couldn't be mad about his ex's behavior. This shit was too much for even the hardiest of mystics, much less a shallow urbanite who knew nothing about the spirit world.

*I'm not going to make it*, Fonsi realized, seeing how Gwendolyn and Arturo were looking down at him. Like he was at death's door. Exactly how he felt. *This is it.*

The silliness he'd endured, for months trying to figure out how to make Raphael happy and be the type of boyfriend he wanted. And then the weeks he'd spent feeling upset, betrayed. Such a waste, and coming to an abrupt, undignified end on prickly high-rise carpet. He refused to spend his last moments of sanity consumed by bitterness. He hoped his ex would survive the ghost invasion and get himself together, try to be a human being who was less haughty, more real.

A jumbled swirl of voices was enmeshed within Fonsi's thoughts, cutting into him like barbed wire. The obsessions of newly released spirits brought to the fore, soft, too loud…

*…I'll burn that goddamned theater to the ground for kicking me out of the production…*

*…gotta send message to Ty…somehow… He'll want me back in his bed… We can try again… He ain't so mean…*

*…pepperoni pizzaaaaaaaaaaaa…yum, yum, yum, yum…sixty damn years since I've smelled pepperoni pizza…*

*…Twelve years and you still ugly…*

*…filthy, smelly, vermin-infested trap…what the fuck was I thinking coming back? I was better off in limbo…*

Dozens upon dozens of apparitions swirling all around with their conflicting emotions. Their longing to reconnect with those they lost or destroy the places they hated. Their rage at discovering the people they yearned to be reunited with were long gone. Fonsi would've once given anything to discern ghostly chatter without having to sleep-trip. He'd gotten his wish, and it was awful.

He was vaguely aware of the big driver dude, Bo, carrying him back into Gwendolyn's apartment. Fonsi couldn't move, could barely speak.

"I'm going to get you a glass of water," Arturo said, or at least that's what he thought Arturo said, his voice drowned out by spectral sounds.

Fonsi grabbed Gwendolyn's arm. "Do the ritual with the others, for the breach. You don't need me."

She pressed her palm against his cheek, kissed his forehead, and ran over to the other side of the living room to Oshun's altar.

Fonsi felt something buzz against his butt. Painful, uncomfortable. He reached into his back pocket, having forgotten that was where he'd put his phone. Saw that it was Robyn.

"Jefe, hey," Robyn said right after their face popped up on the call. "Ohmigod, you look terrible! What happened?"

"I'm fine," Fonsi lied, seeing large statuettes of the twin Ibeji orishas in the background. "Why are you at the shop? I told you to stay home. Protect yourself."

"Yeah, I thought about that, but then I realized the community needed La Playa, needed the resources we offer. So many people were coming through for candles and figurines and ointment 'cuz of the red sky. But then when those lights started streaming down and crazy shit started happening... Yo, everyone just gathered here, to be with each other." Robyn scanned his phone around the store, full of dozens of people. Fonsi couldn't believe his eyes.

"They... wanted to come to the store?"

Robyn smiled. "Yeaaah, Jefe. Cuz of all the hard work you put into this place. People been asking for you, wanting to make sure you're all right. Saying how you treat them like family no matter who they are, how much they spend. That's why I called, to check in, let them know you're okay." Robyn once again placed his phone in front of the crowd. "Ey, y'all, I'm speaking to Jefe. Say, 'Hey, Fonsiiiiiiiiiiii.'"

A league of La Playa customers called out his name in unison, Fonsi somehow able to hear their voices even with the incessant ringing in his head.

"Robyn, I didn't realize..."

"Even Mrs. Johnson and a few ladies from her church are here," Robyn continued. "Did you see 'em? They're keeping everyone's energy up. They said it's best to find refuge in a spot that's 'spiritually bountiful.' That's nice and all, but we also need to be practical considering what I'm peeping out on them streets, so I distributed the machetes we keep in the back."

"But... but we don't have machetes."

"I ordered them a few weeks ago from one of Abuelo's DR connections. You always gotta be prepared in the 'hood, you know that. We're holding it down in case anything tries to make a move up in here."

"Right... right, okay, that's good," Fonsi said. It was painful to speak. "Robyn, I don't have a lot of time, but I just want to say you've been the best employee I could've ever asked for. Superb. And... and a great friend. Thank you for everything you've done for La Playa, for our business. For me." Fonsi welled up. "I'm so sorry, but I'm not feeling well. I gotta go."

"Jefe, wait, where are you? I'll come get you."

Fonsi hung up and turned off his phone. Tears streamed down his cheeks at the thought of not seeing Robyn again. And the people at La Playa. He shifted slightly to see Gwendolyn gathering the others, no doubt sharing instructions on how to create a ritual Guardián style. His cousin, his true inspiration, the reason he'd pushed himself for so many years to improve his gift. His freakin' *magnificent* cousin, who'd brought him such joy as a kid. He could admit that now. Could admit that he should've tried to find her years ago. She was a badass, definitely might repair the breach, though he wasn't sure it would be in time for him.

Fonsi closed his eyes, made his mind small. His head throbbed, his psyche on the verge of snapping from all the energy he was taking in. Something caressed his jaw, and then his cheek. A calloused hand. Fingers.

He opened his eyes. There before him were the faint outlines of a face, skin dark, lips full, the vision clearer than before.

Amede.

"You're here," Fonsi murmured.

*Yeah, this'll do.*

His thoughts drifted, aimless. When he passed, would he embrace true death or dwell within El Intermedio? And what would be the rules if the barrier between worlds remained broken? Would he be able to go wherever he wanted? Maybe he would simply float around with Amede and have hot ghost sex all the time. Probably no limit to where they could travel even as the world turned to hell. Maybe he could see his mother again, try to figure out why she'd done this thing that would ruin so many lives. Maybe he could help her find peace.

It really didn't matter, was way too hard to think.

He felt Amede's lips on his. Light yet full of presence. Fonsi let go of questions and time and floated into the arms of his sweet ghost.

*This'll do nicely.*

CHAPTER TWENTY-TWO

# A GENTLE PUSH

Gwendolyn ran back into the living room from the bathroom, first aid kit in hand for Bo's wounds. He'd taken off his shirt, revealing several keloids on his back, his mountain of muscles tinted by crimson sky from the window. The sight of so much bare flesh reminded Gwendolyn of her last night with James. She still hadn't cried for him, hadn't started to grieve, not really. *I don't have time.*

She looked at her mess of a place and the people gathered around. Her neighbor Molly, the woman in athleisure green, tended to the scratches on Bo's back as he peered around the apartment, head and eyes darting back and forth. *Is he casing the joint for spirits?* Gwendolyn wondered. She didn't have the heart to tell him that ghosts weren't random street punks that he could intimidate, that depending on their power they could walk through walls and have their way with people.

Arturo passed a glass of water to Yvette, who was slumped in a corner on the floor. She cradled her head in her hands, clearly still reeling from being possessed. Gwendolyn was so impressed by Arturo, how the kindness and care he displayed when they first met wasn't an act. He glanced over at her and then averted his gaze, like he was nervous.

Fonsi was a shivering mess on her couch, murmuring a steady stream of gibberish. He had a dopey smile on his face, his hands and arms raised as if locked in embrace. He looked completely out of his mind.

*These ghosts, their noise, they're killing him*, Gwendolyn realized. Her cousin, the only family she had left—she wasn't going to lose him, not after James, not after being reminded of all she'd lost as a child.

She cleared her throat, ready to address the others. "I know I might sound insane," she said, "but considering what you've just experienced, I hope my words will ring true. I'm part of a mystical order whose power is shaped by trust, intention, by connecting with people who believe in what we can do. There's a breach between our world and the spiritual realm that I must repair, and I don't think I can do it alone. I need all of you to sit with me..."

Gwendolyn stopped. She needed to seal the fissure *and* corral countless ghosts swirling throughout New York back into limbo. How many would she have to locate? Hundreds? Thousands? A mind-boggling feat for a trained mystic at the top of their game, much less for someone like her, who hadn't used her gift in over a decade. Who'd been swept into the in-between place so easily and almost taken out by a possessed Yvette.

*This...this is way beyond me. I'm not powerful enough.*

The small group stared her down, looking for answers. Shouts and screams and odd noises from outside continued to echo through the apartment, even with the windows closed. Waves of heat and cold flashed through the living room. Gwendolyn refused to flinch. She needed to show the others she was brave even as sickening reality settled into her stomach and limbs. She wouldn't be able to pull this off, her gifts insufficient. They were doomed, destined to contend with ghosts running amok for who knew how long.

She clasped her hands in front of her. It couldn't end like this. The terror her city would endure. The misery and death. She'd made it back from hell, somehow, and now...

Gwendolyn's gaze once again settled on the statue of Oshun, her powerful, blessed lady.

Something stirred as she recalled the orisha's power. Her blazing grace. Her symbols that permeated dreams. How connected she felt to the orisha when she was at her lowest points. In Panama and the Bronx... in El Intermedio. All the years she tried to escape.

The goddess had been calling to her for so long.

That was it.

On her own, Gwendolyn didn't have sufficient skill or juice to handle the task at hand, but Oshun did. The signs the orisha had been sending must mean something.

"Everyone," she said, "I need you to focus on the statue. Oshun is one of the most powerful orishas of all time, a mighty goddess of love and sensuality and rivers with followers all over the world. This little figure here is just a sliver of who she is, what she represents. I know you may not know much about her, but I need for you to focus on her, on the majesty found in this glorious representation. You must believe she's on our side."

*And she in turn will help me,* Gwendolyn thought even as doubt returned. The goddess had worshippers all over the Americas and Africa and parts of Europe. Could she *really* corral that power and channel it to Gwendolyn? And would she do so after having remained apart from the world for so long, as all deities did in the modern age? What if Gwendolyn's theory was simply her own imagination run amok?

*I'm a Guardián,* she admitted to herself for the first time in ages. *I've been chosen to help others. I've gotta believe this can work.*

Yvette pushed herself up from the floor and rolled up the sleeves of her sweatshirt. "Everything you're saying we need to do, we can try," she said.

Gwendolyn nodded then bowed to the orisha as she picked her up and placed her in the middle of the group. She took a cushion and situated herself next to the statuette. The others formed a small, uneven circle around them.

"Please join hands." The group looked at one another, self-conscious. With bandages crisscrossed around his chest, Bo wiped his palms against his pants before he joined hands with Molly.

"I'm going to fall out," Gwendolyn explained. She turned to Arturo. "Exactly as you saw me earlier. It'll look like I'm sleeping, but don't try to wake me up. Just protect my body." *If this doesn't work, then it really won't matter what happens to me*, Gwendolyn thought.

She closed her eyes and began to murmur under her breath, sending prayers to her blessed lady. She took a moment, wondered how her soul self could reach El Intermedio again without Fonsi's guidance. But as she reached for her talents, she grasped a new reality. As a result of the breach, El Intermedio was all around her now, above and below, permeating the city, its energy filling her limbs.

Gwendolyn chanted rapidly, words coming to her from long ago as she strove to connect with the goddess. She opened her eyes briefly, saw the group around her buried in concentration. She closed her eyes again and reached out to the statue before her with intention.

And then...

A surge of energy erupted within. Gwendolyn grunted and tried to remain still, not wanting to alarm the others, though she felt intense pain, as if she were being assailed with millions of sharp needles. The color behind her eyelids went from black to a bright, dazzling yellow. The air in the apartment was flowery, fresh, so very sweet.

"Ohmigod," she heard someone mutter, "what's happening?" Molly.

The source...Oshun's power, building within her. Gwendolyn whispered another incantation and pushed her spirit from her body, a relief to use her gift, the energy pulsating within her far too much. She saw the blood-red sky, saw the blazing white fissure, far larger than when she'd first touched El Intermedio earlier in the day. Crackling bursts of light nipped at her. She knew what was on the other side, who would be waiting for her. This time she didn't fight, didn't scream as she was drawn back into limbo.

There they were, of course, Madrina and Duarte, still guarding the breach. The two not yet enjoying their freedom as liberated spirits, traipsing through New York high and happy. They were watching for Gwendolyn until the equinox was over, making sure she didn't disrupt their plans.

She had no time to waste.

"Madrina, I'll leave my body permanently," Gwendolyn said. "Join you here in El Intermedio for as long as you like until true death comes. I promise. We can practice our gifts together, as manipulators, even in limbo. Isn't that what you always wanted, to be more powerful, for us to share what we have?" The thought of dealing with her godmother's bullshit again wasn't remotely appealing, but Gwendolyn would do what she needed to do. "Please, we have to close the breach. It's not right, to make so many suffer."

Duarte rushed over to Gwendolyn, grabbed her by her shoulders, the sensation sickening. "You... who the hell do you think you are?"

"You would stay with me?" Madrina asked Gwendolyn, the edges of her body blurring.

Duarte turned to her. "Ignacia, don't listen to this bruja. It's bullshit, not even a real choice. She'll figure out a way to escape El Intermedio. She'll leave you again. Why risk it when we can roam the world however the hell we want?"

"You know all about manipulating people's choices, don't you, Duarte?" Gwendolyn said. She quickly played with the energy of the in-between place, manipulated its crimson colors and textures. Her gift was no longer this weakened, deflated thing in limbo, not with Oshun boosting her power. She gave herself freely to the realm, allowed El Intermedio to see what she held in her heart.

The murk around them morphed, once again shaped by Gwendolyn's suppressed memories. She and Madrina sat cross-legged in Madrina's den, Fonsi out of the house at La Playa. Their ritual where they were surrounded by candles and pictures of the orishas, chanting. Gwendolyn started to reach out to El Intermedio as she always did, even though using her gift left a bitter taste in her mouth after she'd burnt down Presente.

A blast of heat enveloped the den, and then a blinding white light. The two women screamed.

Present-day Gwendolyn used her power to control the scene, slowed it down so her godmother could see. A figure appeared, hands curled, in Madrina's den. A figure with long raven hair and a beard doing the thing that ghosts have done for time immemorial. Haunting a space.

"It was Duarte," Gwendolyn said to Madrina as they watched their past play out before them. "It was always Duarte. He was the one behind our ritual going wrong that night when the house burned. I don't know what talents he's gained as a ghost, how he stayed connected to you after death, but he's the one who grabbed your soul when both of us touched El Intermedio that night. Who murdered you."

Madrina recoiled. "No…"

"Mentirosa! Fuckin' bitch," Duarte yelled as he once again rushed toward Gwendolyn.

She uttered a quick incantation and pushed his form backward with a wave of force. Duarte wasn't a manipulator far as she could tell, couldn't hope to match her no matter what power he'd gained.

He tumbled head over heels as the scene of Gwendolyn and Madrina holding their ritual so many years ago faded, present-day Madrina now staring down her lover, in shock. "You're the one who did this to me?" Her voice was small, feeble.

"Think about it." Gwendolyn spoke quickly. "To create a breach between our worlds requires a certain type of craft. Duarte isn't a Guardián, doesn't have the juice or skill to do it by himself, no matter what power he's able to manifest as a spirit. He needed a manipulator. I don't know if he was trying to grab both of us or just needed someone he could more easily control. This story you shared, that he happened to find you floating in El Intermedio…bullshit. He knew all the time where you were because he was tracking you when he brought you over. He just couldn't reveal what he'd done." Gwendolyn looked away from her godmother, the thought uncomfortable to say. "I think…I think he grabbed your soul because of the relationship y'all had when he was alive. He needed someone he could use."

Madrina's body blurred and her face crumpled, as if she lacked the strength to hold herself together.

"Duarte doesn't give a shit about you, Ignacia." The first time she'd ever called her godmother by her first name. "You're nothing but a means to an end. And I don't know if Duarte gives two shits about the freedom of other ghosts. What if destroying the barrier between worlds is really about him, about *his* freedom? Making sure he can move between worlds whenever he sees fit? If ghosts run around creating mess, what does it matter, long as he gets what he wants?"

Gwendolyn drew closer to her godmother. She knew this woman, had to let the truth sink into her spirit. "He got over on you, Madrina, after fucking you over. After stealing your soul. After destroying your life."

Madrina's face stopped crumbling. Her body stopped dissipating. She swiveled over to Duarte, whose debonair face now had a new look. Fear.

Madrina was still, too calm, too quiet. With no warning, she whispered an incantation and released a blast of power, an arcane energy that tore through Duarte. His spirit began to crumble before he muttered a few words, a shield rising before him. Madrina's second blast deflected off the barrier and filled the surrounding murk with blinding light. And then she let loose another charge of power, and another. The dueling ghosts' bodies became blurry, more intangible. They were using too much power too fast, magicking themselves into nothingness.

Gwendolyn felt a tinge of guilt. Having lived with Ignacia for years, she'd known how her godmother would react upon being wronged. Exactly the distraction she needed.

She pushed herself away from the dueling couple and imagined herself floating above the fissure between realms, still within her line of sight. Gwendolyn grew her spirit as large as she could, reminding herself she was empowered by her blessed lady even though she was terribly frightened. She reached out with her mind, tried to connect with as many ghosts as she could even as she slowly sealed the breach. Tried to hype herself up even though her mission felt beyond her.

Some ghosts, she realized, had simply slipped out of the breach and saw the city as an urban wonderland to explore and exploit. Those entities zipping around just needed Gwendolyn's gentle but firm coaxing, almost as if she were their big sister, or mother, or lover. To be held and seen for who they were when they were flesh and blood, to have their pain acknowledged, finally...*finally*. She represented Oshun, orisha of love, and she would act from love.

She touched them with her power. A caress.

*Come...return...this place isn't for you.*

But it was the other ghosts, the ones who were raging, who were plunging knives into eyes or strangling people in their beds, these were the spirits who required a stronger hand, who needed to be forced back. She grabbed as many of them as she could, usurping control of their forms. They were of the stuff of El Intermedio, and she controlled the stuff of El Intermedio, and she would not be denied.

Gwendolyn sent out her power as far and fast as she could throughout New York, spreading herself too thin, aware she might lose consciousness at any moment. Her mind surveyed the city again and again. She spotted her apartment, saw that Arturo and Bo and the women still had their hands joined together in front of Oshun. Fonsi was still on the couch. There was a badly scarred ghost holding him, caressing him, his head in the ghost's lap. The same ghost who'd tried to help Gwendolyn in limbo.

*Oh Blessed Lady, he's looking after Fonsi.* And that was all Gwendolyn needed to know to leave the scarred spirit alone.

Gwendolyn was tired, but she managed to survey the city once again, barely detecting any remaining ghosts except for a presence she felt in Manhattan, in Chelsea, at the medical center. She followed the thread to a frayed stuffed animal, an otter that had been kicked under a chair, forgotten since being left there only a day ago. She felt something, a pull, the remnants of someone she'd come to care for deeply. He was holding on, barely holding back true death.

Her sweet James.

He'd tethered himself to a cherished object, perhaps not realizing he could freely roam the city with the barrier between worlds broken. She wouldn't seal him back up in the in-between place. She refused.

Gwendolyn thought fast. As the white fissure was closing, she swept her consciousness back into El Intermedio. There were Madrina and Duarte, still fighting, Duarte's body on the verge of disintegrating.

*You vile, disgusting man*, Gwendolyn thought. She grabbed what was left of his spirit as he wailed, as an enraged Madrina battered him with another blast of light. Gwendolyn grabbed what was left of Duarte and placed it into the otter, feeding energy to James's soul. And then she grabbed James's spirit and shoved it back into his body, located in the ice-cold drawer of the morgue.

She left the hospital, knowing she still had work to do. Knowing she had to be as thorough as possible even though her power was starting to fade. Gwendolyn swept the city, not sure how much time she had before sunset, thankful she no longer detected any spirits as Oshun's power left her body, as fatigue brought her down. She sealed the fissure even as she thought of poor Madrina. She imagined Ignacia roaming El Intermedio confused as to where Duarte might have vanished to. Gwendolyn could no longer worry about her godmother. She had to let her go.

Her soul self was now tiny, fragile, barely able to creep back to soft, warm flesh. She opened her eyes to the ceiling of her apartment. The crimson that had been pouring forth from her window, gone. She struggled to look outside, saw nothing but blue sky.

Arturo, Bo, Molly, Yvette...all huddled over her. And then Fonsi pushed through them, his face full of color and life.

"You did it, Gwendolyn," he said. "You did it!"

She grasped his hand and tried to speak. No words came. Instead, Gwendolyn gave a limp thumbs-up and let sleep ferry her away.

CHAPTER TWENTY-THREE

# THE MEDIUM'S TEARS

Days after what was now being called the Ghost Equinox of New York, Fonsi took a rainbow feather duster to the half-empty shelves of La Playa after an extraordinarily busy Tuesday. Since he'd opened the shop that morning, he'd had customers nonstop. He hadn't been able to take a real lunch and barely had time for bathroom breaks since he'd given Robyn the day off after the poor kid had worked the entire weekend by themself. La Playa had never been this busy at the beginning of the week… Well, really, on any day of the week.

When the last customer had left the shop, Fonsi propped up his phone on the counter and watched yet another news update. Scores of businesses throughout the city had been damaged or outright destroyed, though La Playa was unscathed because people from the neighborhood had banded together and made their stand. Robyn and Mrs. Johnson had guided besieged pedestrians to safety while others led prayer circles to frighten ghosts away.

"Ey, Mrs. Johnson can kick *ass*," Robyn said. "There was this wicker chair trouncing hard on this little cutie pie right across the street, and Mrs. Johnson busted out and yelled, 'In the name of Jesus, I rebuke your power!' before she started hacking away at the thing with her machete. Little pieces of bamboo, all over the sidewalk. Then we hauled dude up and got our asses back in the shop, where she kept praying over all of us. She's so dope, Jefe. Abuelo was like, 'Who's that?' licking his lips all hungry, but I told him to back off, she's a widow in mourning. So, you seen how fly the store receipts are?"

Fonsi was happy everyone was okay, especially considering how he had to watch over Gwendolyn, who'd slept for two days straight. After she'd sealed the fissure, Fonsi and the others had no choice but to get her to Harlem Hospital amid so many others who'd been taken to the ER.

"This woman fuckin' saved us all!" Bo had bellowed at medical staff upon their arrival. "You need to get her a bed, now." Fonsi was relieved that they'd somehow found Gwendolyn a room despite the overcrowding. (He suspected the looming threat of a well-placed wallop from Bo made administrative miracles happen.) Over the next forty-eight hours, he refused to leave his cousin's side, with Bo and Arturo returning to visit as the world around them changed overnight. Legions of people suddenly believed that spirits were a real thing. There were still naysayers who thought that what they'd witnessed and survived in New York was an elaborate hoax. But it was hard to deny the truth—over five dozen people killed and hundreds injured in circumstances widely described as "inexplicable" or "demonic" or "ghoulish." So much pain and death from apparitions running rampant through the city for a few hours. But people rallied, especially in the entertainment world. The singer Veronykah Cahmet, whose songs were already regarded as mystical in scope, would be headlining a Barclays Center benefit concert over the weekend to raise millions of dollars for New Yorkers. And Beyoncé was rumored to be working on an R&B/pop track that would be considered the "Thriller" of the '20s.

Pundits from across the world weighed in on what had happened during the Ghost Equinox, with journalists calling upon people from the supernatural community for their analysis. Fonsi smiled as he sat in Gwendolyn's room on the third day of her hospital stay when he spotted Estelle on the overhead TV giving a breakdown on how the spirit world worked.

"I have theories as to why Oshun statues across the world started to glow during the equinox," Estelle said to her interviewer. She was her usual poised, superfly self in pink jogging gear and matching kicks. Long-bearded Humberto Ramos sat next to her and spouted a few words in thickly accented English about the "sanctity of realms" and being freer to "protect your busted asses."

"She's one of our most powerful orishas," Estelle said. "Maybe in fact, our most powerful. I think she chose to reveal herself and intervene to save tons of lives. This is a new day, a new era for all of us."

Fonsi locked up the shop and walked home at a leisurely pace. He took in the garbage crews sweeping trash off the street and the news cameras that had descended on every other corner and the scores of people entering or leaving storefront churches on a weekday. So much of the world familiar yet radically different.

He entered his studio and once again stopped and bowed at his altar to Oshun. Tomorrow he'd set forth an array of treats for all the deities, but her especially, paying close attention to her favorites. He'd taken the orisha for granted, seen her as this outwardly beautiful goddess but frivolous, without taking time to understand her depth, the lessons to be learned from her stories. There was a lot to learn, especially from Gwendolyn.

After showering, he sat on his bed cross-legged and meditated. He felt... odd, suddenly aware of all he'd endured. For the first time in days, he was completely still without any distractions, without having to run around or tend to his cousin or customers.

Fonsi breathed in and out, focused on his center, let his mind roam forth from his body.

He wasn't alone.

"Amede, hello."

Fonsi bent forward as he leaned into the spirit and allowed Amede to wrap his long arms around him. He inhaled and exhaled, relieved to be held.

He began to cry. Once the first stream of tears hit his cheeks, he couldn't stop. He cried, thinking about all that he'd witnessed, all that he'd wished he could change. He thought about how much he still missed his mother even though she'd caused so much pain and loss. How he wished that he'd been enough for her, that she'd cared for him more even though he wasn't as powerful as Gwendolyn. About how hard he'd tried to be the vapid, unfeeling thing that his boyfriends and booty calls wanted him to be. And how hard he'd worked for his clients, to understand the stories of their ghosts. He cried and cried, realizing how much time he'd spent chasing love's illusions without knowing who he was.

Much, much later, during the wee hours of the night, tears dried up, Fonsi felt his body being gently nudged. An invisible calloused hand took his left wrist.

Fonsi rose from his bed and let himself be led into the bathroom. He stopped in front of his mirror.

There in front of him, reflected into glass, stood the finest man Fonsi had ever beheld. His head was completely bald, his skin a deep, dark brown, eyes large and round, lips effulgent. His defined chest and neck and arms and torso, a sculptor's dream. His defined chest and neck and arms and torso covered in jagged scars.

Even though most spirits had the ability to play with their form, this was how Amede chose to manifest himself. Injured. Damaged.

Someone who went through a terrible ordeal. Or at least that was what Fonsi presumed.

He looked at his reflection in the mirror next to Amede's and felt joy at seeing his ghostly lover for the first time. And then…horror. Fonsi's own hair was as wild and unkempt as ever, the circles under his eyes deep, dark. The length of his beard could give Humberto Ramos's a run for the money. Who knew what choices Amede had about how he manifested, but Fonsi was walking around…like this?

"I'm totally jacked up," Fonsi muttered.

Amede leaned toward the mirror and smiled, revealing sparkling white teeth. The glass turned cloudy. He placed his finger against it and wrote a message. Then he caressed Fonsi's face and gave him a kiss.

Fonsi leaned against the sink to balance himself, about to swoon. He read Amede's latest message.

*Beautiful*

CHAPTER TWENTY-FOUR

# NOT READY TO LET GO

I*really* can't believe this is the first time you've had me over. This place is fabulous, girl." Jessica gestured over to the figure of Oshun that dominated the living room's northeast corner. "That sculpture over there, nice touch. Eclectic, mysterious. More, please. Break up the beige in here."

Gwendolyn sat with Jessica on her couch. She'd ordered a full breakfast spread with fruit and bagels and scrambled eggs to commemorate the special occasion of finally inviting someone into her home to chill. It felt wonderful to see her boss and friend sitting there, looking fierce as ever in another wide-legged jumpsuit, this one an understated maroon.

After having spent two days unconscious and two days awake in Harlem Hospital while held for observation, Gwendolyn's official diagnosis was severe exhaustion and dehydration on top of her lacerations. She'd been instructed to take off a few more days from work and drink plenty of water, her harried physician presuming that, on top of the stress of the equinox, overdemanding celebs had run poor Gwendolyn down to the ground. "I know your agency represents that poser Clive Sergeant," the doctor said. "With everything you must've been putting up with, I'm surprised you didn't have a breakdown sooner."

Bo had picked Gwendolyn up from the hospital and practically carried her into the elevator and then her apartment, where Fonsi had doted over her for hours. She was grateful for her cousin's attention, but she needed time to think, to acclimate to this new world since the so-called Ghost Equinox, the day that changed things forever.

Gwendolyn gradually learned about the death toll and injuries along with the millions of dollars in damage inflicted upon the city. She'd felt the weight of it all once again, just for a moment. She felt the weight and let it fall from her shoulders. The self-blame, useless. She'd made mistakes, had regrets, but refused to see herself as a corrupt thing. She had to figure out how she was going to move through the world, how to embrace something closer to truth when it came to who she was.

*Is this what coming out is like?* she wondered as she tried to figure out whom to tell what she could do as a Guardián. The cat was out of the bag with her neighbors Yvette and Molly considering what they'd all been through together, but others… Maybe it would be on a need-to-know basis? Yet the thought of continuing to maintain a mountain of secrets made her skin itch.

She decided she would take her time with what she revealed to Jessica. Unsurprisingly, her boss was getting a crash course in all things ghostly. Sublime had been inundated with requests for representation from people in the supernatural community. "Girl, I don't know what to make of all this talk 'bout 'rampaging' spirits and equinoxes," she confided, only having vague memories of her mother's ghostly voice. "Sounds to me like the powers that be are covering something up, but who knows. I'm not one to ignore opportunity."

Jessica hired a new assistant and waited patiently for Gwendolyn to recuperate, believing she had finally fallen out from overwork. And most of those who'd dropped Sublime for representation had come begging back once they realized that the sabotaged events were merely a precursor to the Ghost Equinox. Even Clive's lawyers had contacted Jessica, explaining that he might've been hasty in blaming them for the Silvercup debacle.

Jessica took a sip from her coffee, wiped her mouth.

"Would you like anything else?" Gwendolyn asked. "Or is it time?"

"On the dot, Gwen. I've gotta get outta here. Octavia De La Cruz's *This Is Your Life, America* appearance is in an hour. Our girl just got signed for the next installment of the *Spooky City* franchise. They're doing an entire segment on what we can learn from horror and fantasy cinema after the equinox, and the producers want to put her film front and center." Jessica rose and grabbed her jacket. "There'll be *tons* of opportunities for the agency. And that lady from Queens you referred to us, Estelle Bailey? A pro. Already got her a couple of talk show spots."

"She'll be great," Gwendolyn replied. "About what this means for Sublime, we'll see."

"Yeah, I know how cautious you are. That was really something, huh, what happened at the office and your events? It's like ghosts decided to fuck with us before everyone else." Jessica laughed nervously and peered once again at the statue of Oshun, which was flanked by a bowl of honey, a large bronze hairbrush, and five vases of sunflowers. And then she turned back to Gwendolyn, her gaze weirdly reminiscent of Detective Zachensky's.

Gwendolyn soon walked her boss to the door. "Thank you…for being your wonderful self, fine lady," Jessica whispered as the two embraced. "We're gonna be fine." And then she dashed down the hallway and took out her cell.

Gwendolyn cleaned up and soon headed downstairs. Bo sat in the black sedan that she'd weirdly begun to see as her refuge.

"Morning, Ms. Montgomery," he said.

"Oh, Bo, I'm Gwendolyn. No more Ms. Montgomery, okay? We're way past that." The man was unflappable, still showing up in his standard suit with his standard demeanor, as if days earlier he hadn't ripped a crazed possessed woman off Gwendolyn's neck. On the first day she'd awoken, she'd explained to a visiting Bo as much as she could about who she was and the belief system that fueled her gift. He listened solemnly, taking it all in, not saying much before he bade her good evening.

Now he sat down behind the steering wheel, silent and still for reasons Gwendolyn couldn't discern. He stared at his hands and turned. "Ms. Montgomery...er, Gwendolyn...I just wanted to say, it's been an honor to be your driver, for us to work together. I'm still sitting with everything that went down at your place, still learning, listening to the news. I'm talking to my sister more, who's into paganism..."

"Ah." Gwendolyn tried to tune in to Bo's energy, to suss out where this was going. "Do you have...questions?"

"No...I mean, yeah, sure, of course, but they can wait. I just wanted to say, when I quit being a firefighter, I felt lost. People don't realize how hard that type of work is on the body, the terrible things you see. I settled into my driver's job, thought my life would be simple. Just get a check, build my pension. But after meeting you, after seeing you in action, what you did up there...getting to be part of that." Bo tapped his chest. "I feel like maybe I've discovered my purpose again. And I needed to thank you." He lowered his head, the soldier who'd completed his mission. "Let's get you to your destination."

As the car drove south, driver and passenger lost in their thoughts, she took in the terrain, the plethora of police units clustered around certain locales. The construction crews that had descended on damaged buildings every few blocks. New York moving and morphing, rolling with the punches even after a catastrophe. The sedan soon pulled up to Sublime's office space. For the first time since she could remember, Gwendolyn wasn't sure what her place with the agency would be. A grand host of Guardianes were meeting in a few days to determine how they should operate as an order considering the circumstances. Gwendolyn knew she'd have to attend, had no idea what would be asked of her and if she could continue working as a publicist. But the work she'd done over the years at the agency, that was part of who she was as much as her mystical past.

Whatever was on the horizon, she would no longer bury herself. Gwendolyn stepped out of the car and tapped on her driver's window. "Bo, I know I asked you to call me by my first name, but there's another name I once went by, back in my home country. My birth name…my real name is Giselda."

✱ ✱ ✱

Five hours later, Gwendolyn lightly rapped on the door to James's hospital room. He was sitting upright in bed reading a shiny graphic novel with spacecraft on the cover. For the first time, it dawned on her that Fonsi and James would probably get along. She tried to convince herself that he'd be fine, that his prognosis was good even though the assortment of bandages covering his body made her queasy.

"Hey, handsome," she said.

"Hey, sexy lady," he said. "Aw, Gwen…" He gave her a light kiss and embraced the humongous panda bear she pulled from a shopping bag. His movements were tentative and small, as if he was tired. Or in pain.

As she placed the bear next to James's otter, which was nestled in a chair, Gwendolyn noticed that two nurses hovered by the closed door, staring through its window. Spooked. She jutted her chin at the duo. "You have fans?"

"Yeah, like every fifteen minutes. It's not every day that staff can say they're attending to someone who'd been declared dead and then ended up banging against a morgue cabinet." He chuckled. "It was freakin' cold in there. When they rolled me out, an orderly was holding this big broomstick above his head and a doctor was holding two scalpels in front of her like swords, like a ninja."

Gwendolyn gave a grim smile. She'd heard as much from Anita about the circumstances of her brother's miraculous resurrection. Another extremely bizarre event associated with the equinox. James's family had gathered around him 24/7, thinking it was a miracle from God that he'd been brought back. Anita had encouraged Gwendolyn to join the family in their celebration, but Gwendolyn politely declined. James and his people needed privacy after his ordeal. And she needed to talk to James privately herself.

"And about what happened at your place, you don't remember anything?" Gwendolyn asked.

James shook his head. "Nope. After I got that snow globe gift, everything went black. I saw your message on my phone way after the fact here in the hospital, saying that it wasn't from you, that I needed to run like hell." He looked at her solemnly. "So what was that about?"

Gwendolyn let out a deep breath. She'd prepared herself as best she could for the big confession, though she still would've preferred to turn around and pretend like there was nothing to admit. She wouldn't run, not anymore.

"James, I'm sorry for what I'm about to say." For the first time in her life, Gwendolyn shared most of her story, revealing her birth name yet again, relaying what she could remember about her time in Panama and coming to the states as a tween and realizing she was a mystic. She meandered and stumbled, cried and blubbered, knowing she was a wreck. Yet she felt such tremendous relief, giving her secrets air to breathe.

She spoke for she didn't know how long. Dusk arrived. Tears dotted her hands, which she held still, folded in her lap. It was so much easier to look at her hands than take in this man whom she'd placed in mortal danger. When she finally looked up, she saw James staring at her so hard that under different circumstances she would've asked if she was covered in pigeon droppings. But there was something else in his eyes and the shape of his mouth. Concern.

Gwendolyn still withheld information. She didn't admit all that she'd done as a teen and certainly wasn't about to reveal to James how he'd been revived. That he really had died. Too much, too fast. But she was as honest as she could be. "At the end of the day, holding back wasn't fair to you," she continued. "You had every right to know who you were getting involved with, so you could make an informed choice. It's what I would've wanted... it's what everyone deserves. I adore you, James Watson, but it was selfish of me, and I'm sorry." She shook her head. "If I'd suspected this was going to happen, I would've run far away."

Silence floated between them for what felt like forever. James continued to take Gwendolyn in, as if he needed time to determine if everything she'd said was true. Or perhaps if their connection was worth the pain.

"I think you need time and space to think things through," Gwendolyn volunteered. She stood up. "It's a lot, and we're still getting to know each other. What I've shared, maybe what we have isn't enough to hold that kind of drama. But whenever you want to talk, no matter what, I'm here."

"I knew," James said.

"You knew?" Gwendolyn paused, incredulous. "About...about my gift?"

"I knew you were hiding something. Those awkward silences we had. When I'd be waiting for you to share something real about yourself that wasn't related to Sublime or entertainment stuff, something personal, you'd shut yourself down. I knew you weren't ready to open up. I guess...I get it now." James studied Gwendolyn's face. "But I also knew, when we were holding each other, in each other's arms on the street, or at my place, I knew you were a good person. So very good. Someone I could love, and, um, well...maybe who could love me? I decided to wait until you were ready to share, that our journey would be worth it. I wasn't ready to let go then, and on the real, I'm still not ready to let go."

Gwendolyn once again sat before Oshun to meditate and contemplate the orisha's mysteries, what the goddess had orchestrated, what more might be asked of her. A Black goddess, making her presence known...exhilarating. She'd heard from Estelle how people around the world had felt compelled to gather and pay tribute to the deity, setting up altars or lighting candles right around the time she'd last touched El Intermedio. How some even claimed that their statues glowed, that the very air around them seemed to come alive with an invisible energy. A circuit of power channeled to Gwendolyn. What once would've been deemed implausible now a distinct possibility.

Gwendolyn couldn't help but wonder why, out of all the spiritual forces out there, Oshun had been the one who'd chosen to act. And she couldn't stop thinking about all the spirits she touched swarming through the city, how it felt to understand their anguish and pain, to provide relief through a magnificent act of love. She suspected many had relinquished their phantom existence, had given up their place in limbo. For a dazzling moment they'd been seen for who they were, for all that they endured, and so they could finally, truly be free.

She was still ruminating when half an hour later she opened the door to her apartment only to be transported back to her youth. Fonsi had shorn down his afro and shaved his beard, his face on full display. Those sharp cheekbones and long eyelashes, far more noticeable.

She pulled him in for a hug, mindful of the large, slim package he held by his side. "Cousin, you look fantastic. What made you...?"

"It was time for a change, suffice to say," he said. "Was rocking the fro for Amede, to try to forge a stronger connection based on archaic Gran Libro theory. I don't think that matters now."

"Is he...gone?"

"Actually, I feel his presence pretty regularly, though I don't know how long he's going to stay." Fonsi chuckled. "I guess I could ask him to try to use a pen or computer and write a long note with his intentions, but...when he's ready." He ran his fingers through his short curls. "That troglodyte style wasn't me. I was walking around bending myself out of shape trying to hold on to a dude...I mean, ghost dude, mind you, but still a dude...instead of being authentic and having faith he'll stick around. I'm not doing that anymore. It's time I figure out who I am first and foremost, honor that. Who'll come will come."

"Well, okay then," Gwendolyn said. Hearing Fonsi's words, her thoughts drifted to James, as they had almost nonstop since she'd left him at the hospital. She'd bidden him goodnight earlier and would check on him first thing in the morning. Exhilarating, to show her fuller self to someone she cared about. To indulge in her infatuation, no holds barred, to see where it took her. Where it took *them*. To express the joy she'd so often buried.

"And to answer the question you maybe don't wanna ask," Fonsi added, "I have no idea if Amede's going to stick around or make his way back to Haiti and the DR or travel the globe. I'm just happy he doesn't have to be tethered to an object, because of your grace, Gwendolyn."

"Fons, there was no way I was going to shunt him back to limbo, not when I saw how he was caring for you. Not after what he'd done for me." She dramatically waved her hand in his face. "And about the fellas, now that they can see that pretty face of yours again, get ready. If you were a client, my boss would *sooooooooo* pimp you."

"Aaaaw, cuz…" Fonsi purred. "The attention I've been getting…feels nice. I have a coffee date tomorrow with this yoga samba dude, Matteo. We'll see." He walked into the living room and gestured to the TV, which was on mute. A clip played of an apparition wreaking havoc in a garden, in this case a four-foot donkey piñata that pounced upon birthday revelers. "Ghost Equinox coverage 24/7," he said. "Nothing else matters in the world anymore."

"They're saying the UN will be creating a special tribunal for supernatural affairs," Gwendolyn said. "To discuss future threats. And the mayor announced that the city's planning to create paranormal police units for each borough."

"Knew something like that was gonna happen." Fonsi stopped and bowed in front of the statue of Oshun. "You're keeping the blessed lady out of the closet?"

"No more closets for her ever again. I mean, I'm certainly not going to run around explaining who we are to everyone, but I'm not hiding my altar. Not when the days of secrecy for the Guardianes seem like they're over. Regardless, you were right, our goddess needs air and light and reverence."

Fonsi passed Gwendolyn the package he'd set against her couch. "For you. From Arturo."

"Huh. How is he? I haven't had time to swing by Faith's."

"Er, well, he's no longer working there, at least for a little bit. Took a leave of absence. He came by the shop today so I could bring this over."

"And he didn't want to stop by himself? Didn't you say he visited the hospital when I was knocked out?"

"Yeah, that was his sense of duty," Fonsi said, hesitating. "After all you did. Arturo is processing everything. He's an incredibly sensitive guy, been grappling with how to deal with this hidden world that's been revealed to everyone, what he just saw with El Intermedio, how that impacts his beliefs... and on top of that, I'm pretty sure he's enraptured by you."

"Oh." Gwendolyn hesitated before tearing away brown paper from the canvas. There was Oshun floating in the background, an almost exact replica of the statuette standing in the living room. And there was Gwendolyn floating in the foreground haloed by sunflowers and bees. The two figures hovered over a glistening river, part turquoise acrylic, part collage made from photos of different bodies of water. The oranges and yellows... all the colors had an uncanny sparkle, as if ready to jump from the canvas.

In florid script at the bottom of the image... *Her Shimmering Spirit.*

"I've started to explain to him how our order works, how works of art can be conduits for our gifts," Fonsi said. "I think he did this to honor your juice. That Oshun has chosen you."

Gwendolyn said nothing, was overwhelmed by what stood in front of her, knowing she would incorporate the image into her altar. She had to reach out to Arturo, give him her thanks.

"There's so much we have to figure out, Fons," she said. "I mean, I spoke to Arturo only because I noticed how he incorporated sunflowers into his work." She held up her ring. "And those buzzing bees. Oshun's symbols. She was guiding me to him, I'm sure, so the two of us could reunite. And when you mentioned the peacock feathers outside my building, the smells…"

"She's been sending us signs. Yeah." He paused. "Hard to dispute. Honestly, I've sometimes struggled with my belief in the orishas, though I have faith in our gifts with all my heart, believe me. I guess…it's complicated. There's a lot to discuss."

Gwendolyn peered at her cousin and tried to read where he was at so she could clear the air. Maybe they'd always have a certain level of awkwardness. Maybe the trust they once had would never be reclaimed. "There *is* a lot to discuss. I'm…I'm ready to talk about what happened the night of the fire," she said. "I already told you what Madrina and Duarte were up to, but I can share more. I know it's important."

Fonsi held up his hand. "We have all the time in the world. Mom and all her pain and madness… That's stuff I'm still figuring out, that I want to figure out, especially how that chump Duarte became so powerful, but for now…" He wiped at his eyes. "…for now I just want to hang with my favorite cousin and gossip about La Playa and Sublime and spout trash about dudes and catch up. What I want more than anything."

The two talked and laughed for hours, and as the witching hour approached, Gwendolyn insisted that Fonsi spend the night, that they do brunch in Harlem the next day. Fonsi agreed, with a caveat. "Before we go to bed, I just want to sit with you as you call forth your gift, like how we used to do in the Boogie Down. For us to be in ritual, without all the pressure and crazy shit. I just want to enjoy your art. For us to feel good."

Gwendolyn smiled. She hadn't used her gifts since she'd repaired the fissure, even though she'd felt energy bubbling under her skin for days. The two sat across from each other on the floor and she made a quick incantation. She thanked Oshun as Fonsi chanted, his grand tenor bouncing off the walls, her hands enveloped in a bright glow.

A kaleidoscope of colors filled the living room. Touching El Intermedio, she felt the living room become cold and adjusted the temperature with ease. A breeze swirled through the apartment. Warm, infused with traces of hyacinth. Effortless. What she'd run from for so long.

That night, even with all the uncertainties and questions she faced, Gwendolyn dared to exult in her gift, dared to remember just how beautiful she was. How beautiful her cousin was, her brother. How beautiful her family was back in Panama, whom she wouldn't forget. And from that place, her shimmer soared.

EPILOGUE

# WAVES

"Here's your sangria, sir."

Felix took his drink and looked out upon the turquoise waters of the Atlantic as he sat at a seaside bar on Miami Beach. Eyes veiled by shades, he pretended to ignore the lanky waiter who lingered by his table and slowly walked away, obviously checking him out. Felix's mesh tank top and zebra print swim trunks left little to the imagination. The waiter's reaction, intended effect. Felix made it his business to pump iron for ninety minutes in the morning and then indulge in half an hour of running early evening, opting to skip cardio if he got in exercise via carnal delights. He was small in stature but mighty in form, his arms and thighs the apple of everyone's eye. He'd just left his latest conquest snoring in a hotel room. No need for goodbyes after getting what he wanted. Felix had blocked the moron's number as soon as he reached the elevator. A thick piece of Mediterranean tourist ass whose name he'd already forgotten.

At the bar, Felix stared down at his phone, looking at a video clip of Estelle dropping knowledge on a morning talk show. His former mentor who'd helped him understand his medium gift as a kid, finally able to speak freely about their traditions. He was transfixed by the news that

# EPILOGUE

had come from New York about the Ghost Equinox. Felix felt an odd longing to be back in his hometown, to be among other members of his order during tumultuous times, even if he was technically responsible for the crisis. Even if he'd distanced himself from other Guardianes ages go.

Felix had once been surprised that there were practically no Guardianes to be found in Miami. Members of his order seemed to be always clustered in nexus cities, places inhabited by people with roots from all over the world, places like New Orleans and New York and Panama City and Salvador. Miami seemed ideal for Guardián activity, but that wasn't the case. Felix had long ago stopped wondering why. Such circumstances were fortuitous, exactly what he needed to create his own order, to build his agenda with no prying eyes.

He rose and walked down the steps from the bar so he could feel sand beneath his toes. He needed to get closer to the ocean and clear his head, let go of the disappointment. His plan, a failed disaster despite years of strategizing.

As a medium back in New York, he'd spent so much time in conversation with Duarte once he'd been killed, directing him on how to quietly build his power as a ghost and sabotage the ritual between Ignacia and Giselda. To get Ignacia to the in-between place and deceive her into creating a breach. The Ghost Equinox was supposed to sow discord, usher in a new era of chaos so his people could swoop in and provide stability, becoming saviors for citizens terrorized by spirits. And now that dream was gone.

Felix knew he had to return to his hometown, find out how that simpering-excuse-for-a-medium Fonsi had been involved. Find out more about that cousin of his, Giselda or Gwendolyn or whatever the hell she was calling herself. There were rumors circulating she was the one who sealed the breach. She was back somehow, now the grandest manipulator Guardianes had ever seen.

# EPILOGUE

It didn't make sense. How'd she become so powerful? And then, Estelle's mention of Oshun? Disorienting, confusing...*infuriating*, really, after all his plans. Felix let the sound of the waves carry him away, and then he grabbed hold of himself. Obsessing was silly. He'd figure out things soon enough, including how to handle Ignacia's adopted goddaughter.

Gwendolyn, exulting in power, running the show? That wouldn't do for what Felix had in mind. Simply wouldn't do at all.

# ACKNOWLEDGMENTS

Dear readers, thank you for undergoing this journey with me, for diving into a story that I hope will get folks talking. I'm beyond grateful for your support, your thoughts, and your time, and for being part of the collective literary community that I adore.

To my visionary editor, publisher, and friend Krishan Trotman, from the bottom of my heart, thank you for believing in this project, for your unyielding care, for providing editorial guidance that was kind, critical when necessary, and refreshingly nuanced. For helping me find my voice and confidence. This book would not exist without you, and I'm so extremely grateful for everything you've done.

To the super damn fly Legacy Lit team—Mahito Henderson, Amina Iro, Tara Kennedy, Maya Lewis—thank y'all for being such a pleasure to work with, for your dedication to the process, for putting up with my legion of questions, and for infusing your combined professionalism with joy.

To the production team, including Emily Andrukaitis, Tareth Mitch, Taylor Navis, Diane Miller-Espada, and Janice Lee, thank you for getting the manuscript into tip-top shining shape, for creating a package that's streamlined and modern. And to cover artist Natasha Cunningham and designer Dana Li, I don't have the words to convey my gratitude for what

## ACKNOWLEDGMENTS

y'all came up with. A stunner that mixes stark elegance with the ethereal, with a phantasmic slice of mischief. (I smile.)

To renowned authors Diane Marie Brown, Sarah Beth Durst, Rachel Howzell Hall, Veronica G. Henry, Rasheed Newson, and Luanne G. Rice, thank you, thank you, thank you for your kind words of support, for inspiring me with your majestic prose and narratives, and for taking time to read this story. I'm so grateful and appreciative.

To my beta readers, my boys Leroy Bryant, Daniel St. Rose, and Jens Rauenbusch, thank you for your thoughtful, moving critiques, for taking time to discuss the text, and for simply being wonderful human beings. I continue to learn from the shining examples each of you put forth into the world.

To my family and friends in general, I'm not able to list everyone here but you know who you are. Thank you so very much for your support through the years and for being exemplars of thoughtfulness and decency, with a special shout-out to my Tía for her unwavering love and Carmen King for helping introduce me to the joys of books at an early age.

And to the readers once again, there are so many more stories to come. Let's remember to always embrace the fantastic and love as much and as far as we can.